JAY CROWNOVER

Recovered

Getaway Series

Runaround

Escape

Shelter

Retreat

The Saints of Denver Series

Salvaged

Riveted

Charged

Built

Leveled (novella)

The Breaking Point Series

Dignity

Avenged (crossover novella)

Honor

The Welcome to the Point Series

Better When He's Brave

Better When He's Bold

Better When He's Bad

The Marked Men Series

Asa

Rowdy

Nash

Rome

Jet

Rule

RUNAROUND

Runaround
Copyright © 2018 by Jennifer M. Voorhees.
All rights reserved.
Congress Cataloging- in- Publication Data has been applied for.

This is a work of fiction. Names, characters, places, and incidents are products of the author's imagination or are used fictitiously and are not to be construed as real. Any resemblance to actual events, locales, organizations, or persons, living or dead, is entirely coincidental.

All rights reserved. Printed in the United States of America. No part of this book may be used or reproduced in any manner whatsoever without written permission except in the case of brief quotations embodied in critical articles and reviews. For information address Jay Crownover LLC 1670 E. Cheyenne Mountain Blvd. Box# 152, Colorado Springs, Colorado 80906.

Cover design by:
Hang Le
www.byhangle.com

Photographed by and Copyright owned by:
Wander Aguiar Photography
www.wanderbookclub.com

Editing by:
Elaine York, Allusion Graphics, LLC/Publishing & Book Formatting
www.allusiongraphics.com

Proofreading & Copyediting by:
Bethany Salminen
www.bethanyedits.net

Interior Design & Formatting by:
Christine Borgford, Type A Formatting
www.typeAformatting.com

THE
GETAWAY
SERIES

RUNAROUND

NEW YORK TIMES BESTSELLING AUTHOR
JAY CROWNOVER

Dedicated to everyone who freaked out or got a little hot about Escape being a cliffy! Come on now . . . I wouldn't do you dirty like that!

PROLOGUE

WEBB

TROUBLE TAKING OVER MY LIFE was nothing new.

We were old friends, and we went way, way back. Sometimes we had a good time . . . a really good time. Trouble could be a lot of fun if you knew how to play with all of the sharp, enticing edges of it. Sometimes trouble and I had a falling out, and I tried to get my act together, telling myself I was going to do better, be better. But, like the most talented and determined of lovers, trouble always came calling. And like the weak bastard I was, I always gave into the temptation. Always put my hand directly in the flame, even though I knew I was going to get burned.

Trouble was familiar.

Trouble was so easy to slide into, and I couldn't ever walk away. Most days I didn't know who I was if I didn't have trouble trailing after me, dogging my every step, luring me into dark corners toward bad decisions I knew would hang around my neck like a dead weight for the rest of my life.

Today, trouble had the worst timing imaginable when it decided to show up. I was acting right and had been keeping my nose clean. I landed a job on a friend's ranch in the middle of nowhere Wyoming, foolishly thinking I'd put enough distance between us that it wouldn't be able to find me. I should've known better.

Trouble was crafty and persistent. Trouble never let go. Trouble had its claws dug so deep into my skin, I'd ripped flesh and bone away when I ran the last time I'd attempted to leave it in the dust.

Trouble wore a lot of different faces. It came in all different shapes and sizes, so I never quite knew what to look for or when to run.

Today I was at a wedding, a celebration of life and love. I was surrounded by happy people, smiling children, and my family. I also couldn't take my eyes off the only thing in the world I'd ever encountered that tempted me more than trouble: a woman. A beautiful, brave, smart-mouthed woman, who made it clear she didn't have the time of day to give me. Tall, blonde, with shrewd green eyes set in a face that told a story, Tennyson McKenna was not a woman who suffered fools, or lovesick city boys, lightly. She wanted nothing to do with me, which made her smart and told me she had good instincts. Her blatant dismissal and outright hostility did nothing to cool the heat that pooled low in my gut whenever I caught sight of her. Every rejection she fired my way only made the challenge of chasing her infrequent smiles and rare laughter all the more thrilling. I wanted her. So much so, I forgot that I already had a mistress who liked to come calling when my back was turned. Trouble was a tricky bitch with a nasty bite. Trouble showed up in the form of a swarm of black-garbed FBI agents waving around a warrant for my arrest and making a scene on a day that was supposed to be goodness and light.

Trouble was splashy and loud this time. It was the center of attention when all eyes should have been on the bride and groom. Every instinct I had was to fight, to push back, to tell trouble now was not the time or place. However, when trouble came with a badge, armed to the teeth, I knew the only thing I could do was to go with it quietly so that the people who mattered could try and salvage what was left of their special day. I'd done this dance more times than I could count. I knew all the steps, even if trouble was singing a new tune this time around.

A big guy looked at me like I'd crawled out of the sewer. He was from the Colorado Bureau of Investigations, the division responsible for this part of Nowhere since Wyoming had so few residents and such a low crime rate for federal offenses. He informed me that my picture was on surveillance footage and my DNA was found several armed bank robberies throughout northern Wyoming and Montana. I didn't say anything. I didn't defend myself. I didn't declare how the evidence was impossible because I knew it wouldn't do me any good. I listened quietly while they read me the rights I already knew by heart. Trouble made sure I had my back against the wall. It was smug and confident, and it had me right where it wanted me.

I went quietly, my older brother not so much. Wyatt was the only blood family I acknowledged. He was the only person in the entire world I gave a shit about. Up until a few months ago, when I stumbled upon the woman who made my heart race. For once, Wyatt had been the one tangled up in trouble's sticky web, and when I'd gone to get him out, I found myself in the middle of a place I never wanted to leave, surrounded by the kind of men and women who made me regret giving trouble free rein in my life up until then. Wyatt was a DEA agent, one of the good guys. We'd always been as different as night and day, but he'd never stood by and let trouble roll over me. It was his life's mission to keep me from getting crushed under the weight of my poor choices and desperate decisions.

"Don't say a goddamn word, Webb. Keep your mouth shut until I can figure out what's going on." He was in full protector mode, taking on the CBI like it was something he did every single day, as they loaded me into the back of one of their black SUVs.

I wasn't going to say a word, but I wanted to. I wanted to

shout over everyone trying to pull rank and the threats being tossed back and forth. Ten asked me what I had done. She was watching the events unfold with narrowed eyes, and her bottom lip tucked between her teeth. She already believed the worst about me. I'd never really given her a reason not to. But it burned to see the doubt and question in her eyes as I was led away. I wanted to believe that I'd have the upper hand, that trouble wouldn't win this round, but I was in deep, and I could feel the thump of my heart hammering as I tried to breathe through the mess I was in.

The drive to downtown Denver was long and boring. Occasionally the big guy in charge tried to pepper me with questions, but Wyatt said not to talk. The only person I wanted to say something to was likely never going to believe me anyway. I kept quiet and watched the only place that ever really felt like home drift away.

It was late at night by the time the feds tossed me into an interrogation room. This was not my first rodeo. Sadly, I knew the drill as well as I knew my own name. A federal crime like armed robbery was no joke, and these guys weren't playing around, but all the standard operating procedures were pretty much the same as every petty crime I'd ever been hauled in on.

I kept my shit together, played it cool. I acted unaffected and bored, mostly because I was. I knew Wyatt was out there somewhere raising hell and trying to get me released. All I had to do was bide my time and be patient. I was winning the game until a new player put his pieces on the board.

When he walked in, I knew he was different than the guys who dragged me off the Warner Ranch. This guy wasn't dressed in black tactical gear. He didn't smirk and swagger like he knew something I didn't. He simply walked into the small, barren room and took a seat across from me. He was dressed in a suit similar to the one my brother had worn to the wedding, but I knew enough about men's fashion to know that his cost double what Wyatt was willing to drop on his threads. He also had an expensive haircut, and he was wearing a gold watch that managed to look both sophisticated and pretentious at the same time. This was no wet-behind-the-ears agent. This was no brutish field agent. This guy had climbed his way up the ranks and wasn't afraid to let me know they'd called in the big guns to shut me down and trip me up.

Without saying a word to me, the man opened up a manila folder he'd carried in with him. A moment later I was staring at a crystal clear, black and white photo obviously taken inside of a bank. The man in the center of the image was making no effort at all to cover his face or conceal his identity. In fact, it looked like he was staring directly at the security camera. He had a gun in his hand. He held it like he knew how to use it. He also had a smirk on his face and a taunting challenge in his eyes.

Shock and disbelief loosened my tongue. "What the fuck? What kind of trick is this?"

I reached for the photo, hands shaking, sweat starting to bead on my forehead and slip down the back of my neck.

The smirk, the tilt of the eyes, the cock of the chin, the way he stood: they were all a perfect image of me. I was staring at myself robbing a goddamn bank. I sucked in a breath so quickly it hurt. My fingers shook as I touched my own face in the picture.

I looked up and stared at the stone-faced FBI agent. "That isn't me." But it sure as hell looked like me. That was my face, my body, my everything. I would bet every measly dime I had to my name that his hair was the same blond and his eyes were the same blue as mine.

The FBI agent didn't say a word. His silence was a weapon, where mine had been armor. I tapped a finger on the photograph. "It looks just like me, but it's not. I swear to God, that is not me."

But it was my face, and they said they had my DNA at the

scene. Trouble was playing to win this time. It didn't want to let me go. It wanted to bury me so deeply there would never be a day I was free of it. Desperately my eyes scanned over every inch of the photo, mind racing, pulse pounding. I was dizzy, and I felt like I was going to hurl all over the table. This was a nightmare, and no matter how hard I pinched myself, I wasn't waking up.

Between blinks, my eyes flicked over the date-stamp on the corner of the image. A tiny flare of hope lit up in the center of my chest. Frantically I pointed at the tiny orange numbers and looked at the FBI agent who still hadn't said a single word.

"If that was the date of this robbery, I have an alibi." Relief made the words rushed as they stumbled over one another. "I was in Denver with Tennyson McKenna and Lane Warner looking for a runaway teenager. There was even a cop there. Denver PD sent her in when Ten found the kid. I was nowhere near a bank in Wyoming or Montana. I'm telling you, that isn't me."

The FBI agent finally moved. He put his hands on the table in front of him and leaned toward me. "You have an alibi?"

I felt my eyebrows wing up and I nodded slowly. "That's what I just said. My boss's brother ran into some trouble, so I drove down to Denver with a neighbor, Tennyson Mckenna, to help track him down. I was in Denver for several days. Ten is a forest ranger up in Sheridan, and like I said, there was a female police officer involved in trying to track the kid down. Talk to them. They'll tell you I was nowhere near this robbery." I had no explanation as to why the man in the picture had my face, or how my DNA ended up at a crime scene miles away, but I knew Ten was the only thing keeping me from spending the foreseeable future behind bars.

"Are you romantically involved with either alibi witness?" The agent's voice sounded curious, and there was something else in his tone I couldn't place. "Is either woman likely to lie for you, Mr. Bryant?"

I blinked and shook my head. "No. The cop was married, if I remember correctly, and Ten thinks I'm a stupid kid. She tolerates me because she has to, not because she wants to."

The agent leaned back in his chair and gave me a look. "I didn't think you would be her type. You're too young. Reckless. Impulsive. Your criminal record is impressive, and you lie too easily."

Startled by the sudden change in the direction of the conversation, I slumped back in my seat and stared at the other man stupidly. "Excuse me?"

The FBI agent reached across the table and snatched the picture. "You have an identical twin out there somewhere, Bryant?"

"No." Even though people often said Wyatt and I could pass for twins. I frowned. "Not that I know of. But neither of my folks stuck around very long, so who the fuck knows what kind of siblings I got out there? Also, how do you know what Ten's type is? Do you know her?" She'd been an FBI agent herself for a stint long before I came crashing into her life. It was likely her path had crossed with this man in her former career.

The agent cocked an eyebrow at me and moved toward the door. "I was engaged to her for two years, so even if she tries to lie to me to cover for you, I'll know. Sit tight, Mr. Bryant. You aren't going anywhere anytime soon."

The door clicked shut with a sign of finality, leaving me to stew. Fuck trouble, and fuck me for never being able to get away from it.

CHAPTER 1

TENNYSON

THE FIRST TIME I LAID eyes on Webb Bryant he was frighteningly pale from blood loss and nearly delirious from a raging fever. He'd been sporting a hole in his shoulder from a bullet wound and was terrified his brother was dead somewhere in the vast Wyoming wilderness. It was my job to protect and patrol, one I focused on diligently, but Webb was admittedly distracting. I thought he was going to pass out at my feet, a city boy in way over his head. He didn't. He never wavered or stumbled in the unfamiliar terrain and unknown situation . . . not once. He'd impressed me with his resilience and his determination to find out what had happened to his older brother. He'd also caught my attention with those burning blue eyes and shock of blond hair, which gave the misleading impression that the man had a single angelic quality about him. Every long, lean line of Webb Bryant oozed playful mischief and bled the promise of wicked things done in the dark . . . or during the bright light of day. He didn't seem like the shy type. Even injured and out of his mind with frantic worry for his older sibling, he was the most charming, most flirtatious man I'd ever met. He sent every defense mechanism I had into overdrive, and there wasn't a second that slid by where I didn't remind myself he was not my type in the slightest. Besides, once the Warners and I had both the Bryant brothers straightened out, I figured I wouldn't have to dodge Webb's advances ever again. He would ramble on to his next adventure and be out of sight and mind.

I breathed a sigh of relief when he went away. He was too tempting. It was too enticing to give in to every single promise made by his easy smile and glinting eyes. Webb was several years younger than me, a man who was obviously lost and still trying to figure out who he wanted to be when he finally grew up. I was a woman who knew exactly who she was and who she would never be. I was never the type to chase after the bad boys, the wanderers, the reckless. No, I fell for the steadfast, the sturdy, and the solid. I gave my heart to the kind of men who held the world up and buffered everyone around them from the raging storm.

I handed my heart to the oldest Warner brother, Cyrus, when we were just kids. Coming to terms with the fact the stoic and serious cowboy would never feel about me the way I felt about him had been one of the hardest things I'd ever had to do. We shared similar dreams, knowing our lives were so much bigger than the ranches that had our family's bloodlines entrenched in the soil. We both wanted more than Wyoming, and for a long time, I honestly believed we were on the road out of our tiny town together. It didn't happen that way. Sure, we both got out in our own time and in our own way, but we both ended up back where we started. Cy was taking his return home in stride. He was far less resentful about his homecoming than I was. In fact, the wedding Webb was dragged out of two short days ago was Cy's.

I thought it was going to be hard, damn near impossible, to watch the man I'd openly loved from afar for most of my life promise his forever to someone else. It wasn't nearly as bad as I envisioned. Mostly because Cy was stupid happy with his fiery city girl. He'd never been that happy with me, before we left or when we both admitted defeat and came back home. He'd never loved anyone like he loved his Leo, so the sting of watching him put a ring on someone else's finger was minimal.

I would gouge my eyes out with a rusty spoon before admitting to anyone, especially myself, that since the start of the wedding most of my attention had been on Webb instead of the happy couple. To my surprise, my heart didn't feel nearly as trampled as I thought it would. It was too busy stupidly racing over the man I believed I wouldn't see again and knew I should keep my distance from.

The blond man with a penchant for trouble hadn't stayed gone like I predicted. Nope. He'd shown up right when Cy needed help on the ranch and offered to stick around. Webb claimed he wanted to learn a new skill, seemed he'd taken a shine to the rough way of life in the Wyoming backcountry and wanted to play cowboy for a while. Cy couldn't say no, and as badly as I wanted to, I couldn't stay away. I was caught in an endless game of cat and mouse, and some days I wasn't sure if I was the predator or the prey. I tracked Webb out of the corner of my eye for months. I expected him to up his game and try to lure me to bed, knowing the wedding was going to lower my defenses. Never in a million years would I have predicted he was going to be led away from the festivities in handcuffs. He was a wildcard, as unpredictable as the wind, but I had a hard time wrapping my head around him being a master criminal.

For one thing, a crime like armed bank robbery took major planning and preparation. Webb was more a fly-by-the-seat-of-his-too-tight-pants kind of guy. For another, the man had been on my heels since returning to the Warner property. I couldn't shake him loose, no matter how much attitude and disdain I tossed his way. It was impossible he had the time to rob banks all over the damn state and beyond, only to be back in my pocket hours later, flashing that panty-dropping grin of his.

I wanted to chase after the black SUV. I wanted to scream at the guy snapping the cuffs on him that he had the wrong man. However, in another life, I was a fed. I knew they wouldn't have picked up Webb if they didn't have the evidence to back up their actions. Besides, who was I to Webb Bryant? A passing fancy. His current curiosity. I had no grounds to march into the Denver field office and demand anything. Instead, I'd grabbed the older Bryant boy and demand he pass along any information he managed to pull from the agents who took his baby brother. Wyatt was DEA: a different part of the alphabet soup that made up the various branches of law enforcement, but he was more likely to get news on Webb than anyone else.

I spent a sleepless night and a restless morning waiting for any word. It was noon the following day when Wyatt called and told me Webb was using me as his alibi. He ran down the dates and through the seemingly rock-solid evidence the feds had against Webb. They had his face and his DNA. He'd left a baseball hat behind at one of the banks, a bandana at another. Wyatt could neither explain the identical match to his brother, nor could he answer me when I demanded to know if anyone had collected fingerprints at the crime scenes. Identical twins could share a face, and they had matching DNA, but no one had fingerprints that were exactly the same. Wyatt was too frazzled and concerned for his brother to think clearly. I didn't have the same problem. Sure, I was concerned about Webb, but I was more pissed about the fact he was obviously being railroaded and set up and no one seemed able to stop it.

I assured Wyatt I would get my ass to Denver as quickly as possible to verify Webb was with me during one of the robberies where they had him on film. Before I swept into the field office, I stopped by the hotel where we'd crashed on the date of the robbery and asked to see the surveillance footage. When I asked if the feds had already been by, the security guy looked at me like I was crazy and told me no way. The laziness of the investigation into Webb's involvement really pissed me off and reminded me why I was no longer an FBI agent. They had the evidence. They believed it was Webb. There was no other scenario they could piece together, so they were going to close the file and move onto the next case, even if the man they had in custody was innocent. That narrow, rigid thinking was one of the worst parts of being a federal agent.

When I walked into the field office, I was full of fire and righteous indignation. There was no way Webb had been in two places at the same time, and I was bound and determined to make someone listen to reason. When I was led into one of the familiar, empty rooms to give my statement, the last person in the world I expected, or wanted, to walk through the door, did.

Gage Gordon was the Assistant Deputy Director of the Criminal Investigations Division of the FBI. He was my former boss and my ex-fiancé. It'd been almost three full years since I last saw the man, and I honestly hoped I would never have to lay my eyes on him again.

I sat back in the uncomfortable metal chair and tapped my fingers on the table in front of me. "Did you ask for this case?"

Gage settled in the seat across from me, his familiar gaze assessing. He was a handsome bastard, in a polished kind of way. He didn't look much different than the day I'd thrown both my job and his platinum and diamond monstrosity of a ring in his face. When we'd first gotten involved, I couldn't ever quite get my head around why someone like him was interested in someone like me. I should have listened to those instincts.

"No. I didn't ask for it. But when the director asked me to oversee it, I didn't say no. It's been a long time, Tennyson. You look good." A grin tugged at the corners of his mouth, and I wanted to smack the smile off of his face.

I hated it when he called me Tennyson. I was Ten. Always had been to the people who mattered to me. It should have been the first red flag when Gage refused to abide by my wishes to use the shortened version of my name.

"He's innocent, Gage. You've got the wrong man in custody." I wasn't about to get pulled into any of the old games I used to let this man play with me.

Gage leaned back in the chair across from me, calm and certain as can be. "The evidence says otherwise."

I rolled my eyes, not bothering to hide my irritation. "Evidence only tells part of the story. You really think Webb just took off his hat in the middle of a robbery and left it behind? He just absently left his DNA? He planned multiple robberies but didn't bother to try and hide his identity at all, but oh, he didn't leave any fingerprints? None of that adds up, Gage, and you damn well know it." I pushed the still from the hotel security camera, complete with a time stamp on it, across the table in his direction. "Not to mention that he wasn't lying about being with me at the time of the robbery."

In the picture, I was standing next to the tall, handsome, blond man. We were leaning in toward one another, Webb's head bent down, my chin tilted up as we walked across the lobby of the hotel. It looked intimate. We looked like a couple headed up to the room we shared. There was no way to know Webb had been intently telling me he knew all too well what happened to a young kid on the streets with no one to turn to for help. My heart was breaking for the child the man next to me had been, but there was no denying it was Webb in the picture. There was also no getting around the fact there was clearly something there, hovering between me and the younger man. I knew Gage could see it. I saw the recognition flare in his eyes and his jaw clench. For all the things he was, stupid had never been one of them.

Gage tapped a finger on the picture in front of him, eyes lifting to mine. "The cop verified he was in Denver at the time of the robbery as well." He didn't sound at all happy about that fact.

I grunted in a very unladylike way and crossed my arms over my chest. "Because he was. I don't know who was robbing that bank in Wyoming, but it was not Webb Bryant. I can round up at least three more witnesses to corroborate that Webb's ass was right next to mine in that hotel in Denver."

A dark eyebrow winged up and the smile he'd been playing with died. "What happened to your one true love? You couldn't hightail it back to Warner fast enough when you walked out on me. You decide he was too old and boring for you, as well, so you moved on to a younger cowboy with tighter jeans? Were you looking for someone whom you could boss around? Someone who would let you take charge?"

I gritted my teeth and counted backward from ten so I didn't jump across the table and wrap my hands around his throat. He'd always been a condescending prick, but it seemed like he'd grown even more patronizing. Still, he was a good interrogator. He knew exactly what buttons to push to get a reaction.

"Cy is a happily married man. I'm sure you know that. I wouldn't put it past you to have sent your boys in during the wedding on purpose. You never could keep your knee-jerk reactions in check." He'd treated me like a doll, a trophy. He acted like I didn't have two brain cells to rub together and pretended the only reason I was part of his unit at the agency was because I was blonde and had a nice rack. He never, not once, took into consideration how hard I'd had to work to earn my badge and title.

"Bryant's pretty young." His other eyebrow lifted. "Do you know how extensive his prior criminal record is?"

I sighed. "He's not mine, so none of that matters." But I did know all about his transgressions, and there were times he *did* feel like mine, but Gage didn't need to know any of that. Webb never tried to hide who he was or where he'd been. He was technically young, but the man had lived a lot and lived hard in his years. He was no innocent lamb, and despite his glorious, golden good looks, he was obviously no angel.

Gage leaned forward in the chair, a frown pulling at his mouth. "You seem pretty attached."

I threw my head back and lifted my hands to pull at my hair in aggravation. "What I am, is annoyed. You have the wrong guy. Get off your ass and go find the guilty party. I know it's been a while, but I figure you can't solve a crime without getting off your ass and doing some . . . I dunno . . . investigating."

"I don't remember you having that mouth on you." He climbed to his feet and gave me a narrow-eyed look.

I barked out a sharp laugh. "It was always there, you just never listened."

He gave a grunt. "You do realize how unbelievable it would be if this kid has an identical twin he never knew about trying to set him up? Things like that don't happen in the real world. Even if he gets out, there is a good chance he's going to end up right back here."

We stared at one another locked in a silent battle. I knew Gage was going to cave first. He walked out of the room mumbling something about getting a status update on Webb. I needed to find Wyatt so we could have a chat. I didn't think for a second that Gage was going to put any effort or resources into tracking down the man with Webb's face, which meant someone with a vested interest in keeping Webb Bryant out of jail was going to have to do it.

There wasn't a question the person who was going to do it was me. I was the best tracker the FBI had ever seen, and against my better judgment, I was very invested in keeping Webb out of trouble.

CHAPTER 2

WEBB

IN A PERFECT WORLD, THE powers that be would simply believe me when I said there was no way the man in the picture was me. They would take my alibi—a cop and a former FBI agent for Christ's sake—at face value and let me go. Of course, the world was far from perfect, and lady luck didn't owe me any favors. I ended up cooling my heels in the federal building's holding center for four days before they let me go. By that time, my brother was fit to be tied and had hired a top-notch lawyer for me. He was the only person they'd let in to see me. I knew from him that both the Denver police woman and Ten had verified my whereabouts on the day of the last robbery. I also knew Wyatt was already doing his best to track down our mom so he could ask about the fact I obviously had a twin she never bothered to tell either one of us about. Having confirmation that an identical twin did indeed exist from the woman who birthed us would go a long way in proving exactly how my face and my DNA ended up in a place where I had never been. I wasn't holding my breath. My mom was tricky and damn sneaky. She'd bounced in and out of our lives since we were kids, and she'd been pretty much missing in action from the minute Wyatt took responsibility for raising me. She was always on the run from something, so tracking her down was never going to be an easy task.

The lawyer also mentioned how Ten was trying to find the man who had my face. He told me she was going toe-to-toe with the FBI agent in charge of my case. Apparently, she was making a lot of noise, maintaining it was impossible that I was guilty. Now, that was something that made me breathe a little bit easier. I could still hear her asking what I'd done when I was being led away from the wedding. I could still see the questions in her emerald green eyes, the doubt and the uncertainty. The fact she was here at all, championing my cause, was a miracle. Knowing she was pushing back at her former fiancé on my behalf was something else entirely. It gave me hope. Not necessarily hope my happy ass was going home anytime soon, but there was a small, bright spot in the center of my chest that glowed hot and bright at the thought of Tennyson McKenna not being as indifferent to my considerable charms as she pretended to be. If she cared at all, even in the smallest way, well, that was more than I'd believed possible.

I wanted to see her. I wanted to see my brother. I wanted out of this damn building so I could figure out what the fuck was going on in my wayward life. There were answers out there, and I needed to go find them. My mom owed me an explanation, and so did the man committing federal crimes and trying to pin them on me. It was obvious the other me had to know I existed. I couldn't figure out another reason for him to rob banks without trying to hide his identity. His moves were bold as fuck and served a purpose. It was planned. I needed to know how he knew about me when I had no clue he existed until I was taking the fall for him. The longer I spun the information around in my head, the more impatient I became. I'd paced a hundred miles in the small holding room, mind racing, questions building. The FBI had yet to formally charge me with anything, so I was holding out hope someone was going to show up and set me free sooner rather than later.

I got my wish on the fourth day. I had no clue what time it was since there were no windows or clocks in the small, industrial space. The door opened and my lawyer walked in, followed by the FBI agent who used to be engaged to the woman I couldn't get off my mind. Truth was, I had no idea what Ten had ever seen in the stuffed shirt. The guy was a total tool. His head was so far up his own ass it was a wonder he hadn't suffocated yet. He treated me like I was something gross stuck to the bottom of his shoe every single time he'd come in to interrogate me, so I'd taken great pleasure in pissing him off every chance I got. I wasn't intimidated by his badge or title. I was angry and jealous he'd had his hands and mouth on Ten, even if it had been years ago, so I let those feelings guide my responses. I wouldn't give the asshole the satisfaction of seeing me sweat.

"You're getting released within the hour, Mr. Bryant." My lawyer sounded pleased; the FBI agent looked like he'd been forced to suck on a lemon.

I lifted an eyebrow and crossed my arms over my chest. "What's the catch? I gotta wear one of those GPS ankle bands or something?"

The lawyer grinned. "No. You are free to go. There won't be charges filed right now. Not until the FBI can figure out a way to explain how you managed to be in two places at once. Without fingerprints to distinguish *who* was on the surveillance from the bank in Wyoming, there isn't much they can do. Your brother is here to take you home."

The FBI agent with a chip on his shoulder scowled at me. "Don't do anything impulsive, Bryant. We still have a string of robberies someone is responsible for. We're not going to stop until someone is locked up and punished for those crimes." That someone was obviously supposed to be me.

I could read between the lines. He still thought he could pin the armed robberies on me. They were letting me go, but I wasn't foolish enough to think they weren't going to be watching me. This guy had a hard-on for me. I was sure it was only in part because he actually believed I'd robbed those banks. I bet a good chunk of his desire to see me rot behind bars had to do with the fact his former flame was going to bat for me. Agent Gordon didn't seem to like that one bit. I moved a step closer to him, lifting an eyebrow in challenge. I watched his jaw clench in response as I taunted, "Good luck finding my prints in a place I've never been, Agent Gordon. That'll be a really good party trick." I flicked my gaze over to my lawyer and lifted my chin. "Let's go."

They let me change back into my street clothes so I felt more like a normal man and less like a prisoner. But I knew that the feds were still watching every move I made.

I could practically hear Agent Gordon's teeth grinding to dust as my lawyer led me past him and out into a long, boring hallway. I followed the quiet, older man silently into a busy office area. I let out a slow, long breath when I caught sight of Wyatt. My older brother was leaning against a desk, arms crossed over his chest, his face set in hard, unimpressed lines. We looked a lot alike, but Wyatt had grown up way too fast and taken on too much responsibility far too young. He rarely smiled and always looked too serious, if you asked me. The moment his eyes hit mine I could see relief burn through the blue. His big frame sagged on a huge sigh. He pushed off the desk and stomped across the space separating us. He paused long enough to shake my lawyer's hand, and there was no missing the furious glare he shot over my shoulder in Gordon's direction.

I was roughly pulled into a hug tight enough to crack ribs. I returned the squeeze and briefly closed my eyes. It was so easy to pretend Wyatt would take care of everything like he always did when he put himself between me and the rest of the world. He gave me a solid pounding on the back and tilted his head down, his gaze searching mine to make sure I was all right.

"You okay, little brother?" His voice was gruff, none of the East Coast shine coloring it that he'd picked up over the years working in the DC area.

Wyatt and I had been born in a small parish outside of New Orleans. We'd stayed in Louisiana up to middle school, but then Mom had hooked up with a new fella and suddenly we'd been uprooted and moved to sunny Miami. Florida lasted as long as I was in middle school, but by the time high school rolled around, we were on the move again. We'd ended up in Las Vegas for a while, and then Oregon. When Mom dragged us to San Diego and tried to move us not even two months later, Wyatt put his foot down and told her we weren't going. He was barely sixteen then, and Mom hadn't looked back when she walked out the door. We were officially on our own from that moment on, just trying to survive. Wyatt was always looking for permanence and security. He was the one who was relentlessly searching for a forever home and family. I always believed I had enough as long as I had him. It was only one of the many ways in which we differed.

"Get me out of here, and I'll be fine." I turned to the lawyer and thanked him profusely. He told me he'd be in touch and to stay out of trouble. I didn't bother trying to explain that trouble tended to find me despite my best intentions.

I followed Wyatt out of the building, biting my tongue, so I didn't fire a million questions at him all at once.

"How are Cy and Leo doing? I feel terrible that I ruined their wedding reception." I liked my boss and his new bride. More than that, I respected the hell out of the whole Warner gang. Cy didn't have to take a chance on me. He knew about my questionable past and my lack of experience in ranch work, but he took me on anyway. I wasn't the Bryant looking to grow roots and settle down, but somehow, without even trying, I'd found a place where I felt like I belonged. He welcomed me into the fold without question, and how did I repay him? By ruining what was supposed to be one of the most special moments of his life. I wouldn't be surprised if he fired my ass and banned me from the ranch for life.

"He's worried about you, not the interruption of the reception. They all are. Cy's called me once a day for an update. They're flying out tomorrow for their honeymoon, so you can call him and fill him in on everything before he whisks Leo away to paradise for a week." Wyatt paused next to a rental car and pushed the fingers of one hand through his messy blond hair. "Ten has been in and out of this office for the last couple of days. She's like a pit bull. I can't believe the feds let her go. She's the one who laid out the fact that if they tried to charge you with the conflicting evidence, any good lawyer was going to bring up the lack of fingerprints at the scene. There is so much reasonable doubt threaded throughout this case that it would never hold up in court. She's a hell of an investigator, and she is clearly worried about you."

I felt a smile pull at my mouth. "She's a good person to have in your corner."

Wyatt nodded. "That she is. She's also determined to find the guy on the surveillance footage."

I blew out a breath and leaned a hip against the side of my brother's rental car. "Any luck tracking down Mom?"

Wyatt shook his head in the negative and frowned. "How could she have had twins and I didn't know about it?" He sounded angry, and I knew it was all directed inward. He firmly believed it was his role in life to protect me from everything, even myself. It was killing him that he hadn't seen something like this coming. But how could he?

"You were four when she brought me home, Wyatt. None of this is on you." I clapped him on the shoulder. "This is all on her, and on the asshole with my face. Of course, I would be the one to have an evil twin." I snorted.

"I remember her being pregnant. I remember her belly being big, and some guy coming around to check on her. I remember being excited I wouldn't be alone anymore when she decided not to come home at night. I don't remember any mention of there being two babies. You would think that would be something she'd try to prepare for."

"A normal mom would prepare. Our mom," I rolled my eyes up at the sky. "I'm lucky I made it home at all. She could have easily left me at the hospital and made me someone else's problem. I wouldn't put abandoning a second baby, or even selling it on the black market, past her." If that were the case, I was indeed the lucky twin because the man standing next to me always watched my six, even when he wanted to kick my ass. "Last I heard, she was hanging around a motorcycle club in Texas. She called looking for some cash."

Wyatt narrowed his eyes at me. "You give it to her?"

Wyatt didn't talk to the woman any longer. Wanted nothing to do with her. I didn't blame him. She'd stolen his childhood from him, but worse than that, when he came out to her when he was in his teens, she'd tried to make him feel like there was something wrong with him. It took Wyatt a long time to come to terms with himself and his sexuality because of the damage our mother inflicted. I had a harder time totally turning my back on her. Not because I believed she deserved forgiveness, or kindness, or a moment of my time, but because I knew if I didn't step in and help her out occasionally, she was going to harm more innocent people. She was destructive and vindictive that way.

"I wired her a couple hundred bucks. I sent it to a town called Loveless. I doubt she's still there. She said the money was for a bus ticket." I met Wyatt's angry glare. There were some things we were never going to see eye to eye, and I learned to live with that long ago.

Wyatt swore under his breath and tugged on his hair. "Gives us a place to start, I guess. I got a couple of rooms in a hotel close by. Let's get going. We can get a plan together tomorrow."

I nodded but reached out to stop him with a hand on his shoulder. "Where's Ten, Wyatt? I need to talk to her." Needed to thank her. Needed her to believe me. Needed her to help me.

My brother gave me a knowing look. "She's staying at the same hotel."

I grinned and slipped into the passenger seat. As different as we were, Wyatt knew me better than anyone, and I would be forever grateful for that.

CHAPTER 3

TEN

"**I**'M REALLY GLAD YOU'RE HERE, Ten." That voice. It shouldn't send a shiver of awareness down my spine. I didn't want it to send my stomach tumbling. I hated how it took nothing but the low, smooth rumble of his voice to light up every nerve in my body and how it made me hyper-aware of each inch separating his body from mine.

I lifted my gaze as Webb settled in the seat next to mine at the hotel bar. He didn't look any worse for wear after spending several days in FBI custody. He did have dark shadows under his shockingly bright blue eyes, and his usual grin looked like someone had slapped a dimmer switch on it. None of his typical fun and flirty charm was present. In fact, this was the most solemn I'd ever seen him.

One of the cocktail servers swung by the table when she noticed I had a guest. I would've been impressed with the level of service and attention to detail if I hadn't seen the girl's head whip around so fast the second Webb stepped into the bar that I worried about her neck. He had a kind of magnetic pull, an aura around him which was impossible to ignore. I should know. I'd been trying to pretend I was immune to all that was Webb Bryant for months. I discreetly rolled my eyes as the server simpered as Webb ordered a whiskey on the rocks and a plate of sliders. When she bounded away, I expected him to watch her go. She was young, cute, and clearly willing to take his mind off his shitty week. He didn't so much as flick an eyelash in her direction. Instead, those laser blue eyes locked on me and the sincerity in his heartbreaking gaze hit me in the center of my chest like a punch. I wasn't at all sure what to do with that feeling. Ignoring it seemed like the best option, if I was able.

I picked up my vodka and soda, pulling my gaze to the condensation on the outside of the glass. "I wasn't going to let the FBI railroad you when I'm your alibi. I knew you didn't do what they were accusing you of."

"What if you weren't my alibi?" His voice lowered, and I could feel the touch of his gaze on the side of my bent head. "If I weren't with you for that final robbery, would you be so certain of my innocence?" I could tell by the tone of his voice that my answer mattered a whole hell of a lot.

I wasn't about to lie to him. Sighing, I swallowed the rest of my drink and set the glass on the table in front of me with a thunk. I lifted my eyes to his and told him, "No, I wouldn't have been so sure. The evidence they have is compelling. It wouldn't be as cut and dry if I hadn't been with you at the time of the robbery."

Some of the light went out of his burning gaze, and the faint smile he'd managed to maintain died. His handsome face went blank, all emotion bleeding out, leaving me staring at a stranger. I didn't know who this blank, frozen version of Webb was, and it irritated me that I was the one who forced him to the forefront.

The adorable waitress popped back up at the side of the table. She practically put herself in Webb's lap when she dropped off his drink. She barely acknowledged me when I ordered a refill, and I had to grit my back teeth to stop from snapping at her when Webb's patented panty-dropping smile flashed in her direction before she walked away. I didn't realize how much I'd gotten used to that look being aimed in my direction until it was gone. I wasn't jealous. Nope. Not me. I wasn't jealous at all.

I blew out a breath of frustration and traced a drop of water down the side of my glass. "I'm going to find the person who did rob those banks. It's the only way Gage will let go of the idea of you being the perpetrator. He'll keep trying to pin those robberies on you, no matter what. All he cares about is closing the case and looking good to his superiors. He doesn't care if an innocent victim gets hurt along the way." I was far too familiar with how troublesome Gage Gordon's single-minded focus could be.

Webb took a drink and leaned back in his seat. His cotton shirt pulled tight across his broad chest and I realized Wyatt must have brought him a change of clothes. He wasn't wearing the black suit the FBI had picked him up in. The man looked good in his wedding finest, but he looked even better dressed down in faded jeans and a simple black T-shirt. He didn't need much to add to his natural charisma.

"That guy is a piece of work." One of his burnished eyebrows lifted and a small frown pulled at his mouth. "Not too sad things didn't work out between the two of you."

His words startled a laugh out of me. I put an elbow on the table and rested my chin in my hand as I watched him closely. "I'm not all that sad about it either. I would have been perfectly fine never having to breathe the same air as Agent Gordon ever again in my life."

The waitress slid into our space once again, dropped a plate of food in front of Webb, and purred that she would be happy to get him anything else he needed. There was a heavy emphasis on the *anything*. Luckily Webb didn't seem inclined to take her up on the offer. Instead, his focus stayed on me as he gave me an honestly puzzled look. "Can't quite figure out how a tool like Gordon ever talked you into his bed. He must have a way with words."

I narrowed my eyes at him. "What makes you think I wasn't the one who went after him? You don't know me nearly as well you think you do, Webb."

I bristled as he smirked at me from across the table. It wasn't his easy, careless grin, but it was better than the void of expression stamped all over his face before. "I guess I can't picture anyone jumping from a guy like Cyrus Warner to a douche like Gordon."

My eyebrows shot up to my hairline. Webb and I weren't exactly friends. I wasn't sure what we were. But we definitely weren't close enough for him to be privy to all the intimate details of my romantic history. I was a fiercely private person on the best of days. I didn't like anyone picking apart my past, especially when all the pieces were laid out, it didn't make the prettiest of pictures. But clearly, Webb knew just enough to make him dangerous.

"Maybe Gordon appealed at the time because he was the exact opposite of Cyrus Warner." It had taken me a very long time to realize exactly why I'd fallen so far and so fast for someone like Gage, when every instinct I possessed was screaming at me it was a terrible idea to get involved with him. "We all make mistakes."

Webb polished off the food in front of him and pushed his plate away. I was waiting for another interruption from the bubbly waitress, but Webb lifted a hand and subtly waved her off. He crossed his arms on the table in front of him and leaned toward me. "Oh, I know all about mistakes, Ten. I live my life between the one I just made and the one I'm about to make next. I'm not judging you. Just trying to figure you out." Some of the light lit back up in his brilliant eyes. "Been trying to do that since we first met. You don't make it easy."

No. I didn't. I wasn't sure I'd even figured out what made me tick, and I'd been after it a whole lot longer than Webb. But this conversation was fast approaching an area I wasn't ready to navigate, so I needed to switch the direction before we both said things we weren't ready for. "We don't need to know how the other works to keep you out of jail. What we need to know is how this person who has your face found you. He picked banks in Wyoming and Montana for a reason, and not just because they were located in remote locations. He had to know you were nearby. It wouldn't do him any good to hold up a bank in California when you're hundreds of miles away. He needed it to be plausible that you traveled to a location close to where you're currently living. So, who knows you were working on the ranch? Whom did you tell you were coming back to Wyoming?" Not me, obviously. If I'd known I would have been better prepared for the impact he had on my defenses.

The waitress snuck in to grab the empty plate and asked if we wanted a refill. Webb declined and asked for the check. The young woman's disappointment was palpable, and I fully expected the bill to be delivered with her phone number scrawled across it somewhere. But the gorgeous man sitting across from me had narrowed his focus entirely on me and the questions I fired off in his direction. I could see him rolling through a mental list of people he might have updated about his whereabouts. I got the distinct impression Webb didn't stay in any one place too long, so I doubted he was the type to cultivate deep, meaningful relationships along the way. I cringed when I realized I was silently judging him right after he promised me he wouldn't hold any of my poor choices from the past against me. He might be younger than me, but there were times he'd shown a hardened maturity that made me feel like a naïve idiot when I was around him.

"Wyatt knew. He's the only person I regularly keep updated. I'm sure he told Grady." Grady was Wyatt's former partner. "The Warners knew. I asked Cy directly if I could come fill in for Sutton when he left with Emrys for California."

I thought that through for a moment. "How did you know Sutton was leaving the ranch?" I wasn't aware the Warners kept in touch with Webb after the showdown in the woods. Not that Cy was in the habit of running things by me like he once had.

Webb lifted a shoulder and let it fall. I forced myself to look away from the way his muscles bunched and flexed enticingly. I wondered how the bullet hole had healed, if he had a scar. It wouldn't take away any of his appeal if he did. A scar or two would only add to the uncontrollable bad boy vibe he worked so well.

"I had Wyatt check up on everyone for me. Cy told him Sutton was in some trouble with the law so I decided to head back to the ranch to see if I could help out. Wyatt was pissed when he heard what was going on. I think he had words with the sheriff. The vibe between the two of them was so cold at the wedding, I could see my breath."

All the Warner brothers had run into a spot of trouble recently. Sutton, the middle brother, had been falsely accused of murdering his ex-girlfriend who was also his daughter's mother. The sheriff of Sheridan, Rodie Collins, was an old friend. I'd known him almost as long as I'd known Cy. He was tight with all the Warners, so I bet having Wyatt chew his ass hadn't helped an already difficult situation in the least. Plus, there was the clash of local versus federal law that always resulted in a pissing contest when dicks were whipped out.

I tilted my head to the side and started picking through all the bits and pieces of information laid out in front of me. "So Wyatt might have mentioned to Rodie you were coming back, and Rodie could have passed that info along to anyone who asked." I grimaced. "That's not good."

Webb grunted. "I also told my mother. She reached out asking for some cash, and I told her I was on the move. She asked where I was going. I told her I was headed to a ranch in Wyoming. Jesus. What if the guy tracked her down? He could have pretended to be me and she wouldn't even have known the difference. I haven't seen her in years. We're practically strangers. He could have lied to her so easily."

His words pierced my heart. I wondered if he knew how sad he sounded when he mentioned his mom. "That's probably the most likely scenario. Maybe he tracked her down first and was just as surprised as you to find out he had an exact double out there in the world." I frowned at him. "You need to touch base with your mother and ask her about it. Wouldn't hurt to ask about a twin either. If we can get her to give Gordon a statement, it would get him off your back for a little bit, if not for good."

Webb sighed heavily and lifted a hand to his forehead. He dragged his palm down the center of his face, and I noticed he suddenly looked exhausted. He blinked at me slowly and shook his head like he was trying to clear it. A stray lock of gold hair flopped loose and dangled in front of one of his eyes. I felt my heart stumble and my fingers literally itched to reach out and push it back where it belonged. I fought and refrained. I had a sinking feeling if I ever put my hands on Webb, he wouldn't be able to pry them loose. I wasn't going to be one of the people who passed in and out of his life, borrowing him. No. If he ever let me, I would own him. I'd keep him. I'd force him to stay still, and those thoughts absolutely terrified me. I'd never wanted someone like this before, not Cy, not Gage, no one.

"Wyatt's been trying to get ahold of her since I was taken into custody. She's not a normal mom, Ten. She doesn't know what the word means. She runs from us the same way she runs from the law, and whomever she's done wrong that particular month. Getting answers from her won't be as easy as it seems." He sounded both frustrated and defeated at the same time. I didn't need to know him inside and out to see Webb was at his limit.

I snatched the bill from in front of him. Sure enough, there was a phone number scrawled in big, loopy handwriting across the bottom of it. I scrawled my name and room number to take care of the bill before he could protest, and possibly before he could catch sight of the phone number. Nope. Not jealous at all. "We have to start somewhere. Get some rest. We can work on a game plan in the morning."

He nodded slowly. "Thanks for dinner."

I climbed to my feet, pausing next to his chair, forcing him to look up at me. Despite knowing better, I reached out and pushed that rebellious lock of hair off his forehead. I heard his breath catch as I felt mine still. "I'm glad I'm here, too, Webb."

There was no other place I wanted to be until I knew he was no longer neck-deep in trouble, even if I could see things were about to go totally sideways for me.

CHAPTER 4

WEBB

I DIDN'T SLEEP WELL.

It had nothing to do with the knowledge I had a brother I'd never met, a twin no less, one who was out there committing serious felonies and angling to get me locked up. It wasn't because the brother I did know about was snoring like a locomotive in the bed across from mine. My restlessness didn't stem from the fact I'd turned down the pretty waitress from the bar when she immediately slipped into the chair Ten vacated. The young woman was pretty, flirty, obviously interested in keeping me company for a couple of sweaty, fun hours, but I couldn't say yes. More than that, I didn't want to take her up on her offer. No, the reason I couldn't sleep had everything to do with the way Ten stopped and pushed my hair out of my eyes before leaving me alone in the bar.

It was the first time she'd ever touched me simply because she wanted to. I wasn't bleeding to death, or falling on my face as I tried to navigate my way around the uneven terrain of the ranch. She wasn't helping me. She'd put her hands on me willingly, and the tiny, soft brush of her fingers burned all the way through my body. I felt the heat in places which had nothing to do with my forehead. The immediate, intense reaction would have been embarrassing if she'd stuck around long enough to notice the effect she had on me. I was no saint or shy virgin. Actually, the furthest thing from either of those. I'd learned very early on in my youth how to use my looks and my charm to score a free meal and a warm place to sleep. For the most part, the women who moved in and out of my life were a means to an end. And I always tried to let them know up front they were there because they responded to me and were willing to meet whatever need I currently had. I wasn't made to be anyone's hero or the answer to anyone's prayers. I was there for a good time and a few hours of normal in a world filled with the opposite, nothing more and nothing less. I wasn't the one who ended up discombobulated. I wasn't the one left longing, wanting, waiting. Tennyson McKenna didn't play by my rules. Of course, I'm not sure why I ever expected her to.

When she told me point blank she would have doubted my innocence if I hadn't been attached to her hip during one of the robberies, I was surprised how much the admission hurt. She'd never gone out of her way to pretend or play like she found me anything but annoying. I didn't think she was twisted up in knots over me the way I was over her, but hearing how she believed I could actually pull a weapon on a room full of innocent people stabbed at one of the few soft spots I still had. I wasn't a good man by anyone's standard, but the only person I'd ever purposely hurt was myself. I grew up watching my mother give zero shits about anyone but herself, and those hard lessons had burned a few holes of humanity into my soul. I might blow through life with little regard for the people and places I left behind, but I was careful not to involve anyone else in my ongoing dance with disaster.

Sure, I had a rap sheet, a criminal record as thick as a damn Bible. There were times I did things I regretted in order to survive, but I'd always done my best to make sure my crimes were victimless. I'd been picked up for a variety of things in my teens: solicitation, assault, shoplifting, possession. I'd been a lot better about not getting caught when I got older, and the last time I'd had a run in with the law was when I was busted running an illegal poker game for a guy out of Vegas. I was the one who took the fall, and since I wouldn't give over the name of the man in charge, I sat behind bars for a couple of months until Wyatt finagled some kind of deal and managed to get me out. No, I wasn't a good guy, but I wasn't a bad one either. I hated that Ten believed the worst, but then she touched me like I was something special, and it sent all the anger and resentment building inside of me flying into a million pieces. She messed me up in a way no one ever had. Sometimes I felt like *she* was playing *me*. Since I was the master of game, it pissed me off that I couldn't figure out what moves to make to get ahead of her next diversion. Game or no, I wasn't accustomed to losing.

Since I was already up, I hopped in the shower before Wyatt stopped snoring. While the warm water worked some of the tension out of my shoulders, it did nothing to lessen the way my cock throbbed and pulled tight. I'd been under lock and key for close to a week. There hadn't been an opportunity to take care of business under the watchful eye of Ten's ex, and I wasn't about to let this opportunity slip through my fingers, both literally and figuratively. Knowing my brother was a fairly light sleeper, I clamped my bottom lip between my teeth and slicked my hand around the heavy length of my cock.

It was so easy to close my eyes and remember the way Ten's fingers felt brushing across my forehead. I felt like I'd been waiting for her to touch me all my life. I was dying to feel her hand on me, her mouth equally as much. I'd been in this position before, my hand wrapped around my cock, Ten on my mind, as I pictured all the dirty, sexy things we could do with one another. That was one of the reasons I was undeniably attracted to the tall blonde. She was just so . . . capable. Tough as nails, fearless, and strong, she held her own in any situation, and I couldn't remember ever being as impressed as I was around her. She was the type of person who gave as good as she got, and I wanted her to unleash everything she had on me. I knew she would go just as hard as whomever she ended up in bed with, and for months in my fantasies, that man was me.

It was me who had Ten's long ass legs wrapped around my waist as she writhed and panted underneath me. I was the one with his hands in her long, pale hair. I was the man she watched with those jade-colored eyes. I got to have my fill of her perfectly milky and unblemished skin. I got to drown in the taste of her. I was sure it was a mixture of sunshine and something sweet. I would try not to die from utter pleasure the first time my body slid inside hers. I knew she would be hotter than an inferno and so fucking soft. Ten was a strong woman, her body tight and fit. I would offer up a limb to feel all those lean muscles straining and pushing against mine. I would give up everything to watch her come apart in my hands. She was so structured, severe even. All I wanted was to see her unravel bit by bit because of me.

Behind my eyelids the scene played out, picking up speed and heat. At one point in my imagination, Ten was on her knees in front of me, and my dick was so deep in her mouth I could practically see the outline in her throat. It was filthy and so good, my hand squeezed around the base of my erection so I didn't shoot before I was ready. I wanted a couple more minutes to play with the tip, imagining Ten's tongue sliding against the leaking slit and tracing the long line that ran underneath. It was the vision of her brushing her hands softly over my balls, the same way she'd touched my forehead, that made it impossible to hold back my orgasm.

It was good. It always was when I thought about her. I let my head drop under the water and sucked in a breath to get my breathing under control. It took a few seconds to remember I was supposed to be in the shower getting clean. I rushed through the rest of washing up and groaned when I heard Wyatt moving around on the other side of the door. I was pretty sure I'd forgotten to be quiet there at the end, but I was well past the point of being embarrassed. Wyatt knew I was harboring something which felt so much bigger than a youthful crush on the pretty forest ranger. He'd mentioned more than once he didn't think I had a chance with her. I was determined to prove him wrong.

I exited the bathroom dressed in jeans and nothing else. I was rubbing a towel over my wet hair, so I didn't realize someone else was in the room until I heard Ten's voice.

"I called Rodie last night. I asked him if someone called around to see if Webb had been in Sheridan recently. He told me no one called him directly, but he said he would ask the rest of the deputies to see if any of them had heard anything. He also told me he would keep an eye out for anyone who looks like Webb hanging around." She made a noise as I dropped the towel to my shoulders. "Maybe you should get a tattoo or something, so it'll be easier to tell the two of you apart."

Wyatt was dressed in a pair of cargo pants and a black thermal shirt. He sat on his bed, and there was a tall cup of coffee in his hand and a box of doughnuts in front of him. Ten was sitting on the edge of my bed. She had a pastry in her hand, but it seemed forgotten as her gaze roved over my bare chest and low-slung jeans. I quirked an eyebrow in her direction and watched as she swallowed hard, turning her attention to her doughnut. Trying to subtly recover from her ogling, she mentioned, "I forgot about the scar from the gunshot. I'll call Rodie and tell him you have a scar on your right shoulder if he needs something to determine identity."

Liar. She was paying attention to the way I looked without my shirt on. I hid my smile as I moved deeper into the room.

Wyatt yawned and sleepily grumbled, "Your sheriff is an idiot."

Ten bristled and pointed at my brother with her doughnut. "Rodie was a Recon Marine. He isn't *just* some backwoods, small-town sheriff. He cares about his town and the people in it. I've worked in law enforcement, Wyatt. I know not everyone with a badge operates that way."

Wyatt grunted but looked away. "Thank you for bringing breakfast. You and Webb were both up early."

I turned my back on both of them so I could find one of the shirts Wyatt brought for me. I tugged the dark gray Henley over my head and pushed my fingers through my damp hair. I knew it was going to dry sticking up all over the place, but I had bigger things to worry about.

I plopped down on the end of Wyatt's bed and dug through the box of doughnuts. I took a cardboard cup from Ten and inhaled the addictive aroma.

Ten cleared her throat. "I didn't sleep well last night. I hate it when there's a puzzle I can't figure out."

I lifted my eyes to her and cocked my head as we silently regarded each other. She had faint, dark smudges under her eyes, and she looked a shade paler than she normally did. I wondered if she'd been up thinking about me the way I'd tossed and turned thinking about her.

The tiny frown lines between her eyebrows had me think she was wondering if I'd left the bar alone. It was on the tip of my tongue to assure her it had been me and Wyatt in this room, but something held the words back. I didn't want her to think the worst of me when I'd never given her a reason to. I owned the mistakes from my past, and I would own the ones I was bound to make going forward.

"If we don't have anything to go on in Wyoming, our best bet is to head to Texas and try and track down Jolene, or at least that motorcycle club she was hanging around last I heard." Wyatt sounded like he would rather eat glass. He hadn't seen our mother since the day she left home when he was right around sixteen or seventeen. I knew it went against everything inside of him to actively track down Jolene Bryant.

I reached out and clapped a hand on his shoulder. "You don't have to do anything else, Wyatt. I can go to Loveless and trace Mom's steps. You've done enough, and I'm not talking about right now. My entire life you've always been there making sure I never fell too far, protecting me from everything and everyone. Let me protect you from Mom." I felt him stiffen under my hand, but he wasn't quick enough to hide the flare of relief that sparked to life in his eyes. "Besides, you don't need to miss any more work or hurt your reputation by being tied to a federal bank robbery investigation. I've got this. Trust me."

He was going to protest. I could see it before he got the words out. Luckily, I had reinforcements. "I'm going to go with him, Wyatt. I'll see this through till the end. I'm not going to let Gage Gordon bully another innocent man into a conviction. I don't have a place to start with the twin, but I bet I can track down your mother with a solid lead. It's what I do."

"I don't need a babysitter." I scowled at both of them.

In unison, they both fired back, "Yes, you do."

"What about your job? How can you take off for an undetermined amount of time?" My brother used his cop voice on Ten, but she appeared to be immune.

"I have a ton of vacation and sick days saved up. And right now things are slowing down before the summer vacationers start to show up. Plus, I helped break up a nationwide sex trafficking ring a couple months ago. My boss isn't going to hassle me for taking a few personal days. He always tells me he's so glad I came back and how overqualified I am to find lost hikers and monitor fire dangers." She grinned. "He knows he's lucky to have me."

I could see Wyatt struggling to relinquish control. He'd been the one watching my back for so long, it couldn't be easy for him to hand that task over to someone else, someone who wasn't blood-related. I squeezed his shoulder harder and forced him to look me directly in the eye.

"You don't have to see her. I don't want you anywhere near her. Let me shield you for once." He was practically vibrating under my hand, but I could see he was going to cave. Our mother tried to destroy him, and if she got another chance, who was to say she wouldn't succeed?

"You have to keep me updated every step of the way. And you have to promise to call me if you get in trouble, any kind of trouble." Wyatt's voice was gruff, and there was a faint tremor buried inside of it.

I nodded. "I promise. I'm not going off half-cocked. I have to figure this out. The only person who gets to fuck my life up is me. Not some cheap imitation of me."

He laughed like I intended. We simultaneously turned to look at Ten. She was regarding us both with curious eyes.

I lifted an eyebrow in her direction. "We doing this?"

After a minute she dipped her chin in agreement. "We're doing it."

Holy shit. We were really going to do this. I was about to dive headfirst into the nightmare of my childhood, and I was taking the woman I was certain might define my future with me.

What could possibly go wrong?

CHAPTER 5

TEN

I WAS PRACTICALLY BENT IN half. My head was down, if my hair hadn't been pulled up in a messy knot on the top of my head, the ends would've brushed the floor of the airplane. My eyes were pinched shut, and the friendly, male flight attendant kept coming by to see if I needed another drink. At least that was his pretense. I was pretty sure the reason he was focused so intently on our aisle was because of the man sitting next to me. It seemed both sexes were putty in the blond man's hands. I had no idea how Webb schmoozed both of us into the first class cabin, but I was eternally grateful.

 I wasn't a good flier. I hated the confined space and the feeling of people stacked on top of more people. I felt like I couldn't breathe from takeoff to landing. The freak-out started as soon as I got through security and usually lasted until I reached my destination. Webb must have noticed something was wrong, because he'd started working to get us upgraded when we checked in. The drinks in first class helped some. What really made a huge difference was the warm hand on the center of my back rubbing slow circles and the deep voice uttering quiet reassurances every couple of minutes. I figured he would tease me. I was supposed to be fearless and brave. I wasn't supposed to fall apart and turn into a quivering mess over something as simple as flying.

As he was prone to do, Webb defied all my expectations. Instead of teasing and taunting, he was steady and reassuring. For the first time, I didn't feel like I was suffocating. I was still a shaking, nervous train wreck, but somehow, his unwavering calm and the warmth of his touch kept me from melting down.

"The only two things I'm scared of are flying and needles. I hate going to the doctor almost as much as I hate this." I let out a shaky breath and slowly turned my head so I could look at Webb. His head was bent toward me, his eyes filled with concern and compassion. He was big and broad enough that even the considerably larger, first class seat was dwarfed by his size. He didn't appear to have much extra room. However, I found the way he filled the space comforting. Whenever I breathed in, I inhaled Webb's scent. He smelled like pine and something dark and mysterious. It reminded me of the woods where I worked. It took me to all the hidden places far away from everyone where I managed to hide.

"Not worried about spiders or snakes?" There was humor in Webb's tone, and I almost purred when his palm slid up my back and stopped at the neck. His strong fingers gave the tense muscles a squeeze as his thumb pressed a hard line into the top of my shoulder. Had I not been so anxiety-ridden over this trip, I would've melted into a puddle at his feet.

"I work in the wilderness. I run across snakes and spiders more often than I run across humans." Often they were less deadly.

Webb chuckled as he continued to stroke my neck. "I hate snakes. They were everywhere around the swamp near where we lived when I was little. To this day, anything that slithers sends me running the other way."

Taking a breath, I forced myself to sit up straight. I thought the motion would have Webb dropping the hold he had on me. Instead, he used it to tug me closer. Our noses were almost touching, and

I was so close I could see the stray bolts of silver shot throughout his blindingly blue gaze.

"You okay?" His concern was sweet, and it sent my insides into a slow slide. All morning, I'd remembered how he looked when he walked out of the bathroom half naked. I knew he was fit, there was no disguising the way his biceps bulged or the way his strong thighs and perfect ass flexed when he walked. I hadn't been prepared for the more-than-a-six-pack, the honey-colored skin, the light dusting of golden hair that flared across his sculpted pectorals and narrowed down between a perfect V into the waistband of his low-slung jeans. He was a walking wet dream, too hot to handle, and he knew it. He knew I was staring, that I couldn't look away if I wanted to. I didn't. I could've stared at him all day. More than that, I could've touched him for hours. I wanted to memorize every line and dip of his body with my fingertips.

Blushing, I nodded. "I'll be fine. Just keep me distracted." It wasn't a terribly long flight to Austin from Denver. Close to two hours. It shouldn't be a challenge for Webb to keep my mind off the fact I was hurtling through the air in a hollow, metal tube. "You grew up in a swamp? Where exactly?" I needed a distraction . . . I also needed to know more about his past so I could help save his future.

Webb made a noise low in his throat and leaned back in his seat. When the flirty flight attendant swung by to check on us, Webb ordered a bloody Mary and got me another vodka and soda. Apparently talking about his childhood required some liquid courage. Once we had our drinks, Webb looked at me out of the corner of his eye.

"Nothing about my childhood was normal. The first memory I really have is of Wyatt pulling a chair across a filthy kitchen so he could climb on the counter and look for food. He was six or seven at the time, and already worried about how he was going to keep me alive. Our mom was never around, and when she was, it wasn't good. Some people shouldn't be allowed to have children; Jolene Bryant is one of them." His deep voice dropped an octave, and there was a harsh rasp to it which indicated how hard this topic was for him to talk about. My heart throbbed painfully, thinking of the two little boys having to scavenge for food and fend for themselves. "We lived in a small parish outside of New Orleans until I was around nine. Mom had a small house, a shack, really, built on her family's land. It was far enough out of the way, there weren't nosey neighbors or too many visits from the law. It was also close enough to the city that Mom never had a problem finding trouble. Wyatt and I played in the swamp pretty much every day. It wasn't like Jolene bothered to buy us toys or take us anywhere. I don't know what she did that was bad enough to have her family turn their collective back on her, but she packed Wyatt and me up in the middle of the night and ran like the hounds of Hell were after her."

"Sounds terrifying." I couldn't imagine what it was like to lose everything at such a tender age for no apparent reason. My family had been on the land bordering the Warner's ranch going back to Manifest Destiny. Our roots run deep. So deep it was almost impossible to pull them from the Wyoming soil. It'd felt like I was going to die when I struggled to pull mine free so many years ago.

"The first time it happened, I was scared to death. She wouldn't tell us where we were going or how long it was going to take to get there. She made us leave the little we had behind. Wyatt was so angry. No one interfered with him taking care of me in the swamp. He was scared someone was going to separate us, that someone was going to notice what a shit parent Jolene was. All we had was each other, and he wasn't about to let me go." Webb seemed to sink into the memories. His gaze went a little unfocused, and the hand resting on the back of my neck stopped gently rubbing and tightened to a nearly painful hold. "We didn't stay in the new place very long. Jolene set up a pattern of behavior. We would blow into a new town, she'd find herself whatever kind of trouble she could, and we'd leave in the middle of the night. We never stayed in any one place for more than a couple years."

He sighed and leaned his head back on the seat. "Wyatt hated it. Hated changing schools, trying to figure out how to survive in a new place over and over again. When he was a teenager, he told Mom we weren't going with her anymore. I was just a kid, and he'd been more of a parent to me than she ever had. He got a job delivering pizzas and tricked Mom into signing a lease on a crap studio apartment in the ghetto. He moved both of us in and promised me we wouldn't have to move again. Jolene drifted in and out of our lives for a couple of years after that, Wyatt started talking about joining the military, and I did whatever I had to in order to make sure I stayed with my brother."

He let his hand fall, but I caught it in mine before he could curl it into a fist to match the other one clenched on his leg. I brushed my thumb over his knuckles and watched as a muscle twitched in the curved line of his jaw.

"Mom popped up one afternoon when Wyatt was at the apartment with his boyfriend. He was a nice kid, liked Wyatt, despite all the weirdness of our home life and the fact he was pretty much raising me. It was his first sense of normalcy. It was the first time he'd let someone other than me in. Jolene lost her mind. She was a fucking nightmare, but she was also at her core an old-school southern woman brought up in a very narrow-minded way. She flew off the handle. Scared the crap out of Wyatt's boyfriend, threatened to kill him, told him she was going to burn him alive. He bolted and never spoke to Wyatt again. But Jolene had plenty to say. She accused Wyatt of being unnaturally attached to me. Called him a pervert and a pedophile. She came unglued when he told her point blank he was gay. She tried to attack him, but by then, both Wyatt and I had filled out and learned to fight back. He kicked Jolene out of the apartment and told her never to show her face again. She left, but not before promising to have Wyatt arrested. He never did anything wrong, but he freaked. This time when we went on the run, it was just me and Wyatt. He dropped out of school, and both of us spent a lot of hard months living on the streets avoiding any kind of law enforcement and authority figure."

I couldn't stop the gasp that tumbled out. My fingers tightened on his hand involuntarily, and I knew the minimal color I'd gotten back in my cheeks was now gone. "You were homeless? As teenagers?" It was horrible and so unfair. My insides twisted uncomfortably thinking about everything both Bryant boys had been through.

Webb nodded. "Yeah. Wyatt was scared Jolene had convinced the cops to arrest him. We were young and stupid. At the time it made sense. Eventually, Wyatt got his GED and joined the Army." He cleared his throat suddenly and shifted his eyes away from mine. I watched in amazement as a hot, red flush worked its way up his neck and into his face. "By then I'd hooked up with a woman who was a lot older than me. I'd learned how to use what I had to get what I needed. She didn't care if I was barely educated and a petty criminal. All she cared about was the fact that I was pretty and could fuck all night."

I tried to keep my expression bland but I was slightly horrified by his confession. I was angry he was put in a position to be victimized in such a way, even though I doubted he would see it in that light. He would call it surviving. His confession helped me see his careless flirting in a whole new light. He wasn't used to being taken seriously by the opposite sex, so somewhere along the line he'd stopped trying to forge any kind of real connection with anyone.

"I promised Wyatt I would be fine. He'd already given up so much for me. I refused to weigh him down any longer. I stayed with her until I managed to squeak through high school. By then she was bored and looking for another toy anyway. Wyatt figured out his path in the Army, and I never regretted doing what I had to do to get off the streets and send him off. I guess I'm still looking for the road I'm meant to be on. I never stopped hopping around from place to place, and unfortunately, Jolene's knack for finding trouble seems to run pretty strong in my genes. I hate that I take after her as much as I do."

It was a lot of very heavy, dense information to process at once. I copied his pose, sort of flopped back in the seat, eyes not really seeing as my mind whirred in a million directions. I knew Webb's journey to Wyoming hadn't been an easy one, but I had no idea just how rough the road he'd traveled had been.

"I used to dream about leaving home." My voice cracked a little, so I reached for my drink. I was still holding Webb's hand. I had no intention of letting it go. "My brothers never understood it. Why I wanted more than a constantly struggling ranch and a place with a single honky-tonk and one street light." I gulped when I remembered the endless hours I'd spent arguing with my various family members about my future. "It was easy to let them believe I was chasing after a boy. For them, it made more sense for me to leave because Cyrus was leaving. None of my family could understand the need I had for a life of my own. When I left, I told them I wouldn't be back, and I believed it."

Webb turned his hand over, so our palms were pressed together. He laced our fingers together, and I felt the warmth from the simple gesture shoot up my arm.

"Coming back was the hardest thing I've ever had to do. Most days I feel like a stranger in the house I grew up in." It was uncomfortable and awkward. I told myself I was going to get my own place, but then I was admitting I was staying in Sheridan, that I was giving up on a different life. Every time I told myself I was going to look for a place away from my family's ranch, I talked myself out of it. "I think I had an idea of what would happen when I came home. Cy's first marriage had ended, we were both single, and we were both back in a place we didn't want to be. I was sure this time things were going to work out. I honestly thought we would leave together once and for all."

Webb nudged my shoulder with his. When I forced myself to meet his gaze, I was surprised by the flash of sympathy I saw reflected there. "Didn't work out that way, did it?"

I shook my head. "No. I don't think it was ever meant to. Watching him with Leo, Cy was never like that with me or his first wife. She really does bring out the best in him. It isn't about where he is when he's with her. It could be Antarctica or the middle of Castro in San Francisco. As long as he's with her, it's the best place on the planet. I was tied directly to a place he could never get away from, and when we were together, neither one of us ever forgot where we were or where we'd been." I sighed and offered him a weak grin. "Our childhoods couldn't have been more different."

He lifted our joined hands and pressed a light kiss to the back of mine. It was a small touch, a barely there brush of his lips, but the contact sent flames of awareness and desire shooting up my arm.

"I wouldn't wish Jolene on my worst enemy. Both our childhoods left us wanting. I'm grateful yours didn't force you into a position where you had to do questionable things to keep your head above water. I think it's pretty special you've always been one of the good guys . . . good women . . . good people. I haven't met many people like you along the way." He shrugged after running through all the options.

His consideration made me smile. "I've never met anyone like you either, Webb. Every time I think I have you figured out, you throw me a curveball and I'm back to square one."

His pale eyebrows shot up and the grin he was wearing turned into something seductive and sexy. "If you want to round the bases, Ten, all you gotta do is ask. You don't have to put that much effort into scoring with me."

I felt myself blush and tugged my hand free. I smoothed my damp palm down my jeans. This man got to me so easily. He set me off balance and scrambling to get myself under control.

"You are such a flirt, Webb." I tried to keep my words stern. They were breathless instead.

"I am. But when I say that stuff to you, I mean it." He turned his shoulders a little so he was facing me as much as the small space allowed. "Did I ever tell you, I thought you were a dream the first time I saw you? I was delirious, in pain, worried sick about Wyatt, and suddenly the prettiest girl in the entire world was standing in front of me, looking pissed as hell. I couldn't figure out how I'd conjured you in the middle of the woods like that. You took my breath away, and I've been trying to catch it ever since."

No one talked to me like that. No one said those kinds of things about me, especially a guy who had his pick of bed partners. I wasn't anyone's first choice or the kind of woman they gave up everything for. My sharply honed defenses snapped into place, and my spine stiffened, so I was sitting straight as an arrow.

"Listen, I want to help you. I'm here for you, and I will not let Gage pull his typical bullshit on you, but I'm not in any position to be your next sugar mama. I can barely take care of myself most days. I definitely don't want to take care of someone else." The admission faded out to nothing as Webb jerked back around in his seat and leaned as far away from me as possible. His jaw locked into a furious line, and I swear I could hear his teeth grinding together and his breaths whoosh in and out in angry puffs, making his nostrils flare.

"First of all," his words bit out hard as nails. "You aren't that much older than me." Six years felt like a lot for some reason, but

I knew it would be insignificant if our roles were reversed. Cyrus had several years on Leo, and one of my brothers had married a woman a decade younger than him. Our age difference was an easy excuse to deflect him when I was feeling particularly weak. "Second, if you'd been paying attention at all over the last few months, you would've picked up on the fact that I'm the one trying to take care of *you* for a change. You're too stubborn to see what's right in front of you, Ten. It's easier for you to keep me at a distance, to give me the runaround, so that's what you do."

I wanted to retort that he had no idea what he was talking about, but just then the pilot came over the intercom, telling us we would be landing in twenty minutes. The entire flight had slipped by unnoticed while Webb opened the doors to his past for me.

I dropped my head and panted my way through the landing, this time without the comfort of Webb's touch and the sound of his soothing, rumbled promises that it would all be okay.

It wasn't easy to keep him at a safe distance. I worked at it very hard. He would never know how difficult it was for me to fight against his allure every minute of every day. And I doubted he would believe me if I told him I was doing it more for him than for me. I didn't know how to be someone's dream girl. I was far more used to being the woman men settled for when they couldn't get the one they really wanted. I was the one usually getting the runaround, not the one giving it.

CHAPTER 6

WEBB

WE BOTH ONLY HAD CARRY-ONS, so it was easy to grab our stuff and get through the Austin airport. We trudged to the rental car area, picked up the SUV I'd rented and drove the first fifty miles east, toward Loveless, Texas, without exchanging a single word. The tension pulsing between the two of us was like a living, breathing thing. I could feel the thorns of unease wrapped around us and the chill against my skin. Out of the corner of my eye, I could see Ten tugging on her lower lip as she purposely refused to look in my direction. For a split second, after she accused me of looking for another sugar mama when I turned my attention to her, I'd seen her desire to snatch the words back. She hadn't. She also hadn't offered up an apology, which was both frustrating and annoying.

I hadn't shown her my soft, unprotected underbelly only to have her stab a knife into it and twist. I didn't shake all my skeletons out of the closet so she could judge me for them. Those bones were dusty and long forgotten.

The fact of the matter was, I'd always gravitated to people who were older than me. Wyatt was my best, and often my only, friend. He was four years older, but we were both wise beyond our years. When I was young and hungry, I recognized I was looking for a supportive figure in the older women who took me in. Sure, they wanted sex, but I was in it for totally different reasons. As an adult, I didn't blindly let anyone offer me comfort and care, but I still drifted toward women who had a little more experience and were savvy about all the cruel ways the world worked. I like maturity and independence in the women I chase, and in the ones I let catch me. I wasn't bullshitting Ten when I told her she was the kind of woman I dreamed about: unquestionably beautiful, but so much more. I liked that she was a fighter, a woman who stood her ground and refused to be swayed. I was also totally into the way she kept resisting me. I liked the challenge. Until she went from carefully evading me to forcefully pushing me away. I wasn't going to apologize for my past to anyone. Not even her. It would be the equivalent of saying "sorry I survived," and while I had regrets, I wasn't disappointed I'd made it this far. I was pretty proud of the fact, considering how much trouble loved me.

"It looks like there's a fairly decent motel on the outskirts of the town. We should stop there and see if we can get a couple of rooms since we don't know how long we'll be here. We need a base of operations." Ten looked up from her phone, and I nodded to indicate I heard her and agreed. "I think it's best we split up and hit the ground running. I can go talk to the local law enforcement and see if they know anything. If your mom attracted trouble as easily as you said, there's a chance they ran across her while she was in town. You take the motorcycle club she was hanging around."

"Not all motorcycle clubs are involved with criminal activities. Most are good men who just need an outlet, like to get together to ride, and show off their bikes." I wasn't sure which category the club called Sons of Sorrow fell into. I'd looked them up briefly when Jolene mentioned whom she was staying with, but I needed to do a little research before I rolled up asking questions. I knew they were primarily based in the West and throughout the Southwest. The biggest chapter was in Denver, and the president was somewhat of a local legend in the surrounding area. If I'd had more time, I would have tried to track him down and work my way into a formal introduction, which would've lessened the likelihood of me getting my ass beat by a bunch of badass bikers.

Ten sighed quietly and jerked her head up so she was staring straight out the windshield, not looking in my direction at all. "I didn't suggest you go talk to them because of that. I know most bikers are decent people and they do a lot for their communities. I suggested you go talk to them because no matter how enlightened and politically correct certain members may be, it's still a boys' club. There is no way I can walk in there and get the same answers you can."

Oh. She had a point. They would take one look at her and those endlessly long legs and lose all ability to speak, just like the rest of the heterosexual male population. They probably wouldn't want to let her go.

"Fair enough. I've had my fill of people wearing badges lately anyway. Knowing my luck, I'd end up behind bars as soon as I walked into the sheriff's office." I tapped my fingers on the steering wheel, turning my head slightly when she muttered my name under her breath.

"Webb," she cocked her head to the side and looked at me hesitantly out of the corner of her eye. "I'm sorry I said what I did on the plane. I don't think you're looking for an older woman to take care of you. It was a low blow to turn your words against you when you were so open and trusting with me."

"My past isn't pretty, but there isn't anything I can do about it. I know exactly where I came from and I know exactly who I am because of it. I'm long past the point where I'm ashamed of what I had to do to survive. What pisses me off the most is you not believing I could be into you for any other reason than to have you take care of me. It's like you are completely oblivious to how stunning, smart, and strong you are. How can you not recognize your own value? How do you not see how special you are? You have men falling at your feet everywhere you go, but you step over them without a second glance. I thought I was making headway, getting you to see me because I refused to give up, but I'm just another obstacle you're skirting around."

I watched as she put an unsteady hand on the center of her chest and pushed. It was almost like she was trying to keep her heart in place. She blinked a couple of times, then let out another long, slow breath.

"You said I'm one of the good guys." A tentative smile flirted with her mouth as she repeated my stumbling statement. "But it's not really true. I'm selfish. I'm stubborn to a fault. And unlike you, I deliberately hurt people to protect myself. You said it yourself, even when you were doing things you didn't want to so you could stay alive, you did your best not to hurt anyone who was innocent. That's not me. I worry about myself, and I generally have no trouble walking away from the casualties. Does that sound like a good person, someone special?"

No. It sounded to me like she was confused and seeing herself through someone else's broken filter.

I tightened my hold on the steering wheel and made note that the exit for the motel was only a few miles up the road. Everything out here looked the same. Flat. It wasn't all that different than certain parts of Wyoming. Even the cattle and fences lining the sides of the road were pretty familiar. It was like a completely different world once we left the outskirts of Austin. At least Ten and I would fit in fairly well. There was nothing worse than rolling into a small town and being immediately identified as an outsider. The chances of getting information out of anyone dropped dramatically when they believed you were an interloper there to judge a different way of life.

"It sounds like you've been hurt and you're willing to do

anything to avoid having it happen again. We've both done things when we're desperate and afraid. I'm not going to question why you do what you do, Ten. But you need to know I have no plans to hurt you. Hurting you is the last thing I think about when it comes to you and me." I took the exit and swerved into the parking lot of the motel a moment later. It was right off the main road, and the building looked like it had seen better days. It was weather-beaten and a bit rundown, but there were plenty of cars in the parking lot and no police tape in sight, so it would do for a couple of days.

"I don't understand why you're thinking about us at all. I thought I made it pretty clear nothing was ever going to happen between us." Ten huffed out the statement in obvious aggravation, but as always, there was no real heat or refusal in her tone.

I wasn't one of those guys who believed every 'no' actually meant 'yes.' I was aware enough to know I wasn't every woman's cup of tea. I'd faced rejection in my life, just like everyone had. The only reason I couldn't take Ten's words at face value was because the words she said never quite lined up with what she wasn't saying. There was the way her gaze lingered full of longing when she thought I wouldn't notice. There was the way she always seemed to find me, no matter where I was working on the ranch. Even if it was simply so she could walk away, she still seemed drawn to me, which didn't fit at all with her insistence that nothing was happening between us.

"You're clear as mud most days. It's okay, though. I like to get dirty." I stopped the SUV in front of the motel office and turned to her with a grin. "Do we need two rooms?"

Ten threw open her car door and gave me a sharp look. "Yes, we do. I'll take care of it."

I didn't bother to argue. Wyatt was the one who paid for our plane tickets to Austin. They weren't cheap since they were last minute. I knew he felt guilty heading back to his regularly scheduled life when mine was immersed in chaos. The tickets were a small way he could remain involved while keeping his distance from Jolene. I was going to have to call him and let him know we'd reached the first stop on this bizarre scavenger hunt.

Ten came out of the office a few minutes later, tossing a wave over her shoulder. She climbed back into the SUV, handing over the card key. "I got directions to both the sheriff's office and the compound where the club hangs out. The guy behind the desk mentioned the guys who are part of the club are mostly friendly. A lot of them are former military. He said you shouldn't run into trouble if you aren't looking to *start* trouble when you head out there." She sounded relieved by the revelation.

We took a few minutes to go to our separate rooms and toss our stuff down. It was a basic room, but clean, and everything on the inside looked ten years newer than the exterior led one to believe. I shot my brother a text, letting him know my plan for the day. I got back a short:

~ Be careful.

I promised Wyatt I would, then sent Ten a message letting her know I was ready to get the show on the road. She met me at the SUV. We agreed I would drop her off in town at the sheriff's office and then drive out to the compound. She seemed slightly nervous when we discussed splitting up for the rest of the day. It was the only option we had, though, so she didn't say anything. She was silently tapping away on her phone as I drove back on the main road into Loveless.

The town wasn't much to talk about. It actually reminded me a lot of Sheridan, the closest "big" town to the Warner Ranch. There was one main road dotted with shops and various other businesses. There was a bank, one bar, and not much else. It was no thriving metropolis, even if it was a sight bigger than home. People would call it charming and quaint. I called it tiny and tight knit. If my mom blew through here with her typical destructive ways, there was no way the people here hadn't noticed.

The sheriff's office was located at the far end of the main street. It was a newer building, one of the few painted a color other than white. There were several big pickup trucks parked out front as well as SUVs with police decals on the sides. I rolled to a stop and turned to tell Ten good luck schmoozing the cops, but before I could get the words out, she reached across the space separating us and put her hand on my bicep. Of course, I flexed the minute her fingers made contact. I wasn't about to let an opportunity pass me by.

Ten's golden eyebrows shot up, and a half smile twisted one side of her mouth. "I've seen you without your shirt on; I'm already impressed." She showed me her phone. "I was texting a former coworker who works in the National Gang Unit of the FBI. They keep a running database of pretty much every organized unit of people across the country. I asked her for the 'must-have' info on the Sons of Sorrow chapter down here. She quickly emailed me the skeleton profiles of everyone we need to know."

I leaned back in surprise. Ten was scary efficient and wicked connected.

"The president of the club is a guy they call Shot. Apparently, he's the youngest son of the founder of the entire club, a man called Torch, who operates the main charter out of Denver. The father has a questionable history with the law; the son seems to be either more law-abiding or better at not getting caught. He's another former Marine. Left the service five years ago, reconnected with his old man when he got out, joined the club, then moved down here to start his own chapter when the Denver guys got into some trouble involving an overzealous prospect. If you can't get to him, the second-in-command is a guy called Top Hat. He was in the same unit as Shot and seems to follow him pretty much everywhere he goes. His record is less spotty, and he was dishonorably discharged, but the file is sealed so she can't tell me what he was kicked out for." She paused to catch her breath and her expression twisted into one of concern. "You need to be careful, Webb. These guys all know how to use a variety of weapons, and from the sounds of it, they've all been in a position to take a life before. If they view you as a threat, there is no telling what they'll do to you."

Instead of feeding into her fear, I smirked and asked, "I wonder how he got the nickname Top Hat."

She smacked the bicep she was still holding and whipped around to push the door open. "Take this seriously. Be careful, Webb."

I reached out and caught a loose piece of hair which had escaped her messy bun. I tugged on the silky strand of hair until she looked back at me. "I'll be careful. I promise."

Finally, she nodded and slipped the rest of the way out of the car. I better make it back in one piece or she was going to take me apart, and not in a fun way. She cared, and it was becoming more obvious just how much. I could see it in every move she made. I was just waiting for her to recognize it.

It took a little over thirty minutes to drive out to the property where the club was located. I had to follow a long, barren dirt road back to a ranch property. The road was lined in barbed wire, and there was a variety of livestock wandering the fields. If I didn't know any better, I could have sworn I was driving home.

The compound was more like a working ranch. There was a big, one-level house set back from the road and the fields. There were several barns, what looked like an airplane hangar, and a huge variety of vehicles and motorcycles scattered all around the various buildings. The only thing that kept it from looking like a regular—if expensive—family home was the huge fence that circled the property. It was industrial and appeared to be impenetrable.

This was not a place you visited without an invitation—only that's exactly what I was doing.

I gulped and acknowledged I was both impressed and a bit nervous. I let the SUV roll to a stop in front of the fence and slipped out of the car. I didn't see a gate or a way to signal that someone was waiting outside of the fortress. Confused, I plowed a hand through my hair and looked for a box or something to call inside.

"What are you doing back here? Didn't we tell you we hadn't seen her in months when you came looking last time?" A faintly distorted voice seemed to come from the sky and made me jump about a mile in the air.

Feeling like an idiot, I struggled to gain my composure as my gaze finally found a camera pointed directly at me. I put both my hands on my hips and tilted my head. It would've been nice if I could see who I was talking to, but I would take what I got.

"You've seen me before?"

The electronic voice buzzed with annoyance. "Are you stupid?"

I chuckled. "No. I'm confused. I've never been in Loveless before today. Did the other guy who looked like me want to know where Jolene Bryant was?"

There was a long pause, and the voice squeaked again. "How could you never have been here before when I just saw you not that long ago?"

I threw up my hands and let them fall. "Evil twin. I'm not even kidding. Jolene is my mother, and apparently there was a lot she didn't bother to mention when I was growing up. I really need to find her. Can you tell me what you told the other guy?" I paused, figuring bikers wouldn't mind good manners. "Please."

Another long moment passed, and the voice crackled again. "Hold on a second."

Not sure what to expect, I fell back a step, looking up at the giant fence and wondering about the Oz hidden behind it. I wondered if I was about to meet the Wizard, and was admittedly a tad bit underwhelmed when a man slipped through a gate I hadn't noticed a few feet away.

He was shorter than me but made up for it with a Mohawk that stood a couple inches off of his shaved head. It was dyed a startling shade of green and seemed totally out of place on the ranch. He was dressed in shredded jeans, combat boots, and a black wife-beater, which was covered by a leather vest. His cut, I knew enough from watching Tv to know what they were called that, appeared to have been run over a million times and worn to death. The patch on one side said 'Rave,' the others read 'Secretary' and 'Combat Veteran.' He didn't look like any veteran I'd ever seen and I immediately liked that about him.

He hooked his thumbs in the front pockets of his tight jeans and gave me a considering look. "You aren't fucking with me? You really aren't the same dude who was just here looking for the same woman?"

I shrugged. "Nope. Two different people, same face. I like your hair."

He seemed momentarily taken aback before he muttered a quiet 'thank you.' He narrowed his eyes at me and told me flatly, "I'll tell you what I told him. Jolene only hung around for a week or so. She didn't like to follow the house rules, and no one gets to stay if they don't follow the rules. She was hooked up with one of the old-timers. They rode in from Denver, he left, she stayed behind until the Prez made her leave. She didn't say where she was going, and no one around here cared enough to ask."

I sighed and dragged a hand down my face. "Sounds like Jolene. She called and asked me for money for a bus ticket, but she didn't tell me where she was going, either."

"You might wanna try talking to the folks at the church in town. Those ancient busybodies know everything going on in

Loveless. If your mom was on the run, she might have needed help, and that's a surefire place to get some. I didn't tell the other you anything. He put off some bad vibes. The Prez wanted him gone. He even sent some guys out to make sure he left town. Thought it was weird he'd be back after that kind of send-off." He scratched the side of his nose and lifted a dark eyebrow in my direction. "You really got an evil twin?"

"Unfortunately. He's out there somewhere trying to pin a string of armed bank robberies on me. I'm trying to track him down and figured my mom was a good place to start. Probably a good thing you ran him out of town. He seems to be nothing but bad news." And I already knew that's all my mom was.

"Check with the old biddies." He jerked his chin in the direction of the dusty road leading into the property. "Next time, don't roll up unexpected. That's a good way to get hurt."

I nodded. "Shouldn't be a next time. Hey, if anyone in the club hears from Jolene, would you mind passing the info along? I would sure appreciate it."

The guy with the green hair and careful eyes nodded in agreement. I jotted my number down on the back of a receipt I found in the rental and he took it from me. It wasn't until I was driving away that I realized how tightly my ass cheeks were clenched together, and how sweaty my back was.

Note to self . . . bikers were not people you want to mess with . . . even if they weren't the scary, outlaw kind. Old church ladies were much more my speed. If they knew anything about Jolene, I could charm and flirt it out of them in under five minutes.

I knew my strengths.

CHAPTER 7

TEN

SHERIFF CASE LAWTON WAS A distractingly attractive man. No, really . . . he was disarmingly good looking and had a deep voice with a Texas drawl that I could listen to all day.

I'd had to ask him to repeat what he was saying twice. It should've been embarrassing, but I was too busy trying to figure out why the guy sitting across from me, the one who was so very much my type, didn't flip a single switch. I should've been flirting, smiling back, trying to figure out a way to get up close and personal with the beautiful man, but I wasn't.

He was tall, way taller than me, which was rare. He had short black hair tucked underneath a black cowboy hat and intelligent blue eyes set in a face meant for movie screens and expensive underwear ads. Handsome didn't quite cover it. The man was gorgeous but didn't sacrifice an ounce of masculinity or rugged appeal. He also had a serious, blunt way about him, which I appreciated. Authority and control practically oozed out of his pores. Before Webb tore through my life like a tornado, every single thing about the big, southern sheriff would have had my hormones sitting up and taking notice. He was very much the kind of man I'd always envisioned building a life with, a man so much like Cyrus Warner that it was scary coincidental.

Only today, I appreciated everything he had working for him and didn't mind the view in front of me at all, but I wasn't spinning wild fantasies about him, and I wasn't trying to picture what he looked like without his denim shirt. Okay, so maybe I did when I first sat down, but that was it. My mind was mostly on Webb and how he was fairing with the bikers. Not everyone found him charming and appreciated his smart mouth. I wanted him back in one piece. Worry was making me antsy and blowing my concentration all to hell. The cop sitting across from me obviously noticed.

"I don't think you have to worry about your friend. The club is mostly nonaggressive, all things considered. I doubt they'll even let him through the gates. That place is a goddamn fortress." Case Lawton had a good voice. Deep, with a tinge of a drawl, it was a little bit raspy and kind of rough. It suited him, and I wondered if the single women in this town broke the law on purpose just so they could end up in his handcuffs.

"You seem pretty nonchalant about having a motorcycle club operating so close to your city limits." Most law enforcement officers didn't take too kindly to groups that were potentially problematic. They were a headache no one wanted to deal with.

The sheriff leaned back in his chair, and the corner of his mouth kicked up in a grin. Damn, the man was potent, but still, not even a flicker of attraction sparked to life. When I was alone, I was going to have a very strongly worded talk with myself. There was no way I was letting Webb Bryant ruin me for any other man.

"As long as they don't break the law, which they haven't, there isn't much I can do about them moving into this area. I went to high school with a few of the members. They were good guys back in the day. Don't imagine they've changed much. Not much around here does." He steepled his fingers together and placed them under his chin. "I notice when someone new blows through town. The woman you're asking about was here for a few weeks.

The club kicked her out when she tried to score. They have a strict 'no drugs on the compound' policy. The guy in charge, Palmer Caldwell, is far from stupid. The guy was Special Forces; he's a decorated sniper. He knows if the compound gets raided we can shut the entire place down if we find so much as a joint, so they keep the ranch squeaky clean."

I nodded as if I understood the finer points of running a motorcycle club. "How do you know Jolene Bryant was trying to score?"

His dark eyebrows lowered a little, and his mouth flattened into a hard line. "One of my deputies picked her up. She was drunk, causing a scene outside the bar and she let it slip they'd eighty-sixed her. We put her in the drunk tank for a night and turned her over to the church the following day. There are a bunch of old-timers who run a sort of halfway house out of the basement for the lost souls of Loveless. They might be able to tell you where she was off to. All I can tell you is that Jolene demanded a phone call the night we put her in lockup. She called someone and demanded they wire her money for a bus ticket out of town. She didn't plan on staying."

I nodded again. "She called her son. He's the one trying to track her down."

The sheriff frowned and leaned forward slightly so his forearms rested on the edge of his desk. "The son. Now that you mention it, I think I remember the woman rambling about her son. It wasn't anything good, if I recall correctly."

I made a noise and shook my head. "From everything I've learned so far, Jolene is a garbage parent. She all but abandoned her boys when they were teenagers, and she appears to have had a baby no one even knew about. Which is why we're trying to find her. The missing baby is causing all kinds of problems as an adult." If I ever met the woman, there was a good chance I was going to strangle her.

Case tilted his head and considered me thoughtfully for a long minute. "What about the dad? If the mom isn't around to give you the answers you need, maybe you should look across the other side of the genetic aisle."

I blinked at him like an idiot. I'd been so focused on Jolene, it never occurred to me to ask Webb or Wyatt about their father. They clearly had the same one. They looked too much alike not to.

"He's never mentioned his father. It never occurred to me to ask. I don't think he's in the picture." But what if he was? Maybe Jolene wasn't the only who could assure Gage that there was indeed a twin out there. Even if we didn't track down the dad, we could feasibly find a birth certificate or someone who was present when they were born who could attest to the fact Jolene gave birth to twins. "I've been chasing down lost hikers and working to prevent forest fires for too long. I've lost my investigative edge." I wanted to smack myself in the forehead, but my super sexy company kept me from making a further fool of myself.

Sheriff Lawton let loose a full-fledged smile, and it was killer. He was dangerous, and not just because he was huge and armed. "I'm sure it would've come to you. You seem pretty sharp. Sometimes when we're close to the problem, it's hard to see the whole thing because we're standing right on top of it."

I sighed and climbed to my feet. "It's more than I had when I left Colorado." I stuck my hand out for him to shake and thanked him for his time. My eyebrows shot up when he gave my palm a little squeeze. His blue eyes glittered at me, and his smile shifted from friendly to speculative. "The man you're traveling with, he's just a friend?"

Holy shit. The interest in his eyes was clear. And, good Lord, did I want to be tempted. I was only in town for a short time, and he knew that. He was looking for temporary and quick. He was after something fun and easy, both things I excelled at. Only, there was nothing. Not the smallest blip of excitement or anticipation.

Sure, I was flattered, but my insides weren't on fire and tying themselves in knots the way they did whenever Webb carelessly flirted with me.

I tugged my hand free and forced a smile touched with remorse. "He's a very *good* friend. It was nice to meet you, Sheriff. You were a big help."

He took the dismissal with good humor, walking me to the front door of the station and pointing me in the direction of the church. It was across the street, located in the center of a small park. A familiar SUV was parked out front. I pulled my phone out of my back pocket and noticed Webb had both called and texted several times. His last message stated he was headed to the church and for me to call him whenever I got a chance. I was so glad he was back, unscathed, I let out an audible sigh of relief. I thanked the handsome sheriff again for his time and practically ran the distance to the church.

When I pushed through the ornate wooden doors, I was immediately stopped by an older man. He asked what I was doing, and when I explained I was looking for my friend, he smiled and pointed me toward a stairway. "He's entertaining the girls. I don't think they've laughed like that in years. Your fella is quite the charmer, isn't he?"

I agreed and moved to the stairs. It took every bit of my self-control not to skip down them two at a time. Webb was okay. He was still breathing. Nothing bad had happened to him. I still couldn't stop the painful need prickling under my skin, to see for myself that he was intact.

The stairs dumped me out into a wide-open space. There were several beds pushed against the far wall, a tiny kitchen against the opposite one, and a long wooden table dividing the room in two. Webb was sitting on one side of the table, his back to me. On the other side, there were three women in their eighties. All of them had towering gray updos, and they were all laughing so hard they were holding their sides and wiping at their eyes. As I approached, one of them reached out and patted the back of Webb's hand. It was a very sweet gesture, but Webb totally melted my heart when he caught the weathered, fragile hand in his much larger one and brought it to his lips for a kiss.

I must have made some kind of noise, because four pairs of curious eyes turned in my direction. I placed my hand on the back of Webb's neck and let my fingers drag through the short hair on the back of his head. "Sorry I didn't answer the phone. I was in a meeting with the sheriff."

He smiled up at me, and I swore all three of the elderly women let out a collective sigh. "No problem. Esther, Gladys, and Amandine have been keeping me company. They've been filling me in on all things Loveless."

The woman in the middle, whom I assumed was Gladys, smiled at me and adjusted the huge glasses perched on her nose. "Case Lawton, the boy is hopeless. Every woman with a single daughter within a hundred miles has tried to get that boy to settle down since his divorce. All he does is work. Not that it's an easy job. His father left a mess when he was finally voted out of the position."

I offered what I hoped was a friendly grin. "Being a cop is a hard job, and it takes a toll on families and relationships. It takes a pretty special person to put up with the demands of the job. Maybe the sheriff hasn't found the right person yet."

The Golden Girls all tilted their heads and gave me a considering look. Before they could grill me on how I knew what it was like to be involved with someone who risked their life every time they walked out the door, Webb caught my hand and pulled me to sit down next to him.

"Esther remembers Jolene. She spent a couple of nights here

before moving on. The ladies tried to help her out, but apparently Jolene was determined to get out of town. She was worried someone was after her." Webb gave me a knowing look, and I wanted to kick myself for noticing his eyes were so much bluer than the sheriff's. "She also had some choice words to say about Wyatt. Amandine has a son who is gay, so she didn't appreciate Jolene's less-than-progressive attitude."

Amandine had some dark brown in her mostly silver hair. She was still a lovely woman, her skin hardly wrinkled or papery at all. Her scowl was pronounced as she snapped, "You are supposed to love your children no matter what. Your job as a parent is to bring them up and teach them how to be good people. It isn't to judge who and how they love. I'm here to help anyone who may need it, but I was not fond of that woman." A speculative gleam lit up her gaze. "You never did say if your brother was single or not. My Max is quite a catch. He's so handsome; he looks just like my Gerald."

I snickered as Webb chuckled. "I don't think Wyatt's in the market for a relationship right now. Sort of like your sheriff: he works a lot and his job is dangerous. He goes undercover pretty frequently. Honestly, Jolene didn't set up either one of us to be the best at relationships."

The women all turned their eyes toward me. The one who hadn't spoken yet gave me a little wink, then said, "All it takes is the right person to turn it all around. As for your mother, she hightailed it as soon as she was able. She didn't say where she was going, but she did say she wanted to go somewhere no one would ever think to look for her. She seemed genuinely worried someone was after her, but people on drugs, their minds aren't always right."

Webb cleared his throat and gave me a look out of the corner of his eye. "Someone was looking for her. The guy at the gate of the motorcycle club mentioned someone swinging by not too long ago looking for Jolene. He gave up the info because the guy asking after her happened to look an awful lot like me. Seems she's been pretty popular lately. And her mind was never right, long before the drugs."

The women all made noises of sympathy and tried to offer both of us tea and muffins. Webb politely turned them down, and after making each of them blush when kissing their cheeks, we said goodbye and made our way back to the SUV. Webb was quiet, obviously thinking, as he drove us out of town back toward the motel. When the silence got so thick I felt like I could no longer breathe through it, I asked, "Webb, what about your dad? If Jolene is in the wind and we don't have a starting point to look for the twin, isn't he the next logical option?"

Webb's jaw clenched, and a muscle started to tick in his cheek. "I don't know who my dad is."

"I figured, but obviously you and Wyatt have the same one, and you said the parish you grew up in is small. Someone has to know who he is. Wouldn't he know if you were one half of a set of twins?" I could tell the questions were upsetting him, but I had to keep pressing onward. "What about your birth certificate? Wouldn't his name be on that?"

The tick fluttered faster, and Webb's knuckles turned white on the steering wheel. "Wasn't born in a hospital. Mom had us at home with the help of one of my aunts. I didn't have a birth certificate until it was time to go to school and Jolene was forced to get one. Pretty sure she left the father's spot blank."

I sighed and reached out to run a soothing hand down his arm. The muscles were tense and hard as steel. "What about Wyatt's? His might have the name of your father on it. Whoever it was, he was obviously in Jolene's life for a little bit of time considering there are four years between you and Wyatt." I petted his forearm and ran my thumb over the back of his tense hand. When had it gotten so easy to touch him? When had I started needing the contact? And why did such a simple touch have fireworks shooting off in the center of my chest? "I'm not sure where else to go if we don't go back to the start. Jolene is smart enough to use cash, and we can't pinpoint where she went when she left Loveless. I can ask another friend in the FBI to run a check for any arrests nationwide that match Jolene's description, but that makes our haystack twice as tall as it already is."

After a long, strained moment, Webb finally let out a breath, and I watched as he forced himself to relax. "I'll call Wyatt and ask him about his birth certificate once we're back at the motel. I need a minute, and then I want to shove some food in my face. The bloody mary from the plane isn't cutting it anymore. I'm starving."

Now that he mentioned it, I was aware of a hollow ache low in my gut. "I could eat. I'm sorry I keep pushing you further back into places you obviously don't want to go." My words trailed off in a whisper as he turned his head to look at me. Those blue eyes of his were hot and bright enough, I felt as if the heat could weld me to the spot.

"I've spent my entire life moving so fast the past could never catch up to me. I guess it's time I slowed down enough to deal with everything I left behind. Can't move forward with that anchor weighing me down."

He flashed his familiar smirk and I settled back in my seat once again wondering how he knew so much more than me. I needed to pay attention. There was a lot I could learn from Webb Bryant. I needed to stop being terrified of the doors he was kicking open and the light he was shining into my relatively dreary life.

CHAPTER 8

WEBB

"I NEED TO TALK TO you about something we both promised never to talk about." As greetings went, I could have come up with a better one, but giving Wyatt a chance to think and formulate a response wasn't a good idea. He could be an evasive bastard when he wanted to be. "I need to know about our father. Aside from knowing we have the same one, I know nothing. Not his name, not where he was from, or where he might be. I have no idea what his connection to Jolene is, or why he never had anything to do with either of us. Jolene is totally in the wind, and the other me was trying to track her down as well. I'm hitting dead end after dead end. It's time for a new plan."

The silence on the other end of the phone was deafening. I thought Wyatt hung up on me until I looked at my phone and saw the call was still connected. I heard him suck in a breath and I could picture him pacing back and forth in his boring office back in DC.

"We don't talk about him for a reason, Webb." It wasn't often my brother let the strain and frustration of our youth bleed through. He was always a tough guy, the stoic one who did what he had to without complaint. In this moment, I could hear every instance of pain and hurt he'd been through at the hands of others when he was too young to fight back. "We agreed to let sleeping dogs lie when it comes to the man who is no better than Jolene. In fact, if it's even possible, he's worse."

I flopped back on the bed in the center of the motel room and stared up at the ceiling. I pressed a hand over my eyes and tried to push back a headache I could feel knocking on the center of my forehead. "I know, but what if he knows about the other brother? Someone out there has to be able to tell the FBI that Jolene had twins, and maybe he knows where the other baby went. If he does, that could give me a place to start figuring out who he is and what he wants with me. I know you don't want to touch our childhood with a ten-foot pole, and I sure as hell don't either, but I don't have a choice. I have to go back to the start to get to the end of all of this." I was pleading with him, desperate and not ashamed to show it.

Wyatt's sigh was gusty enough to make my ears ring. I had to wait through five minutes of swearing and name calling while I listened to him kick stuff around his office before he finally gave me anything useful. "I fucking hate the guy, Webb. Hate him. I wanted to kick his ass for knocking Jolene up with me, but then he did it again. He wasn't around. Ever. He didn't care that Jolene left me alone. He didn't bother to check and see if I was alive, even though he knew how messed up she was. He was too busy playing the perfect family man with his *real* family to give a shit about his mistress and bastard son stuck out in the swamp." Wyatt's voice cracked, and he cleared his throat loudly, coughing to try and cover it up. "He can burn in hell for all I care."

I waited as the sound of something breaking tinkled through the phone line. It was a good thing Wyatt had seniority. He was less likely to get his ass chewed after his tantrum. "Who is *he*, Wyatt? And why did Jolene keep him around? We both know long-term is totally against her usual pattern of behavior."

"Mathis Bernard. He was the son of one of the founding families who settled in that parish. They were some of the first sugar cane farmers in the area, so old money. He and Jolene knew each other when they were younger. Our grandparents worked for the Bernard family. Jolene's mom took care of the house; her dad did maintenance or something. All their kids played together and grew up together, but the class division was never forgotten. Jolene and Mathis had a long history of messing around; it was the worst kept secret in the parish. No one was surprised when she got knocked up before graduating high school."

I grunted and gave up trying to push the headache back. "Jesus, there are more siblings out there?" Jolene had Wyatt when she was twenty, so the baby she was carrying in high school wasn't him.

"No. The Bernards paid her to not have that one. When she wanted to be particularly cruel, she would tell me she wished I was the one she got rid of. She would say, 'I bet the first baby wouldn't have ended up a goddamn queer.'"

It was my turn to swear long and loud. I wanted to break a bunch of stuff, too, but everything in the motel was secured down, so I didn't have the option to throw a tantrum like Wyatt had. Instead, I silently cursed my mother to a fate worse than death. She deserved that and so much more.

"I think she kept Mathis around because he was familiar, and he gave her money. She isn't capable of anything as basic as love and affection, so all I can figure is greed as her motivation. Plus, Bernard was forced into a marriage with a woman he barely knew. They put on a good front, but I don't think it was a very happy home. Jolene was easy, available, and she was never going to ask for anything more than cold hard cash. She was the perfect mistress." He grunted, and I could almost picture him rolling his eyes.

"After I came along, he sent her money more regularly, not that she ever used any of it to make sure I was healthy and cared for. It was a good thing she stayed on her family's property those early years. There were enough cousins and aunts around I never starved or froze to death. I often wondered why she didn't just drop me on Bernard's doorstep so he had to deal with the consequences of their actions. I asked him about it when I was a teenager. Tracked him down before I shipped out on my first deployment. Thought maybe he would change his tune when he realized I was trying to do something with my life, how I was very different from Jolene. I had idealistic ideas, like maybe he would keep an eye out for you, maybe he would give a shit I was getting ready to go to war. I should have known better. I asked him why he pretended like you and I never existed. He looked me dead in the eye and told me 'you don't.' We were nothing to him. Not even an afterthought. He threatened to call the cops—most of whom were in his back pocket and corrupt as hell—if I didn't get off his property. He shut the door in my face, Webb. He wasn't interested in where we'd been or how we'd survived. He literally hadn't given either of us a single thought in all the years we'd been alive. Didn't care if we lived or died."

It was a lot to take in. Everything in my past was. I didn't know the man, hadn't given him much thought when I was on the streets doing what I had to do. Wyatt had always been both mother and father when I needed someone, and I always knew an absent stranger would never compare to the unconditional love and acceptance my older brother gave me. But hearing my father was as much of a disaster as my mother . . . that hurt. It shouldn't have been so hard for our parents to love us. We were just kids. Taking care of us was really their only requirement, and they both failed spectacularly.

"I don't need him to acknowledge me, Wyatt. I'm not searching for validation or acceptance. I just need him to tell me if he knew Jolene gave birth to twins. Once he does, I'll spit in his face and walk away." I bit out the words with more confidence than I actually felt. I was the one who still had a soft spot for my grifter mother, and my older brother knew it.

"I don't think it's a good idea." Wyatt's voice got quiet which meant he was deadly serious. "I've stood behind you no matter what you've done, Webb, but this . . . this is going to go bad. I can feel it." Wyatt had good instincts. It was how he managed to stay alive so long in a life plagued by danger and violence. I couldn't discount that he was probably right.

"If it goes bad, Ten will be there as backup. She's not going to let me do anything stupid." At least, I hoped she wouldn't.

Wyatt sighed again. "You put a lot of faith in a woman who can barely tolerate you most days."

My brother's dry tone forced out a laugh. The chuckle made my head throb and my eyes water with a mix of pain and humor. "Yeah. I trust her more than almost anyone, except for you. I know you want to keep me from getting hurt by all the same things that hurt you, but it's not possible. Some knocks I just gotta take without you there to hold my hand. This is a fight you have to let me win or lose on my own."

Another long silence drew out between us, but finally after a long, tense moment, Wyatt mumbled, "Bernard moved his family to New Orleans a few years ago. I was working an op after Katrina and remember seeing an article about him in the local paper. The family puts on a show of giving back to the community, so he shouldn't be too hard to find if you're determined to do this."

I made sure my voice didn't waver at all when I replied, "I'm doing it."

Wyatt offered a few more gruff words of warning before hanging up. I tossed my phone on the bed next to me and pressed my palms into my eyes. The headache thumped even harder, the beat angry and unsteady. I needed to eat, and I needed a good night's sleep. I was running on fumes and tired of banging into brick walls every time I turned around. There was only so much abuse I could take before I broke.

There was a light tapping on the door, sending my gaze to the digital clock near the head of the bed. Ten and I agreed to meet in an hour to hunt down dinner. She'd given me an extra couple of minutes, and again I wondered how she could be so perceptive. She must have known the conversation with Wyatt wasn't going to be an easy one, and I was going to need a minute, or five, to get myself together after it ended.

Pushing to my feet, I shoved a hand through my messy hair as I lumbered to the door. I pulled it open just as Ten was lifting her hand to knock again. She gave me a startled look and pitched forward with the momentum of her next swing. I caught her, and her hands flattened on my chest. I caught the fresh scent of soap and shampoo, indicating she'd used the time we'd been apart to shower. Her skin was silky and soft under my palms as my hands slid down her arms to keep her steady.

"I love it when you're excited to see me, Ten. Doesn't happen very often." I made sure I put a little extra something in my words so she knew I was playing with her.

I figured she would scramble to put space between us, pushing me away like she always did. I was shocked into utter stillness when, instead of shoving off me, her hands drifted over my chest and wound around my neck. Her fingers pushed through the short hair on the back of my neck, and I had to fight not to shiver like an untried teenager.

"Are you okay? I've been worried about you all day. First, you dealt with a group of bikers on your own, then you had to talk to your brother about something that is clearly a sore spot for both of you. And I don't know if you've seen it yet, but Gage has released one of the surveillance pictures to the media, so your face is all over the national news. The conniving bastard didn't bother to clarify the man in the picture isn't you, so going forward things might get tricky if we run into law enforcement. You haven't gotten a single break since the FBI let you go." Her emerald eyes gleamed with concern and her mouth was soft and so fucking close. I wondered if she had any idea how tempting she was, how irresistible I found her. I wasn't known for walking away from the things in life that were bad for me; she was a prime example of that. I bet she didn't even know she was my favorite kind of trouble to get into.

I dropped a hand to her waist, letting it slide around to her lower back. Ten wasn't as good at hiding her response to the contact between us as I was. I felt her entire body quake and watched her pupils blow wide, nearly obliterating the pretty, vibrant green.

"I'll be all right, Ten. I've gotten used to getting kicked around and having to get back up. The trip down memory lane hasn't been the most fun I've ever had, but I couldn't ask for a better co-pilot. In all seriousness, you've made the journey almost bearable so far."

She shook her head, sending the scent of flowers and something sweet dancing toward my nose. Her grip on the back of my neck tightened as she lowered her gaze. "I haven't done anything, and my objectivity is all shot to hell." She dropped her forehead so it rested against my chin. "You confuse me, Webb, and I don't care for it."

A puff of laughter escaped as I lifted my other hand to her face. I cupped her cheek and used my thumb to trace the elegant line of her jaw. "Nothing to be confused about. What you see is what you get with me. I haven't made it a secret that I want you, Ten. Haven't kept quiet about the fact that I'd like to get to know you better, either. You'd see through any bullshit I tried to sell you, so I've kept my intentions crystal clear." Which was an entirely new game for me. I was learning the rules of honesty and transparency with her as I went along.

Ten pulled her head back so we were eye-to-eye. "I guess what's confusing is the way you make me feel. I'm not someone who gets taken in by a pretty face and practiced words. I'm not sure why I can't walk away from you."

I wasn't sure either, but I was pretty happy about it. "Even if you managed to figure out how to walk away, there's a good chance I would follow you. You are the only woman, hell, the only person, I've ever come back for in my entire life . . . aside from my brother. That means something. We don't have to figure it out right this minute, but I'm not going anywhere until we do."

She gave a jerky nod, but I wasn't really sure if it meant she agreed with me or not; she looked so uncertain. Before I could ask, she scrambled my brain and sent all the blood in my body flowing south toward my cock, when she tilted her head back and lifted up just enough to brush her parted lips across mine. It was barely a kiss, but it packed one hell of a punch. She stole my breath and my hands clenched in the fabric of her shirt. She made my knees turn into water, and had my dick turning into an iron spike behind my zipper. It was probably the most innocent, delicate kiss I'd ever received, but it shook me all the way down to my bones. She was already the one woman I'd been unable to forget; now that I had a taste of her she was going to be lodged deep inside the few undamaged places near my heart where my minimal good memories were kept.

She was out of my embrace before I could fully comprehend what happened. My lips tingled and the light, fresh scent she'd brought with her was still caught in my nose, which were the only indications she'd been as close as she was. I blinked, and she was a couple feet away looking at her phone, acting like something significant hadn't just happened.

"There's a steakhouse in almost every direction. Welcome to Texas. There's also a diner we can walk to. You pick. I could eat anything at this point." She looked up at me and narrowed her eyes. "Once I get some food in my face, we're going to go over everything that happened today. I want to hear about the bikers and what Wyatt said that put the tragedy in your eyes I saw when you opened the door."

I grumbled good-naturedly and went back into the room to grab my wallet and phone. "Let's walk to the diner." I could use the fresh air and time to figure out how to explain that finding my father might be worse than trying to find my mother.

Talk about the family reunion from hell.

CHAPTER 9

TEN

DINNER WAS A SOMBER AFFAIR. Webb didn't go into a ton of detail about what transpired between him and his brother, but he did reveal that Wyatt had known for quite some time where their father was. I could tell he was frustrated with his older sibling, but not surprised. Wyatt seemed determined to protect Webb from everything he could, even if the younger man was no longer a child and had proven smart enough to make sharp decisions when he had all the applicable facts. Webb didn't sound thrilled with the prospect of coming face to face with his father, but we both agreed it was the only logical next step. We also agreed we might as well drive instead of spending the money on another flight since it was only six hours or so away.

We ate quickly and quietly. There had been so many heavy conversations and revelations the last few days, it was evident we both needed a little bit of a break. The silence between us wasn't uncomfortable or strained; it was actually kind of nice. I wasn't fending off his flirtatious overtures and internally arguing with myself to resist. With his shiny, pretty veneer stripped back, it was easy to see Webb was a much more complicated man than he presented to the unsuspecting world around him. I was starting to wonder if the cheeky flirt was a role he'd learned to play when he was younger, because the introspective, serious man happily devouring a massive plate of biscuits and gravy was the real Webb Bryant. He resembled the man who'd shown up when I told Webb I wasn't sure I would've believed in his innocence if I hadn't been with him during the last robbery. I didn't prefer one over the other. Both versions made my nerves vibrate under my skin and sent my heart careening dangerously out of control. I liked that he had multiple sides to him. Trying to figure him out kept me on my toes, which not many people did. I found so many of them boring and predictable.

I still couldn't believe I kissed him.

It wasn't like I was shy or reserved when it came to asking for what I wanted from the opposite sex, as long as it was about meeting my sexual needs. Talking about how I felt, or didn't feel, wasn't something I did. I'd learned that lesson when I poured my heart out to Cyrus Warner, telling him every dream and hope I'd pinned on his ridiculously strong shoulders. What I wanted and needed from him hadn't mattered, and the pattern repeated with Gage. Despite our differences I'd tried, really tried, to keep the relationship going. I'd practically given Gage a handbook, explaining in minute detail what I needed to be happy with him, but again, it hadn't mattered. Gage had his own way of doing things and he firmly believed his way was best. He wasn't looking for input from his partner. Not in bed or out of it. Now, I knew enough to ask for it harder, faster, deeper, rougher, but I didn't trust anyone with the insanity inside of my heart.

Except for Webb. I couldn't seem to stop giving him a look at every honest emotion he wrung out of me. When he accepted my confusion at face value, saying we would figure it out in time, I couldn't stop myself from stealing the kiss he'd been tempting me with from the start. Webb didn't accuse me of playing games or leading him on. He didn't call me selfish or heartless. He simply kissed me back with the gentlest of touches and flipped my world over. I remembered our argument on the plane and him telling me to pay attention, that he was trying to take care of me. The kiss proved it. Even though I was the instigator and the aggressor, he was the one who turned it into something significant and momentous. It was a promise of things to come. He would do right by me, and I wasn't certain I even knew what that looked like, because none of the men in my past had bothered to try.

I was startled out of my thoughts when Webb ordered dessert to go and handed over a credit card to pay the bill. I opened my mouth to protest, we weren't on a date after all, but snapped it shut when he glared at me. I flushed somewhat guiltily; it was second nature to provide for myself. It was what I'd always done, what I'd resigned myself to a lifetime of doing. I told myself when I was forced to go back home, after things with my career and Gage imploded, I would never put myself in a situation where I relied on anyone ever again. It was supposed to be me, myself, and I for the long run. Only, Webb showed up and sent all those determined plans and promises flying haphazardly out the window.

I followed him back to the motel, working on a mild way to tell him I wasn't going to go back to his room with him. I was very aware I was the one who changed the dynamics of our relationship with that kiss, but I wasn't ready to jump into bed with him. Well, that wasn't entirely true. I'd fought the desire to succumb to the dark want and need he never bothered to hide from the start. Sex I could do, even wanted . . . to lose myself with Webb. It was everything that came after I wasn't ready to deal with. I had a hard enough time trying to figure out if I was coming or going around him as it was. Throw some sweaty, uninhibited, bed-breaking sex into the mix, and I was bound to lose my mind and reservations all together. I wasn't ready to surrender to Webb just yet. Though I felt myself slipping closer and closer to the edge of defeat the more time I spent getting to know him.

When we reached the motel parking lot, Webb took the impending awkward goodbye entirely out of my hands. He dropped a light kiss on the top of my head, wrapped one arm around my shoulders and gave me a tight squeeze. His embrace fell away before it really started, and I found myself fighting the feeling of being dismissed, even though I was planning on spending the night alone.

Once again, I misjudged Webb's startling ability to read me. With a lopsided grin, he reached out and ran the tip of one of his index finger down the length of my nose.

"I know you were going to send me to bed alone tonight, Ten. You've been thinking so loud the last couple of hours it made my head hurt." He bumped my shoulder with his as I playfully narrowed my eyes at him. It was refreshing he could still find a way to lighten the mood and joke around, even with all that was weighing on him at the moment. "I've been waiting for a long time for you to give me the green light to start something. Had no idea you were going to make the first move. Have to say, it was a nice surprise considering all the crap that's been flying my way lately." My breath caught when he unleashed his lethal simile in my direction. He bent down, and I went still as stone as the tip of his nose lightly touched mine. "Next move is mine, Ten, now that you've decided to play. You'll know when I'm ready to make it. Get some sleep. Tomorrow isn't going to be fun."

"That wasn't a move. It was an impulsive decision I'm trying really hard not to regret," I pouted. It was an actual pout, which couldn't be nearly as effective as it once was when I was younger and much more naïve.

"Oh, it was a move, however small, but I think it was a huge one for you. I'll see you in the morning." He tossed a wave over his shoulder as he sauntered off.

I muttered a halfhearted goodnight and watched him walk

away, shaking my head at the cocky swagger and self-assured way he carried himself. He was far more confident about how all of this was going to go down between us than I was. I headed to my own room, tired of my own screaming thoughts. Webb was right, they made my head hurt, too. I doubted I was going to sleep well. I hadn't since Webb was picked up by the FBI. Or, if I was being honest with myself, which was a rarity when I dealt with my thoughts about the man sleeping a room over, I had to admit I hadn't slept well since I'd found him shot to hell on the side of the mountain. Those unmistakable blue eyes of his followed me into my dreams. And now that I knew how strong, defined, and sexily cut his torso and stomach were, I had a feeling the image of Webb without his shirt on would be trailing me into sleep as well.

The long day, on top of the stress of worrying over Webb's well-being and battling my own rampaging emotions, took its toll. I was dead to the world the second my head hit the pillow. The deep, heavy sleep didn't mean I escaped visions of a nearly naked drifter. Webb was there in the dark, all bronze skin, golden hair, and twinkling eyes. I woke up sometime before dawn with my hair sticking to my damp skin, my legs shifting restlessly under the covers, and my hands traveling all over my body chasing a phantom touch. I groaned into my pillow, cursing Webb and my body's traitorous reaction to him.

Since I had a room to myself, and both the time and privacy, I allowed the heady fantasies that had been following me around to run free. With my eyes clamped closed and my body already hovering on the precipice of release, it was far too easy to picture Webb's big, strong body taking up all the available space between my splayed thighs. His shoulders were so wide, they would force my legs to part in a graphically wanton way. I already knew his hair was soft, and his mouth was scalding hot. I wanted to feel both on my skin as he worked himself toward the part of my body already pulling and pounding in anticipation. I could almost feel the rough drag of his fingertips through my sensitive folds, even though it was my own smaller, softer hands touching all the places I wanted Webb's touch.

It didn't take long to fall apart. I gasped Webb's name when I did, bright blue eyes and a wicked smile taunting me as I shifted around trying to catch my breath. Sleep found me once again after the orgasm wrung me out, and I felt surprisingly well-rested the next morning when my alarm went off. Webb and I agreed to meet at the SUV at seven so we could get an early start on the drive to Louisiana. I tried to give myself enough time to round up breakfast so I could surprise him before we left, but Webb was already leaning against the side of the big vehicle when I left the room. He had a fast food bag resting next to him on the hood and a white cup of coffee in his hand.

I couldn't hide the blush I knew was staining my cheeks as I approached him, gratefully taking the coffee cup he passed my way. Proving he was too observant for his own good, Webb arched a blond brow and asked, "Sweet dreams?"

I really had to work not to spit out the coffee I'd just sipped all over the front of his white T-shirt. I coughed a little as I swallowed and lifted a hand to tap against my chest, trying to catch a breath so I could wheeze out, "Are you ready to go?"

He chuckled and nodded, handing over the brown paper bag. "Yeah. Let's do this." My voice was still raspy from the near miss with the coffee.

For the first hour or so we rode in companionable silence. I took a few minutes to tease Webb over his erratic, ridiculous playlist pumping out of the SUV's speakers. He liked everything from old country to classic rock. It was the addition of bubbly, shiny K-pop that threw me off. If he hadn't bopped his head along to the infectious beats, I would've sworn he added the pop songs as a joke. But no, Webb's musical taste was just as irreverent and playful as the man himself.

We stopped for an early lunch, then I offered to drive. I thought Webb was going to fall asleep in the passenger seat, but once we got rolling again, he surprised me by turning the music down and asking softly, "Tell me about Gordon. I like to think I'm slowly figuring you out, but that guy," he shook his head. "I still don't get it."

I sighed, glad I had dark sunglasses on so he couldn't read my expression. I was sure every ounce of regret and anger I still had over my entire relationship with Gage was stamped all over my face.

"When I left Wyoming, I did it with a broken heart. I had it bad for Cy, and I told him so. I thought we were going to go off to college together. I honestly believed we were going to be together forever. I had no idea he didn't even think of me as his girlfriend. I was just one of the many local girls he was killing time with. I had no idea how I could be so blind, but the truth crushed me. Cy went to Boston. I wanted to get as far away from him as I could, so I enlisted in the Army."

"What?! I had no idea you are a veteran." He sounded shocked, and I couldn't blame him. My military service wasn't something that came up in casual conversation.

"Not a lot of people know. I don't talk about it much. I was only in for four years. I went through basic and ended up in Germany. I ended up being as far away from Wyoming and everything I was trying to outrun. I enlisted so I could join the military police. I knew I wanted to go into law enforcement when I got out. I was accepted into the FBI's training program almost instantly. It was my dream job, and I couldn't have been happier with how my life was turning out. I left the ranch, I had a career that mattered, and I was finally over Cy. Gage was in the graduating class ahead of mine at Quantico. He was handsome and sophisticated. He was ambitious, driven, smart as hell, and so different from Cyrus

Warner I couldn't say no when he started to show an interest in me. I was flattered. Gage is from New York. A total big city guy. I thought I'd finally shaken off my small-town roots and evolved into the woman I always wanted to be when he paid attention to me."

I still remember how overwhelmed and outclassed I felt when he started buying me expensive gifts. I didn't have a clue how to act when he wanted to take me to five-star restaurants and the theatre.

Webb snorted. "He's still hung up on you. Pretty sure he kept my ass locked up an extra day or so because of those surveillance photos of us together."

I sighed again and shook my head. It was possible. Just like he released the picture of the bank robber to all major media outlets without clarifying the FBI wasn't hunting Webb down like a dog anymore. He knew how to manipulate almost every situation to his own benefit. "He doesn't like to lose. When I broke things off, he thought I was joking until I moved out of our apartment and quit my job. He couldn't fathom someone like me leaving someone like him."

I thought I heard Webb growl. "What exactly does 'someone like you' mean?"

I snorted. "A backcountry girl with no class and no manners. Throughout the course of our entire relationship, Gage was trying to turn me into his ideal woman, and I let him. I believed that I needed to be someone different in order to finally be happy." I shook my head again. "He tried to change the way I dressed, the way I spoke, even the way I thought about things. He started messing with my work. I've always been good at puzzles and seeing patterns other people miss. I'm also really good at finding people who don't want to be found. Gage was encouraging me to take shortcuts, to bulldoze my way through investigations the same way he did. I don't think he's ever cared about having the right person behind bars, so much as he cares about having a viable suspect to hang suspicion on. He always closes his cases, and his bosses like the way he works. I hated it. We clashed over a kidnapping case we both got assigned. There had been a rash of them in the area, so it was a big deal, the kind of case bound to lead to promotion if it was solved swiftly. Gage believed the father of the little boy was the culprit. Something was definitely off with the dad, but I didn't believe he would hurt his own child. Gage ruined his life. Hounded him at work. Stirred up suspicion with the local media. Turned his neighbors and his wife against him. The guy lost everything. I think he confessed just to get Gage out of his life."

My hands tightened on the steering wheel remembering the tragic, broken man and the way Gage gloated and celebrated over his confession. My stomach hurt with remembered distaste and despair.

"The dad was gay. He had a male lover he'd been hiding from his wife for years. That was his big secret. He didn't have anything to do with his son going missing. It was the goddamn bus driver. He was picking out latchkey kids, ones with working parents, learning their patterns and schedules. It only took me a day to track him down because while Gage had the father in custody, another kid went missing. The bus route was the only thing they had in common. We got the kid back alive, but . . . damaged. The father blamed himself for everything. He committed suicide a week after he was released." The bitter taste of injustice burned the back of my throat, and I felt my eyes burn. "Gage was promoted to Special Agent in Charge the same week. No one seemed to care that he totally dismantled a man's life. He was a closer. I broke up with him and quit my job, but when I did that, I realized I had nowhere to go besides home. It was the last place I wanted to be, but, what choice did I have?"

"And Cy was back as well." He said it without a hint of censure, but I could hear the thread of jealousy underlying the statement.

"Yeah. That was the only part of going back that didn't suck. It was easy to pick up where we left off. I was older and wiser. I knew I wasn't his one and only this time around. I also knew it was up to me to figure out my life, not just ride someone else's coattails." I only had myself to rely on. I was the only one who wouldn't let me down.

"Are you still in love with Cy?" Webb asked the question softly, but the weight of it hung suspended in the space between us.

"I'm not." For the first time in forever, the words rang true when I said them. "I loved him for a very long time, but watching him with Leo," I shrugged. "I had to learn to let go. I think loving him became a bad habit; it wasn't something I did consciously. I did it because it was comforting and reminded me of the woman I was before Gage twisted me into someone I barely recognized."

We lapsed into silence, once again my love life lying like a deadweight between the two of us. Thinking back on it, who was I to say anything about Webb hooking up with a woman old enough to be his mother just so he could get himself through high school? It wasn't like I'd made better choices when it came to my heart and body.

After several minutes, Webb's deep voice rumbled through the interior of the car. "I didn't know you before, but I gotta tell you, Ten. The woman you are now is no one to be ashamed of. You might not be where you want to be, but you can change that if you really want to. What you can't change, what never changed, is the caring, deeply compassionate woman you've always been. You went from the Army, to the FBI, to being a forest ranger. You want to help people. People who often don't want to be helped. I know, because I was one of them when we first met. Your huge heart makes you so special, and both Cy and Gage were blind if they couldn't see it. It's beautiful."

Again, I was super grateful for the oversized sunglasses on

my face. They hid the tears welling up in my eyes, threatening to overflow. I heard all about how pretty I was. How nice my legs were. How amazing I was in bed. I even heard how badass I was on the regular. Yet, it'd taken me thirty-eight years to have someone tell me my heart was beautiful, as though it was the biggest, best part of me. Where Webb was concerned, I felt like I was made of glass and he was looking right through me.

"Those words of yours . . . I never know what to do with them." And it scared me how much I wanted to hold onto them and believe them. I wondered if he could hear in my voice how scared I was of him and everything he made me feel.

"Believe them. That's all you have to do." I guess the sunglasses weren't as effective as I thought because the next instant I felt the brush of his thumb against my cheek, chasing moisture with a heartbreakingly gentle touch.

What in the world was I going to do with the man who had no ties to anything in the world, but wrapped me up in gossamer words time and time again? I was such a goner.

I turned the music back up, humming along to the bouncy K-pop, allowing myself to have fun, because Webb was more fun than anyone I'd ever met. With this man, I was smiling slightly somehow as I blinked away tears.

CHAPTER 10

WEBB

TEN HAD A LEAD FOOT.
    For someone who had been in law enforcement of one kind or another for the entirety of her adult life, I was surprised by the tiny act of rebellion. She drove like she was qualifying for the Indy 500 and assured me if we ended up getting stopped, she could get us out of a citation for speeding. As a result, she shaved almost an hour off our drive time, and we arrived in the Big Easy a little after lunchtime.

When it came to finding a place to crash for the duration of our trip, I told Ten it was better to avoid the general noise and debauchery of the French Quarter. Since we'd both already visited and enjoyed all that New Orleans had to offer, I found a smaller, boutique hotel set back in the Garden District and booked adjoining rooms there. It would be the first time I was in the colorful, wild city while I wasn't specifically looking for trouble. Not that I believed I wasn't going to find my fair share anyway. New Orleans was close enough to what I remembered as my home, it was an easy place to drift to when I had nowhere else to go.

The little hotel was actually a converted plantation. There was Spanish moss draped elegantly on the outside and stately columns decorating the entrance way. Ten let out a low whistle and muttered, "Just call me Scarlett."

I chuckled and told her she could call me Rhett. There was a flash of surprise in her eyes when I caught the *Gone with the Wind* reference with ease. I winked at her and let her know the movie was one of Wyatt's favorites. My badass big brother was a closet romantic. When I was little, and it was just me and him, he used to put on old black-and-white movies instead of cartoons. I was well versed in all the classics: *Gone with the Wind, Casablanca, Roman Holiday, Sabrina,* and *From Here to Eternity.* Even back then I had my doubts that love was as easy as the movies made it seem. Wyatt was different. He was certain there was a special someone meant for each of us. He told me over and over that it took patience and determination to make love work. He had plenty of both. I had very little of either, until I met the leggy blonde standing next to me.

Blushing prettily, Ten led the way into the hotel, checking us both in with ease. She asked if I wanted to wait to find Mathias Bernard, but I knew the longer I waited, the harder this little reckoning would be. The man had pretended as if my brother and I didn't exist for the last thirty-two years, so why give him any more time to avoid facing his mistakes? We dropped our stuff in our rooms and headed out to the office building where Bernard's non-profit was located. It took a little badgering and some pleading to get Wyatt to hand over the info, but eventually he came through. I wouldn't put it past my older brother to show up out of the blue any minute now. Wyatt was always overprotective, but when he knew I was in over my head, he was something else altogether. I was lucky I hadn't spent my formative years covered in bubble wrap.

I let Ten drive us across the city. I was so caught up in my own thoughts, there was a good chance I would have driven us into the murky waters of the Mississippi and not even noticed. She was quiet, letting me sit with my tangled, messy mind until we stopped in front of a sleek, modern building. It stood out garishly amongst all the old, stylishly renovated buildings that lined the rest of the street. It was obvious someone had spent a lot of money on the place, but they missed the mark. It was a building which would have been at home in Manhattan or Chicago. Here in the sleepy, sultry south, it was the ugly stepsister: all flash, no substance or heart.

Ten and I exchanged a look as we both reached for our doors. "The nonprofit is supposed to help inner-city kids. He started it after Katrina when he moved his family here. A guy worried about underprivileged youth can't be all that bad, can he?" Ten's voice was low, and the question was uncertain.

I grunted and pushed out of the car. "Wyatt and I were underprivileged youths. He didn't give a shit about us, even though he had the means to make sure we didn't go hungry. Pretty sure he's as bad as the regular old rich guy who doesn't give back to the community. He wants the family name to look good. This is all for show, not out of any real concern for what happens to trash like me." I sounded bitter and mean. I was feeling both of those things, which meant this conversation wasn't going to go well. I wasn't confrontational by nature, but damn if I didn't feel a huge battle brewing.

Ten put a hand on my arm, and I felt her fingers dig in almost painfully. "You aren't trash. You never were. You were a kid who lost big in the parental lottery, and you're a man who's had to learn how to live on your own terms because of it. The only thing you are and ever will be is a survivor."

She sounded so passionate, so sure, it was simple to believe her. I nodded briefly, letting her know I didn't only hear her but was listening, as well. I took a deep breath, locked my wayward emotions down, and pulled open the glass door. The interior of the building was as slick and modern as the outside. The woman sitting at the reception desk also looked like she should be in a metropolitan city and not the deep south. She had to be sweltering in the long-sleeved shirt and blazer she was wearing.

She gave Ten and me a sharp once-over from behind gold-rimmed glasses. Her upper lip curled ever so slightly when she took in our dusty cowboy boots and jeans. She even cocked her head and studied Webb intently for a long minute without saying anything, and again I wanted to strangle Gage for putting Webb's face all over the TV and Internet with no disclaimer. I was sure the reaction Webb was getting from this woman was exactly what my ex intended. He wanted Webb isolated and shunned. He wanted to make the other man's life harder than it had to be, and it appeared Gage had been successful.

"Can I help you?" Her accent was distinctly east coast, clipped and harsh.

I lifted an eyebrow as Ten rocked back on her heels and crossed her arms over her chest in a clearly challenging stance. "Can you inform Mathias Bernard his son is here to see him? One of them, that is."

The woman's mouth dropped open slightly, and her eyes widened comically behind her glasses. "Umm . . . I know all of Mr. Bernard's children."

I smirked at her. "Are you sure about that?"

She lifted a hand to her throat and blinked a couple of times. "Uh . . . He's not in, and he doesn't see anyone without an appointment. We deal with families in some pretty desperate situations; it isn't safe for Mr. Bernard to see anyone who walks in the door."

I took a few steps toward the reception counter. It was made of marble and felt cool under my palms as I placed them shoulder-width apart and leaned closer to the woman behind the divider. I felt Ten put her hand on the center of my back. She was trying to settle me, to keep me in check. I wasn't sure if I needed her tugging on my leash just yet, but better safe than sorry.

"I'm not desperate, but I am dangerous. I'm not here to hurt the man, but I will shred his reputation without a second thought if he doesn't agree to speak with me. I bet the people who fork over tons of cash at every charity ball would love to know that Bernard has kids whom he never bothered to acknowledge or provide for. He wouldn't look so much like the Saint of the Big Easy if his rich investors knew his own flesh and blood have had to do unspeakable things to avoid freezing to death while sleeping on the streets."

The woman was shaking by the time I was done. She looked past me to Ten for help but clearly didn't get the response she wanted. With quivering fingers, she picked up the phone and started poking at buttons. After a minute she was speaking into the receiver but still looking at me with huge eyes.

"Mr. Bernard, you have a visitor." She paused shaking her head. "I know you don't have any appointments scheduled today, but you really want me to send this one in." She made a strangled sound and put her free hand back at her throat. "He says he's your son." She muttered something under her breath and jerked her gaze forcefully away from mine. "He says if he doesn't speak with you he's going to the press. He seems serious."

She muttered again and a moment later hung up the phone. She cleared her throat and rose, smoothing her hand down the length of her skirt. "He really isn't in. He went to lunch with his wife. He asked me to show you to the conference room and get you some coffee while you wait. He's going to be here in five to ten minutes. If you would follow me?"

She stiffly led us to a room surrounded by glass walls. Ten and I both turned down coffee but accepted the chilled bottles of water she offered next. As she practically ran from the room, Ten called out to her.

"Hey, before you go, I want to ask you something." The receptionist paused, turning her head slightly to look at the other woman. "Have you seen another man who looks exactly like him hanging around recently? Someone else demanding to speak with your boss?" Ten hooked her thumb in my direction.

The receptionist let her gaze wander to where I was sprawled in one of the leather executive chairs placed around the long glass table. Something flickered in her eyes before she shook her head. "No. I haven't seen anyone who looks like him asking for Mr. Bernard, but . . ." she trailed off, and I heard her gulp. "When you see Mr. Bernard, you will understand why I didn't demand proof of paternity or call security. He's a good boss. He is most definitely not a very good man." With those final words, she slipped from the room, leaving me and Ten staring after her in shock.

"Maybe I should've Googled him before planning this ambush." It hadn't occurred to me. I'd lived my entire life without the man, there was no sudden urge to know everything about him, including what he might look like. Plus, I'd been jumping from place to place, distracted trying to find my mother.

Ten made a soft hum of agreement. When I looked over at her, she was already on her phone. When her eyes popped to twice their size and her jaw unhinged, I knew the resemblance must be uncanny. She pushed her phone across the table in my direction.

"It's like looking at Wyatt in fifteen years. His mouth is a little wider. His jaw is weaker, and his nose is so straight and perfect I'm betting he had work done. The man's genes are powerful though. You could be carbon copies of one another. I wonder if your half-siblings look just like you, as well?"

The man on the small screen in front of me did indeed bear a striking resemblance to both my older brother and myself. His hair was more brown than blond, and he had an overall aura of wealth and entitlement that made him appear much softer than Wyatt and I had ever been. This was not a man who knew what it was like to go hungry and live without. I pushed the phone back with more force than required, but Ten was quick and caught it before it tumbled to the floor.

"I hate everything about this. I'm barely dealing with having a possible twin, how am I supposed to comprehend half-siblings out there I won't ever get a chance to know? I feel like my life isn't my own anymore." I'd been on my own so long, dealing with all these new people I was suddenly connected to was unsettling.

"The only person you're responsible for is you, Webb. Don't lose sight of that." Her voice was quiet, but there was a thread of steel running through it. "You don't owe anyone anything, nothing we learn here, there, or anywhere along the way will change that."

My reply was interrupted when the man in the picture on Ten's phone pushed his way into the room. Without preamble, he took a seat at the head of the big table. Not across from me, or even close enough we could speak without raising our voices. "My secretary called me and told me the other twin was here to see me. I should've expected it after the first one found me. I'm going to tell you what I told your brother, I'm not paying you a dime. I have a family, and you are not part of it. You can out me to the press, to the old coots of southern society, drag my name through the mud, ruin my reputation, but I'm not letting you blackmail or bully me. I told Jolene to get rid of both of you. I paid her a fortune all those years ago so I wouldn't have to deal with this kind of annoyance. I'm not scared of you anymore."

I couldn't breathe. All I could do was stare at the man who was responsible for me being born, the man who let Jolene destroy my childhood, the one who didn't want me.

Ten reached for my hand, but I felt like I was made of stone underneath her gentle touch. "Are you trying to tell me Wyatt Bryant asked you for money when he tracked you down before he enlisted?" She sounded incredulous, and it did something to my heart to hear her so effortlessly defend my older brother.

Mathias Bernard frowned and angrily tapped his fingers on

the table in front of him. "The one who went into the Army? No, not him. He went away when I explained he was a mistake. I told him I didn't want him, didn't want any of you. I should've learned my lesson with Jolene the first time I paid her to terminate an unwanted pregnancy. The woman is a nuisance. I swear she got pregnant on purpose just so she could fleece me for money until the end of time." The man pointed a finger with a big ring on it in my direction. "I'm talking about his twin. The one who showed up on my doorstep, scaring the daylights out of my wife and giving my children all kinds of questions I never wanted to answer. Once the secret was out, it no longer held any power. My family already knows about my history with Jolene, thanks to your brother. I have enough money not to care about public opinion. We can always leave New Orleans if we have to."

He was so blasé about everything. Abandonment. Betrayal. Rejection. They all burned hot and angry under my skin, creeping and crawling their way to the surface.

"You knew Jolene was pregnant with twins?" Thank God Ten was there to get the job done, since I was choking on rage and unable to put a coherent thought together. Her questions were sharp and pointed, cutting through the tension like a knife.

The older man nodded, the action reminding me so much of Wyatt my chest felt like it was going to crack open. "Of course I did. She thought I would take one of them off her hands because 'two sounded hard.'" He made quotes in the air with his index fingers. "I told her I didn't want either one, but that woman never listened to anything. She kept one of the babies and left the other one on my goddamn doorstep like some kind of biblical sacrifice, and since she had them at home, no one was keeping track of her crazy actions. Luckily, I found it before my wife stumbled across it. I had one of the housekeepers who'd been with my family since I was young deal with it." He meant he got rid of the baby. His family paid someone to make the other twin disappear.

It. Not him, or the baby, but *it*, as if the small, defenseless human was something less than. This man was a monster. I was suddenly, overwhelmingly grateful I hadn't been forced to deal with his poison in my life. My childhood wasn't easy, but at least it hadn't been infected.

"You gave Jolene money to take care of us?" My buzzing brain seemed to trip over the tiny bit of information in the sea of revelations he was shoving at me.

The older man nodded. "I did. The same amount deposited into three accounts every month until you were all eighteen, plus a scholarship set up for each of you that was accessible if any of you decided to pursue higher education in the future. I made sure Jolene couldn't access either account. I figured if you kids managed to survive her, you could use the money to put toward your futures. I suppose since she couldn't get her hands on any of the funds, she didn't bother to tell you kids about the money. I should have figured that out when your older brother showed up before he enlisted looking like a homeless person. With interest accruing all these years, there is a tidy sum in each account."

Without meaning to, I rose to my feet, hands flat on the table in front of me as I leaned toward the man I would never consider my father. "What about when we were too young to take care of ourselves? Where was the money so we could eat? The cash so we weren't freezing and sleeping on the floor of some roach-infested squat? Where was the money so we could have what we needed for school? You have no idea what we did to survive Jolene."

The other man rose to his feet as well, not intimidated in the least. "I also gave Jolene money. Am I surprised she never used it for her kids? No. But what could I do about it? I had my own family to provide for."

So much. There were so very many things he could've done

about it. "When you told my twin you wouldn't give him any money when he tried to blackmail you, what happened?"

"I told him about the accounts I set up for the three of you. I explained that was the only money he was going to get since it was rightfully his. I explained how to access it, thinking it would be the end of things. As soon as any of the accounts are accessed, the bank has to alert the other two recipients money has been withdrawn. I put that in place in case Jolene separated you kids. Figured it might be the only way you could find each other in the future. When I explained it all your twin became violent, angry. Asked if I'd ever bothered to look for him. When I told him I didn't give a second thought to any of the children I had with Jolene, he became unreasonable. Demanded to know who his other siblings were. I had my *actual* children in the house with me, and I didn't know if he was armed or not. I called the police, but he took off before they arrived. I don't think he knew about you or your brother until that day. One of the reasons leaving New Orleans wouldn't be the worst thing in the world is because he knows this is where my family lives. There was something wrong with that boy."

"Did you even bother to get the name he goes by now?" My voice was raw, aching. I didn't sound like myself in the slightest.

"No. When I say I want nothing to do with any of you, I mean it." His eyes were flinty as steel.

I felt my mouth open and snap closed. I was at a loss for words. My non-father was unbelievable in his callousness. I very well could have lost my mind hearing him refer to his other kids as his actual children, knowing he'd tossed me away like garbage because I was inconvenient.

"He didn't give any indication where he was going after he confronted you? It's imperative we find him." Ten put a hand on my shoulder, pulled me until I was standing and not looming threateningly. Her arm snaked around my waist. If it were a hug,

I would've loved it, but we both knew she was subtly restraining me so I didn't lunge at the insensitive man who wanted nothing to do with me.

"He didn't say anything beyond the threat to take what he was owed. He did ask where I sent Jolene her last check, and I told him it was somewhere in Texas. Now if you'll excuse me, I have things to do the rest of the afternoon. I'll have my receptionist get you instructions for both you and your older brother to access your accounts."

He exited the room without so much as a backward glance.

I was numb, chilled to my bones even though it was muggy and hot all around me. I let Ten practically drag me out of the room and listlessly watched as she collected the information from the receptionist. She gave the woman her cell phone number and asked her to please call if anyone who looked like me came around. She bundled me into the SUV and started to race back across the city.

"He wanted me in jail, so there would be nothing I could do when the bank set out the alert about the accounts being accessed." I was starting to understand how my twin brother's devious mind worked. "Once I was out of the way, he could easily get his share of the money, as well as mine with a fake ID. How would anyone know he wasn't me except for Wyatt?"

Ten sighed. "Seems like a pretty big risk to take. Why not just keep the money from the bank robberies? Why risk getting caught when he could simply take the money that was already his? And what about Wyatt? Surely he would get involved once he was alerted the accounts existed and that yours had been accessed while you were locked up." She nodded. "You need to ask him to put an flag on those accounts when you talk to him next. He needs to know there might be a price on his head, as well, because your twin needs him out of the way as well if the money is really his motivation." She didn't sound so sure about the *why*, but the *how* was starting to become crystal clear.

I shook my head and ran my hands tiredly over my face. I was exhausted. "He wants to punish me *and* Wyatt." I wasn't sure how I understood his motivations so well, but I was certain revenge was behind his convoluted and highly risky plot more so than a payday. The money was a nice bonus, but watching my life and Wyatt's unravel seemed to be at the forefront of his plans. "Jolene kept us. Even though she treated us like luggage and pretty much hated us, she still kept us. He was literally thrown away, tossed out. His resentment, his abandonment issues have to be triple what ours are." And I couldn't fault him for being a little crazed with anger and jealousy. "And Wyatt stayed with me. No matter how badly I fucked up, or how much we struggled, he never walked away from me. This guy hates me, and he hates that even though me and Wyatt had virtually nothing growing up, I had what he didn't."

It was the only reason his hatred made any sense.

Ten whipped around and gave me a hard look. I could see she was turning my words over in her mind, but apparently she was also thirsty for revenge because she practically growled, "I have a friend who works in the IRS. I'm going to ask him to launch an investigation into all of Bernard's business transactions. Nonprofits can be used for some shady stuff and no one, I mean no one, wants an audit. He might have enough money to protect his personal reputation once outed as a scumbag, but his professional one can't take the same kind of hits. I'm going to make his life miserable."

I loved how adorable she was being in order to help me deal with my swirling, confusing emotions. But her cute actions didn't stop the dull throb inside of my chest. How had Wyatt faced our father's dismissal all on his own? It was brutal and heartbreaking, and I'd had Ten there to lessen the blow. For the millionth time, I realized how lucky I was to have Wyatt. He was stronger than anyone I'd ever met.

I was silent all the way back to our hotel. I was so glad we'd agreed to skip the Quarter. There was no way I could function with all those vices right outside my door at the moment. I wanted to go out and be the very version of myself I'd fought so hard not to become. I followed Ten blindly into the building. Putting one foot in front of the other diligently. It was hard, but I managed.

Thinking I was going to faceplant on the bed and wallow until I could get my emotions in check, I didn't realize Ten followed me into my room until the door shut behind her and I felt her forcibly turn me around to face her. She put her hands on either side of my face, holding me still as those emerald eyes of hers glittered up at me like expensive jewelry.

"Webb," her voice dropped to a husky, sexy tone. The sound of it had my senses waking up, and my attention narrowed in on the damp center of her lip where her tongue kept darting. "Life is too short to waste time and energy on the people who don't want us. They don't matter. They don't get any part of you. Save everything you have, everything you are, for the people who want and need you."

I lifted my hands and wrapped them around her surprisingly delicate wrists. Her pulse was thundering under my fingertips. "Do you want me, Ten? Do you need me?"

There was a moment of hesitation in her gaze, or maybe it was fear. I was asking her to admit how she felt about me, no more hiding, no more denying. She hadn't been willing to admit it to herself up until now; telling me made it all very real.

Slowly, so slow time seemed to stop, she dipped her chin in a nod and whispered, "I do."

It was all I needed to hear. I lowered my head and sealed my mouth over hers.

The little I had to give to this woman who wanted me, who needed me, was more than I'd ever given to anyone else. I just hoped it would be enough.

CHAPTER 11

TEN

NOW THIS WAS A KISS.

It wasn't a hesitant exploration of what might be.

It was no scared, featherlight press of lips against lips.

He wasn't kissing me to figure out if it was something he really wanted or needed. He wasn't trying desperately to figure something out.

There wasn't an ounce of uncertainty or caution while he tried to find his way in the dark.

Nope, Webb knew exactly where he was going, and I was the lucky woman along for the ride. His mouth slid across mine full of primitive intent and dark promise. He kissed like he did most everything else, with wild abandon and unpredictability. When I expected tongue, I got the nip of teeth. When I expected a soft bite, I got a silky glide of tongue. I fully anticipated impatient hands tangled in my long hair. What I got instead were warm palms sliding up and down my sides, soothing rather than claiming. He left the conquering and dominating to his mouth. I was trapped in the kiss. Wrapped in thin, unbreakable strands of seduction and sensation. It was a web, woven to be both fragile and unbreakable at the same time. I could feel the velvet drag of it along my skin as Webb spun it around the both of us, locking us together in a familiar dance that felt completely different than any other time I'd done it. Webb had moves I'd never seen before, and I found myself following along blindly because I wanted this experience to be mine and his alone. I liked that I didn't know the steps or the beat we were chasing around the elegant hotel room.

I wasn't the kind of woman who spent a sultry afternoon making love in a renovated plantation. The entire concept of romance was foreign to me. When Gage had tried to woo me, it was more about impressing me and flaunting the things he had to make me feel undeserving. All of his overtures ended up being not romantic at all, in the long run. And with Cy, it was all about convenience and familiarity. We'd known each other for so long, were so similar in too many ways, there was never the need for something special. I'd always been a sure thing for the rough rancher. At this moment, falling completely under the spell of the man in front of me and the setting surrounding us, I finally understood why a little bit of thought and consideration did wonders for getting the blood pumping everywhere but my brain. It was nice to know the person you were with felt you deserved more than a literal roll in the hay or a few minutes of missionary in between cases with barely a word or kiss exchanged.

Webb traced my bottom lip with the tip of his tongue, fingers slipping under the hem of my loose T-shirt and finally landing on bare skin. Bumps lifted across my skin instantly, and I swore a current of electricity hummed through my veins as his fingers trailed across my lower back. I found myself pressing closer to his big body, softness meeting hard resistance as my breasts flattened against the taut plane of his broad chest. Even through layers of clothing, I felt my nipples bead up in eager anticipation. His tongue shifted and licked along the little divot in my top lip. I found myself chasing after the light pressure, his taste coming alive when it hit my tongue and searing itself into my favorite memories.

I wrapped a hand around his jaw and used my thumb to trace his bristly chin. His stubble was darker than the hair on his head, more caramel than blond. When he let it grow in, it gave him a rakish, rebellious air, which suited him well. It also made him look a little bit older, which I wasn't going to complain about. I knew I looked good for someone who was rapidly chasing down the big four-oh. But knowing it and believing it when there was a solid chance everything I was working with would soon be on display for a gorgeous man several years younger than me, one who was a known ladies' man, were two very different things. There wasn't much in this world I found intimidating, but getting naked with Webb Bryant was right up at the top of the list.

"You're a good kisser." My voice was husky, and I sounded kind of drunk. I had to blink to bring his too-handsome face into focus. There was no missing the self-satisfied smirk which tugged at his mouth.

"You ain't seen nothing yet." He dropped his head down, so our foreheads were touching. "I've been waiting for you, Ten. I didn't know it, had no idea I was searching for something, or someone, all these years I've been on the run. First time I saw you, I finally wanted to stand still."

I gulped and smoothed my hands over the width of his shoulders. I liked the strength that was evident in my hands. It would take a lot to move this man. He's proven impossible to ignore. "You wanted to stay in place, and I wanted to run the other direction. We're never moving the same way."

His arm tightened around my waist, and he tugged me up so I was plastered to his front. There was zero space between our heartbeats or the parts of our bodies throbbing and pulsing with need.

"Might not be headed the same way, but we always seem to end up standing right next to each other when we get where we're going. I think that means something. I think *I* mean something to you, Ten. I know you mean the world to me." One of his wide hands landed on my ass, and the other started to glide up my back, taking my T-shirt with it.

I sighed and closed my eyes. I ran the tip of my nose along the length of his collarbone, my breath making his tanned skin damp. "I don't need those kinds of words, Webb. I'm here. I couldn't stay away. I don't need you to give me the usual song and dance."

He tugged my shirt over my head, sending my hair in every direction. Webb used his index finger to trace the satin that covered the rise of my breasts, his touch light and reverent. He used the knuckles of his other hand to tilt my chin so we were looking directly into each other's eyes.

"You might not need the song and dance, Ten, but you deserve both. And you're out of your damn mind if you think I've ever told another woman she means something to me. I've never stayed in one place long enough for anyone to have time to matter. For you, I not only stayed, but I also let myself wonder what would happen if I never left. I want to give you the pretty words, because they're yours and yours alone." He opened his hand so he was holding my face, and lowered his head so his mouth could settle on mine once again. His kiss turned my mind to mush and my knees into water. I sighed against his mouth when his tongue twisted around mine, delving deep and stealing away the last of my resistance and reserve. How was anyone supposed to stay strong when he talked sweet and kissed dirty?

"I'll take them if they're mine." And because I secretly loved I was the only one he'd given them to, he didn't need to know I would keep them somewhere special inside of me forever.

He wiggled his eyebrows at me, and the smirk on his face turned into something far more lecherous and lustful. "Let me kiss you the way I've wanted to since the beginning, Ten." It was a demand.

"Isn't that what we've been doing?" My voice wobbled, and a pink heat worked its way up over my mostly naked chest and across my throat. I was pretty sure we'd been exchanging some of the best kisses of my life up until a moment ago. I watched with wide eyes as he methodically slipped first one bra strap down my arm, then the other. He kissed each of my shoulders, and silently reached around behind me and unhooked my bra. Normally it would've unnerved me to have my nipples pointing so obviously at the man who made them hard and achy, but all I could feel was pride and power when hunger filled Webb's gaze.

The grin on his face turned wicked, and the blue in his eyes blazed hot enough to burn. "That was me making the next move. Now that I have you where I've always wanted you, I'm going to do everything in my power to make you want to stay there."

He pressed forward, which pushed me backward, the back of my knees hit the edge of the bed. I went down with a soft noise. "Where is *there*, exactly? Beneath you? On top of you? Standing right next to you?" The questions were breathless and choppy as Webb's fingers quickly worked on the fastening of my jeans, parting the denim and revealing the soft skin below my belly button. He let out a groan and shifted gears, tugging my boots off so we didn't have a tangled mess of clothing later on down the line. I blinked, and I was naked, laid out before him like a sacrifice, only I didn't feel like I was about to lose anything. No, I was on the precipice of gaining something amazing, all I had to do was follow Webb wherever he wanted to lead me.

"*There* is all of the above. I want you wherever you want to be, as long as I'm part of the picture. *There* is right here, right now. I want you to want to be with me the same way I want to be with you. I'm going to give you every reason you can think of to stay." In the next breath, his mouth hit my lower stomach, leaving a trail of wet kisses and scalding little licks.

I wasn't thinking about anything but his hands and his mouth moving all over my body. His hands skimmed the outside of my thighs, fingertips rough, palms a warm rasp against my softer skin. His wet tongue dipped into the hollow of my belly button and swirled a sexy figure eight up my torso. I was barely aware of the way I let my legs fall open, making room for his impossibly wide shoulders. I was focused on his hands moving across my quivering skin, chasing shivers and creating a trembling wave, which crashed and broke at the apex of my spread thighs. I knew I was already wet and ready. I could feel the way my body throbbed and pulsed in anticipation. When the warmth of Webb's mouth surrounded a puckered nipple, my back lifted off the bed, and my heels dug into his back without my permission.

I gasped his name and felt his grin against my damp breast. When his teeth dragged across the overly sensitive tip, my eyes crossed and I bit down on my tongue hard enough to draw blood so I didn't scream.

"You taste so damn good. I knew you would. I dreamed about it, jerked off thinking about it. Now I know you're even better than I imagined." One of his hands wandered between my legs. I felt his thick fingers tickle the wetness gathered in my soft, hot folds. Webb hissed out a breath of appreciation, and the whisper of it on my most sensitive flesh sent a shot of liquid heat running through my body.

His quiet admission reminded me of my early morning fantasy about him. I didn't dream about the way he tasted, but after the drugging, addictive kisses he kept feeding me, I knew that was going to change.

Webb used his teeth on my breasts, alternating between playing with the tender, pointed tips, and using his tongue to trace and tease the surrounding skin. While I was drowning in the pleasure his talented mouth was leaving behind, he stole my breath and scrambled my brain by sliding his fingers inside the drenched opening between my legs. I wasn't ready for the jolt of fire that shot up my spine, or the way he seemed to instinctively know exactly where to touch, and just how I liked it. He wasn't gentle or tender. He stroked and fondled with purpose. There was no mistaking he was signing his name on my body with every practiced twist and drag of his fingers.

My hips shifted, searching for more, or trying to escape the overwhelming sensations sweeping through my body. Webb was having none of it. There was no hiding from him, from this. His free arm came across my hips, holding me in place as he leaned back far enough he had an up close and personal view of his fingers playing with my pussy.

His blue eyes glowed with a predatory light I'd never seen before. The look on his face was hungry, ravenous even. His cheekbones had twin flags of red showing under the golden hue, and his nostrils flared every time I made a noise or shifted under his hold. His lips were slightly swollen and wet. He looked ready to pounce, to devour me, and I was more than ready to let him.

My breath hitched when his fingers slid in particularly deep. It felt like he was purposely searching out all the hidden places that were bound to make me lose my mind. No one had taken this kind of time and care with me or my body before, and I vaguely wondered why I'd settled for less when there was so much more out there. Webb said he was constantly searching, looking for something or someone to make him stay. I'd done the opposite: settled, accepted what was offered because I had nowhere to go.

"You're pretty when you're all shiny and wet, Ten. I want to put my mouth on every single part of you." He leaned closer, his teeth digging into the soft skin of my inner thigh. I threw an arm over my eyes as my head tossed on the covers.

My head might have been rolling around in the negative, but

the words leaving my mouth over and over again gave him permission to ruin me however he saw fit. "Yes. I want your mouth on me . . . everywhere."

He gave a hum of approval, lips making their way up my leg until I felt the warm press of his lips surrounding my clit. I swore and blindly reached for the back of his head. White lights popped brightly behind my eyelids, and my entire body vibrated as coiled tension tugged at my muscles. Webb's soft hair slid through my fingers as his mouth and fingers continued their thorough assault. I felt his fingers scissor and stretch, pressing against my inner walls as his tongue circled my clit with slow, deliberate intent. He was taking me apart with every flick of his tongue and flex of his fingers, and I didn't want to be put back together the way I was before. I couldn't fathom a life where I lived without knowing how amazing Webb Bryant could make me feel.

He grabbed a handful of my backside and pulled me even closer to his mouth. The edge of his teeth caught my very sensitive clit, and my back bowed in response. My nails dug into his scalp, and my legs shook on either side of his ears. I kind of wished we were in a cheap motel room with a mirror on the ceiling. I bet we looked good together like this, skin on skin, blonde and blonder all tangled together, trying to get closer.

"Webb." His name escaped in a broken shriek which everyone in the renovated house had to have heard. There was no room to be embarrassed though, because he snatched all the air from my lungs and every thought from my head when his tongue slid inside the velvet sheath already being worked over by his fingers. I felt full, filled to the brim with new sensations and unexplored desires. I doubted I could remember what sex felt like before Webb changed it all and showed me how good it could be when you had it with someone who was searching for you.

Wet fingers trailed across my thighs and drew an aimless

pattern on the flat part of my tummy under my belly button. His slippery tongue darted in and out of my fluttering opening as my body begged for more. I bit down on my knuckle, wanting his mouth on mine while his cock moved in and out of me at the same frantic pace. I wanted him everywhere at once, but the single place he was focused on at the moment couldn't take the attention anymore.

The orgasm hit me with no warning. One second I was warm and writhing under Webb's torment, the next I was a ball of fire burning under his mouth and hands. I mindlessly pulled him closer, legs practically clamping down around his ears. A thin cry ripped out of my chest, and my hands shook as they landed on the bed above my head.

Webb rubbed soothing circles with his fingers on my bare skin as he fell back. He pressed his forehead against the inside on my knee and let out a long, slow sigh of satisfaction.

I was a sexed-out mess, delirious on a heady mix of emotion and revelations. It took me a minute to get it together enough to ask, "What about you?"

I expected him to climb on top of me and start chasing after his own release as soon as he had a taste of mine. I wasn't ready for the gentle care he was showing me instead.

Webb chuckled against my skin. "Do you know how many times I've gotten what I wanted in my life, Ten?"

The question caught me off guard. I rallied enough to push up on my elbows so I could look down at where his golden head was bent between my legs. "Not enough would be my guess."

He snorted and lifted his eyes to mine. "This is the first time I have ever gotten something I wanted without having to do something terrible to get it. Nothing feels better than that." He lifted a playful eyebrow and waved a hand in the general direction of his waist. "Haven't come in my pants since I was a teenager, but I guess it's a good thing. When I got my wallet back from the feds, it was missing a little something-something."

I felt my jaw drop and he rose to his feet. I had questions, but I immediately got distracted when he started pulling his clothes off. I was ridiculously proud of the visible wet spot on the front of his jeans. "Are you telling me the FBI lifted a condom from your wallet?"

My mouth went dry when his jeans hit the floor. Of course Webb went commando. I didn't expect anything else. He winked at me and held out a hand. "No. I'm telling you your douchebag ex took the condoms I had in my wallet to fuck with me, or so I wouldn't fuck you. Either way, take a shower with me. I need to clean up and wash away that meeting with my old man."

Still trying to wrap my head around Gage doing something as petty as snatching protection from a suspect's wallet, I let Webb guide me into the small bathroom. It only took a second for me to realize all of my attention should be on the man in front of me and not one from my past.

CHAPTER 12

WEBB

"**D**ON'T MAKE ME GO OVER your head, Gage. How's it going to look when your superiors find out I'm doing your job for you . . . again? The father is in New Orleans. He was easy enough to find. He knew there were twins from the start, even ended up with custody of one of them, albeit briefly. Get a statement and officially clear Webb." Ten rubbed the furrow between her pinched eyebrows. "And get Webb's picture off the damn television, or at least let people know it isn't him. That was a real dick move."

Ten was pacing back and forth in front of the rumpled bed, phone to her ear, as she practically barked orders at her former lover.

"I can't believe no one on your end tried to contact the father when the mother proved difficult to locate. Still cutting corners when you think you have the right person for the crime, I see. I shouldn't be surprised, but I am."

The shower we shared had been steamy and relaxing in more ways than one. I finally knew what it felt like to have her pretty mouth wrapped around my dick, and I knew she went soft and pliant when I kissed and sucked along the long line of her neck. She was incredibly responsive and receptive. There was a deep pool of sensuality running underneath her hard-as-nails surface. All I needed was a tiny crack in the surface to get at all the sweetness which laid molten and surging below the hard veneer. She got to me in a way I wasn't one-hundred percent ready for. Sure, I chased her, practically hunted her like she was prey, a prize fought for and won. But now I had her, beyond keeping her and making her want to stay with me, I wasn't certain what I was supposed to do with her. Ten made it clear, time and time again, she didn't *need* anyone. I wasn't sure what it meant for us that I knew I needed her and really wanted her to need me in return.

Ten ended her call with a growl, and I watched as she threw her cell phone halfway across the room. Luckily all it hit was a decorative chaise lounge, hitting the velvet surface and bouncing harmlessly to the floor. She plowed her fingers through the front of her long hair and resumed pacing.

"God. He is the actual worst. I don't know how he keeps his job. I can't believe I was ever stupid enough to agree to marry him. It gives me nightmares when I think about what my life would've been like if I went through with the wedding." I swore I could hear her grinding her teeth in aggravation with each step she took.

Unwilling to let the past snatch away the really nice things currently happening between us in the present, I rose to my feet and caught Ten by her stiff shoulders. I dropped a kiss on the top of her head, enjoying the way the damp strands felt against my lips. There was one sure-fire way to get rid of the shadows still surrounding me. I had to pull them all into the light so there was no place left for them to haunt.

"Let's get out of here. There's somewhere I want to take you." While the conversation with Bernard had been enlightening in a pretty shitty way, we still didn't have a clear-cut way to locate my long-lost brother or any idea where Jolene might be hiding. Having Bernard admit he knew I was a twin would get Gordon off my back for a little bit, but I'd seen the determined look in the man's eyes when he sat across from me in the interrogation room. He didn't want to let me go, because he knew I was going straight to the woman who left him. He was operating from a place of retribution, not justice, which made him dangerous.

I was thrilled when Ten's arms wrapped around my waist and gave a hint of a squeeze. She'd spent so much time trying to keep me at arm's length, it was nice to finally feel her thawing out, pulling me closer.

"Where are we going?" She was frustrated and annoyed, but for once those feelings weren't because of me, and I pretty much loved it.

I tugged on the ends of her hair and gave her a lopsided grin. "It's a surprise. Just trust me." I wouldn't say it was a good surprise, but it was one I needed to share with her if this thing I'd been diligently trying to grow between us ever had a chance to flourish.

Wordlessly, she nodded. She pulled away from our embrace and moved to pick up her abused phone. "Give me a minute to run to my room and change. I need to pull my hair up, too. If I leave it down and let it dry, it'll be a rat's nest in no time."

"Take your time. I'm gonna run and put gas in the rental and grab us something to eat while we drive." I also needed to ask Wyatt to put some kind of tracking on the bank accounts with the money Bernard had stockpiled for his unwanted mistakes. Not a conversation I was looking forward to. "I'll be back in an hour or so." Maybe it was wishful thinking, but I was also going to stock up on protection while I was out and about. Never had being unprepared hurt as badly as it did when I felt Ten come apart all over my tongue. I could still taste her and picture the look of shocked ecstasy on her face when she finally let go. She was always the most beautiful woman I'd ever seen, but when she dropped her shield and forgot to hide behind her iron walls, she was absolutely breathtaking. She looked like a goddess, an ethereal being I had no right to be touching, no right to be falling for. I was a mere mortal, a man who was flawed and fucked up on a good day. She was something else, and I felt like the luckiest bastard on the planet to be the one she let close enough to touch. Even if she was covered in thorns, I didn't mind bleeding for Tennyson McKenna.

We parted ways, and I rushed through the piddly errands, the stilted conversation with my brother taking the longest. I took the time to find some authentic Cajun food for us to eat as we drove out of town. I texted Ten when I got back to the hotel, and she came running down the steps a few minutes later. It was all too easy to picture her as a tragic southern belle, fighting everyone and everything for the only home she'd ever known, as all she loved burned in the background. Scarlett was tough; Ten was a hundred times tougher.

She slipped into the passenger seat and immediately grabbed for the bag of food I'd placed on the back seat. She peeked inside and shot me a look out of the corner of her eye. "This looks messy. How are you going to eat and drive at the same time?"

I chuckled and got us on the road. We were headed out of New Orleans and across Lake Pontchartrain. It wouldn't take too long to get where we were going. The drive was short, but the journey had been a long and arduous one. If the FBI hadn't gotten involved, and if I hadn't wanted to prove to the woman sitting next to me, currently trying to delicately eat étouffée from a to-go container, that I was a man who could be worthy of her time and attention, there was a good chance I never would've made a trip back. But I needed Ten to see exactly where I'd been, so she could see how far I'd come, how far I was willing to go . . . for her.

She surprised me when she leaned across the interior of the car, and offered me bites of her food from her spoon so I didn't have to juggle the messy Cajun food and try to drive at the same time. I was used to eating on the run. I could've managed, but it was enlightening to watch Ten step out of her comfort zone and be overtly affectionate and sweet. We were both lost in thought as the miles rolled by. I was watching her. She was watching the scenery as it changed from the glitz and relative glamour of the Quarter to the damaged and decimated outskirts of the city. Katrina had been years ago, but there were areas that still looked ravaged and abandoned, possibly to never be rebuilt as the inhabitants had long since fled.

She let out a shaky breath when we hit the Causeway, which would take us all the way across the lake into St. Tammy Parish. Weird flashes of nostalgia and memory swept over me as we charged toward my past with no warning. It felt familiar, yet somehow so very different. Things had changed, but it all still felt the same. The water glinting underneath the roadway felt like it had been there since I was a child, even though I knew it was impossible. Once we hit the outside of the city and the landscape turned dense and far more remote, Ten reached out and put a hand on my thigh. I knew it was hard as a rock and still as stone, because the tension in my muscles was taut enough I was afraid I might shatter if I moved wrong. Clearly, Ten knew exactly where we were headed without me having to say a word.

I was glad we rented a four-wheel-drive vehicle when the terrain shifted from paved, well-maintained roads to the gnarled, slippery paths I traversed as a child. No one in the swamp worried about ease of access. The harder it was for a trespasser to get onto your property, the better. Once it got dark, finding your way out of the mossy, tree-lined landscape was nearly impossible unless you knew where you were headed.

"Who owns the property you grew up on? You mentioned aunts, but never said anything about grandparents." Ten's questions were abnormally loud in the quiet of the car.

I wanted to put a hand over hers on my leg, but they were locked around the steering wheel so tightly I couldn't pry them free. I felt a muscle in my jaw twitch as I was swept up in unclear memories and old resentment.

"My Aunt Clara and her husband own the land. I think they inherited it from Jolene's parents who both passed away fairly young. Car accident. Her dad was driving drunk. Killed on impact and took a young family with them." Jolene came by her chaos naturally, it seemed. "There were five girls in the family. Clara is the oldest, Jolene falls somewhere in the middle. When I lived here, four of the five lived on the property. Jolene had the shack closest to the swamp, Clara and the youngest sister lived in the house with their families, and my Aunt Ana had a trailer closer to the road. They all had a bunch of kids running around, except Clara. I think that's why she had a semi-soft spot for Wyatt and me. She wasn't exactly maternal, and from what I remember, she couldn't stand Jolene, but she always stopped by once a day to make sure we at least had one meal." I shook my head. "Unless Jolene was around, then she stayed away. The rest of the sisters would pop by every now and then, but Clara was the only one who remembered to check on a regular basis that Jolene hadn't killed us."

"Are you sure she still owns the place? This reminds me of the backwoods in Wyoming. I don't want to run across an armed homesteader pissed we're on their property." I knew by the tone of her voice she wasn't kidding. She probably would've preferred to take this trip down memory lane armed with her shotgun.

"You only leave the swamp if you die or if someone runs you off. No one in these parts is going to give up the hold they have on their property. It's usually the only thing they have." I rolled my shoulders and cracked my neck, trying to remind myself I was an adult now. I didn't have to worry about the creepy crawlies and the pitch black darkness, or the monsters hiding inside of it anymore.

"Besides, we can get to where we're going without running into the family. Jolene made sure she set herself up out of the way. She hated anyone poking into her business. I doubt anyone will know we were ever here." I shrugged. "The place was barely standing back then, who knows if it's even still there." It might be rubble and ruin just like my childhood.

Ten made a humming noise and her fingers dug into the tight muscle she was gripping as if her life depended on it. "You sure you don't want to talk to your aunt if she's around? Might be nice for her to see you're alive and mostly well."

I thought about it for a second, but shook my head when a sliver of unease slipped under my skin. "I think I can only handle facing one ghost at a time." I owed Clara a sincere thank you for doing what she'd been able to. But, the little boy who was whisked away in the middle of the night, stolen away from the only family and home he knew, still had a lot of resentment and anger when it came to dealing with the people who sent Jolene running. Logically, I knew my mother probably deserved the boot, but the wounded child I carried around inside of me stubbornly blamed everyone for the way his life had twisted after that night.

When we rounded a sharp corner, the murky water was visible just beyond the flowing sycamore trees. So was the dilapidated and rusted building where I'd grown up. Calling it a shack was generous. Looking through adult eyes at the mashup of old wood, aluminum sheeting, rusted tin, and broken glass, I realized the building was closer to a shed or a pile of industrial rubbish than any kind of habitable home. Bile burned the back of my throat, and something ugly dug its claws into my gut. I forgot all about Ten sitting next to me until she asked me if I was okay.

It took longer than it should've for me to nod. It was hard seeing this place Jolene considered an acceptable place for her children to live. I guess the accommodations, or lack thereof, never bothered her because she was never around. I threw the car door open with more force than necessary and gratefully clasped Ten's hand when she wrapped it around mine as she resolutely started toward the ramshackle structure.

"I didn't need to see this, Webb. I know you're more than where you come from. I could see you were more than you showed the world, from the minute you told me you weren't going to the hospital to get your shoulder looked at, until you knew for sure that your brother was dead or alive. You never fooled me." She gave my hand a squeeze, which I returned.

"*I* needed you to see it. I think I want you to understand why I've done some of the things I had to in the past. Everything I am, everything I do, is to make sure I never end up back here. I've never needed forgiveness from anyone, but I'm not above asking you to recognize how scared and desperate the kid who came from here was." I stepped in front of her, tested the door, and found it unlocked. No one locked their doors this far out in the swamp. I took out my phone so I could shine a little bit of light into the dark, dreary space.

I was surprised to see the interior looked pretty clean, cleaner than when Jolene was in charge of the upkeep. The furnishings were old and ratty, but someone had patched them up, and there wasn't any dust on them. The floors were uneven and cracked in places, but they were free of debris, and it was obvious someone had swept and mopped recently. The windows were broken in places, but there were cheery yellow curtains hanging over them. The inside was in direct opposition with the outside of the small building.

"Someone has been in here taking care of the place," I stated the obvious, letting Ten's hand drop as I walked around the place that held both my worst and best memories.

"It looks like someone has been waiting for this place to have people living in it again. You think Jolene has been back here?" I felt Ten at my back, protective and curious as she took in our surroundings.

"I doubt it. Like I said, I don't know why the sisters ran her off, but it was bad. She had it easy here; I can't picture Jolene making amends with anyone. She doesn't know how to say 'sorry.'" Oh, she could say it, but she never meant it.

"Maybe whomever has been taking care of this place wanted to make sure you and Wyatt had a place to come back to, a place to call home. Maybe they never wanted you to leave." Ten's voice dropped to barely a whisper, and I felt her palm land on the center of my back. The heat from her touch was oddly reassuring, but her words, those hurt my heart. "I have to tell you, Webb, I ache for the little boy who left here, but there is no way I could want the man who was brave enough to come back here more than I already do." I looked over my shoulder at her and was nearly knocked over by the honesty in her eyes. She wasn't telling me what I wanted to hear so I would feel better, she was giving me the truth.

I exhaled, letting some of the tension and pressure which had been building up inside of me out on the long breath. I managed a smile. "Prove it." The taunt was flirty and meant to be a harmless challenge, but I should have known Ten wasn't the type of woman to be goaded without getting an unexpected reaction.

The next thing I knew her hands were on the center of my chest, and she was pushing me back until I went tumbling over the couch. I landed with an oomph, phone falling to the floor as Ten's body suddenly pressed into mine. She practically crawled into my lap, the dim light of the room making her features hard to see, but there was no mistaking the intent in her hands when they started to pull at the hem of my T-shirt. Her long legs straddled either side of mine as she leaned against the bulge which was steadily filling the fabric behind my zipper.

I felt her fingers brush along the line of my jaw, and her lips lightly touched my temple as she whispered, "It doesn't matter where you are or where you've been. I still want you, Webb. I don't want to, but here we are . . . together."

She managed to wrestle my shirt over my head without any help from me. When her mouth touched mine, I tasted her determination to prove something. To me or to herself, I wasn't sure, but I was happy to be the recipient of the point she was making. Her soft hand skimmed across my chest, nails dragging through the dusting of hair between my pecs. I both loved and hated that her face was obscured by shadows. Not being able to read her reactions or see what she was thinking added an edge of something erotic and dark to the way she touched me. All I had to go on was the small sounds she was making and the way her body moved and bent against mine. She kept pressing closer, her hands seemingly intent on touching as much of my bare skin as possible.

There was no way she could miss the hard shaft rising and pressing between her legs. I could feel my cock weeping and throbbing against the back of my zipper. I would bite my own tongue off before I showed an ounce of discomfort though. I wasn't about to break the spell Ten was weaving around me. With her hands on my skin and her mouth playing with mine, there was no past waiting to take a bite out of me, no future that seemed hazy and daunting. All that existed was the present, the moment where she kissed me, touched me, told me without words that maybe she wanted to keep me around.

I sighed in surrender when her tongue slid across mine, and quickly stripped her out of her top and bra so we were the same amount of naked. I'd had her under me once already, but my skin sizzled when I felt the brush of her pointed nipples against my chest, and I liked the feeling of having her over me even more. Ten was a natural when it came to taking charge and being in control.

There was no hesitation in the way she touched me or teased me. Never in a million years would I have dreamed that coming back to the place where everything in my life started to fall apart was going to lead to something I couldn't live without. Maybe I had to go back to the beginning before I could start all over.

Ten kissed me until neither one of us could breathe. Her busy hands mapped out all the lines and definitions of my chest and stomach, while mine reached for her tied-up hair. I wanted it down and brushing across all of my naked skin. She smiled against my mouth when she traced the cut of my abs, and I was eternally grateful I'd always had a fast metabolism and jobs that required lots of physical labor. When her quick fingers unbuckled my belt and started on the fastenings of my jeans, I forgot my name and where I was. All I could focus on was the brush of the back of her fingers against the sensitive length of my cock. I figured there was no need for underwear since she already knew first hand that modesty and I weren't friends.

She went still above me when hot, wet skin kissed her fingers. Her kiss took on a desperate edge, teeth biting, breaths mingling in a choppy pant as she turned her wrist, so the flat of her palm cradled the rigid shaft. I felt my balls tighten in pleasure and my cock pulse in time to my thundering heartbeat. When she dragged her thumb along the line of the thick vein that ran the underneath side of my erection, I barked her name into the kiss and dug my fingers into her undulating hips hard enough to bruise.

I still couldn't see her all that well, but I felt the feathery sweep of her eyelashes against my cheek when she turned her head so she could whisper in my ear, "I know you were never a Boy Scout, but right about now I'm wishing you were, so you knew enough to always be prepared."

I threw my head back on the old couch, letting out a surprised laugh. With one hand I popped open her jeans so I could work the other between lace and soft skin. I grinned when I got a handful of perfectly round and sweetly toned ass.

"I wasn't a Boy Scout, but I was a horny teenage boy once upon a time. If there was even the slightest hint I might get laid, I made sure to be prepared. I'm talking, if a girl so much as smiled at me in the hallway at school, I went out and bought a rubber. Do you really think I would miss a shot at getting to be inside of you again after our last go-round?" I was far too opportunistic for that.

I felt Ten laugh, and a second later she was standing in front of me stripping off the rest of her clothing. She got naked the same way she did most everything else, efficiently and with minimum fuss. She didn't make a show out of it, no production. It wasn't like she needed the fanfare or gimmick anyway. She already had me anywhere, anyway, she wanted me. An extra wiggle here or there was appreciated but very unnecessary.

Her long hair drifted over her shoulders and slithered over her skin. It shimmered platinum in the waning light, and I wanted to wrap my hands all up in it as she rode me until I lost my mind.

Ten pointed at my lap where the tip of my dick was resting against my lower belly. There was a glimmer of wetness on my abs, and I swore I saw her lick her lips right before she ordered, "Pants off." She held out her hand and wiggled her fingers at me in a 'gimmie' motion. "I never thought I would be interested in someone who was such an optimist."

I pushed my jeans down as far as they could go without having to stand up and strip them off. I passed a condom to Ten from my wallet and found my phone where I dropped it so she could have enough light to get the damn thing open and place it where it belonged.

While she messed around with the foil in front of me, I leaned closer to her, wrapping my arms around her waist so I could touch my lips to the bottom of her breast bone. I moved my head from side to side, so my hair rasped along the sensitive undersides of her breasts.

"I don't have faith in many things, Ten. You and me, I've believed in from the start." I felt one of her hands glide through my hair as she maneuvered me back to the reclining position I'd previously had.

"When you say things like that to me, I don't know what to do with you, Webb." She averted her gaze away from mine as she focused all her attention on rolling the thin latex down the length of my straining erection. I was so hard I hurt. So turned on it was getting more and more difficult to think straight and not say things which might scare her off.

"Right now all you need to do is fuck me." And love me. I couldn't tell her that though. 'We'll get to the rest of it when we aren't someplace filled with so many ghosts." When we figured out where this thing between us was going to land, it needed to be just the two of us.

Wordlessly, she resumed her position on my lap. Hard cock met soft opening and we both sucked in a breath. Even though most of the afternoon had been one long, drawn-out day of foreplay, I didn't want to simply rut into her with no thought beyond getting off. I had more consideration than that. That was the old me. She meant more than a mere means to lose myself in the oblivion of pleasure.

Grabbing the base of my erection, I pressed down until the tip could drag through her wet center. She made a strangled noise in the back of her throat when the flared head tapped against her eager little clit. I kissed my way across her chest, stopping every now and then to suck little bruises on her pale skin. Sex, in this place I tried to forget, was bound to come with a tiny bit of pain. Luckily, she didn't seem to mind.

Her hands curled around my neck as she started to rock against me. Every time her hips lowered, she took a little bit more of my throbbing cock inside of her scalding heat. It felt like liquid silk was being wrapped around the entire shaft. I loved the way I could feel her flutter and quiver along every hard inch of me inside her. I loved the way she moaned my name long and loud.

I pulled her closer with one arm around her waist. The other I worked between us so I could toy and tease her puckered nipples. I watched her eyes flare wide, eyelashes flicking rapidly, as she suddenly moved and impaled herself all the way on the heated flesh between her legs. I gasped at the sudden sensation of being encased in velvet and warmth. My thighs shook, and I felt pleasure spool wildly out of control from low in my spine. Desire rushed unchecked throughout my body, and all I could do was move with Ten as she started to lift herself up and let herself fall into a steady rhythm that made my head spin.

Strong, lean muscle moved under my hands. She didn't need my help grinding and riding us both to oblivion. It didn't take long for a light sheen of sweat to cover us both from head to toe, making her hair stick to every visible patch of naked skin. I enjoyed the way it coiled around me. It was like there was some part of her determined to claim me, even if the woman wasn't fully ready.

I groaned when she rotated her hips and used her inner muscles to clamp down on me like a vise. She threw her head back with a gasp as my lips attacked the vulnerable arch of her throat. I whispered her name against her pulse and felt her body quicken in response.

We'd both already experienced body-numbing orgasms today, so I thought it would take longer to set me off. There was something about being this close to her, about Ten finally letting me in, all the way in, that did it for me. I wasn't going to last with her writhing around on top of me, proving to me that where I came from didn't matter, but where I ended up did.

"Close." Was the only warning she got, before my hips were lifting off the old couch and I was erupting inside of her clenching pussy. My hands drifted down her back as I pumped months of want, need, longing, and anticipation into her welcoming warmth.

Green eyes glittered in triumph, and her mouth kicked up at the corners. She was still rocking, moving in a slow slide on top of me, so I worked a hand across her waist and down her belly to get my fingers on her clit. I sighed as they slipped through silky moisture and watched her with unblinking eyes as she moved against me frantically and confidently, knowing exactly what she needed to get there. Her fingers scraped roughly through the bristles on my chin, and her mouth landed on mine with enough force to click our teeth together. It was a passionate, heady experience to have this woman so wound up she forgot to be careful.

Seconds later, Ten came in a rush, her body bending back as she broke apart in my hands once again. Her chest rose and fell with rapid breaths, and her pulse fluttered like a trapped bird at the base of her neck. She was perfect. She made me feel like I finally figured out how to do something right in my life.

We stayed like that until the sweat on our skin started to cool, and the position became uncomfortable. With one final kiss, we separated and started to climb back into our clothes. I was using the light on my phone to find a discreet place to discard the condom when we both stilled at the distinct sound of an approaching vehicle.

Exchanging worried looks, I grabbed Ten's hand and headed for the door just as a familiar voice, heavily laden with a southern Louisiana twang shouted, "Around here we shoot first and ask questions later."

Ten balked and visibly paled when the sound of a shotgun being cocked echoed through the now-dark night. I gave her a tired smile and squeezed her hand reassuringly. I was pretty sure the woman with the gun wasn't going to shoot.

"Aunt Clara, it's me, Webb. I'm coming out, please don't shoot me or my lady friend."

"Webb?" The drawl wobbled. "Jolene's Webb?"

I snorted. "She's never claimed me, but yeah, I'm Jolene's youngest."

There was a long moment of silence, then the sound of something heavy and metallic hitting the ground. A soft sob broke the night air, and I looked over at Ten in shock.

"Webb Bryant, get your skinny ass out here. I've been waiting damn near twenty years to see those baby blues of yours again."

I was frozen. Luckily, the woman I chose to fall head over heels for was strong enough, both physically and emotionally, to make me move. For the first time since we'd met, I didn't mind Ten pushing me out the door.

CHAPTER 13

TEN

EVEN IN THE MURKY DARKNESS, it was easy to see that Webb was related to the older woman standing next to an old, battered pickup truck. Her hair was more white than blonde, and she was shorter and wider in the way many women got as age and years of less-than-healthy living caught up to them. But the neon blue eyes, complete with a mischievous twinkle, and the smile, full of charm and a little bit of trouble, were all Webb. I eyed the shotgun she must have dropped when she recognized Webb. The stout woman left the weapon behind as she rushed to sweep Webb up in her arms.

At first, he was stiff, not seeming to know what to do with the exuberant affection. It only took the older woman's quiet cry on his chest for him to melt like butter. His strong arms wrapped securely around the smaller woman and hugged her back. I could hear him muttering soothing words into the top of her bent head, and my heart tried to knock its way out of my chest in response. Every time I turned around, he was showing me something new, unveiling hidden parts of himself. All those delicate pieces he'd lost to Jolene Bryant so long ago but was finding once again. I'd always been intrigued by the bits and pieces I'd glimpsed before when he let his guard down, but now I was getting the whole picture of who Webb Bryant was, and I couldn't look away.

"I can't believe it's really you. I shoulda' known that idiot sister of mine was going to snatch you and your brother away in the middle of the night when I told her she had to leave. I've been kicking myself in the rear for years for not taking you boys before she could rabbit out of here with you in tow." The older woman pulled back and ran a hand over her damp face. She put her hand on Webb's arms and tilted her head back so she could look up at him. A blinding smile split her weathered face. "You sure grew up handsome, didn't you, boy?"

It was too dark to tell if Webb was blushing, but by the way he rubbed a hand across the back of his neck and shuffled his feet, I bet he was. His reaction was cute and made me smile.

"Turned out all right, I guess."

The older woman snorted and crossed her arms over her ample chest. "No thanks to that mama of yours, I gather."

Webb shook his head. "No, Jolene didn't have anything to do with how I turned out or anything I accomplished. That all falls on Wyatt. He raised me, gave up pretty much everything to keep me out of trouble and off the streets. He's the best of all of us."

The woman sniffed and wiped away a tear. "Maybe you can convince him to come home for a visit. I've missed you boys something fierce. Always kinda thought of you both as my own."

Out of the corner of my eye, I watched Webb stiffen. I reached out a hand and put it on his back reflexively. I knew he thought he wasn't ready for this conversation when we showed up on the property, but he was going to have to have it anyway. I didn't want him to say something he was going to regret because he was speaking through a filter of old hurt. It was becoming clear the Bryant brothers were nowhere near as alone in this world as they always believed themselves to be.

"Why did you make Jolene leave? It was no secret you and she didn't get along, but you had to know what was going to happen to me and Wyatt without you there to act as a buffer. She treated us like luggage until Wyatt got old enough and big enough she couldn't force him to move anymore. I was lucky he refused to let me go and kept me with him. He's the one who tried to give me a home."

The older woman's eyes drifted over to mine, and I saw heartbreak clear as day shining in the bright blue depths. She rubbed a shaking hand over her mouth and looked down at the dirt between her feet.

"I found out about the baby she got rid of, your twin. At first, I thought it was a rumor. One that swirled around the swamp for years. Sure, Jolene was a selfish brat without two working brain cells to rub together, but I couldn't imagine her throwing a baby away. Not as long as Bernard kept funneling money her way. The rumors got louder, and one of the busybodies in town told Ana they saw a little boy who looked just like you when they were on vacation in Florida. Just like you, Webb. I couldn't take it no more. I didn't bother to ask Jolene because the woman doesn't open her mouth without lying. I didn't ask Bernard either since that uppity bastard would never lower himself to speak to a swamp rat like me. But his staff had loose lips, and it didn't take no time at all to figure out Jolene had twins and gave one of them to Bernard to take care of. He gave the baby away like it was a bad Christmas present. I was furious, and so were the rest of the sisters. Jolene might not have wanted the responsibility of another baby, but we always cared about you boys and wanted you around."

She shook her head, and her wrinkled hands turned into tight fists. "I demanded Jolene find her other son. I told her she wasn't going to be allowed to stay on the property any longer if she didn't bring the boy home where he belonged. I also informed her I was going to do everything in my power to get custody of you boys.

Which would have put an end to her free ride with Bernard. It was time you and Wyatt had a proper home. I hated you boys living in this shack with nothing. Damn Jolene."

She huffed out a breath and reached out a hand, placing it on Webb's chest right over his heart. "I didn't know she would run. I thought she was going to fight me tooth and nail but eventually give in. She never wanted to be a mother. It was too much responsibility. Instead, she vanished and took you boys with her. I looked for you, Webb. I really did, but money has always been tight, and Jolene is slippery." She made a sniffing noise, and I watched as tears welled up in her eyes once again. "I thought you boys were dead. But I kept this place just in case. What if you wanted to come home, what if you wanted to remember where you came from. I refused to let your uncle tear it down."

This time Webb was the one reaching for a hug. He pulled the older woman to his chest and rested his cheek on top of her snowy hair. I heard him sigh, and I found myself having to blink away the burn of moisture in my eyes. It was an emotional reunion, and I could clearly see how important it was for Webb to hear that this woman from his past had wanted him for her own, that she hadn't forgotten about him.

"It was never easy, but we made it. We survived Jolene. And I just found out about my twin. All signs point to him not turning out as well as Wyatt and I did, though. He's been trying to frame me for armed robbery, not even caring if he gets caught in the process. He wants me in jail."

A soft gasp escaped Webb's aunt as she pulled back to look up at him. "Why would he do that?"

"Why does anyone do anything anymore?" I interjected with the dry statement. "Money. There's lots and lots of it sitting in a bank with the boys' names on it, and the missing twin is greedy and reckless."

Webb nodded and took a step back so he was standing at my side once again. "Bernard set up trust funds for all three of us boys. Jolene never told us about them. But when the long-lost Bryant went searching for his parents, he planned to blackmail Bernard but found out about the money instead. I figure, rather than taking his cut of the blood money and being happy about it, he wants mine, as well, and Wyatt's if he can figure out a way to get to it. If I'm in jail, all he has to do is walk into the bank with my ID and my face and they'd let him drain the account, no questions asked. It seems like he's an evil son of a bitch, but he isn't stupid."

I nodded and tugged on my lower lip as I considered everything we'd put together the last few days. "He went after Jolene, trying to find the boys. We're not sure if he ever caught up with her or not, but somehow he figured out Webb was in Wyoming. He's been setting up an elaborate plan for a while now to get Webb locked up." I cut a look at the man standing next to me. "Wyatt is in law enforcement, he's a much harder target to go after, but I'm not entirely convinced this guy isn't going to go after him next. Why take a third of the money when you can have it all? He just needs to get the other brothers out of the way." Webb was convinced he wanted revenge and the money was secondary. I was leaning toward agreeing with him since the twin didn't hesitate to commit a federal crime when he already had a nice stash of cash he could access with very little effort on his part. He wasn't wired right anyway you looked at it.

Going after a federal agent was pretty much a death sentence, and the older Bryant was hyper-alert as it was. I planned to push my concerns about the older Bryant at Webb until he promised to tell Wyatt to watch his back. I didn't like that we were dealing with an unknown entity who had already proven to be extremely dangerous and cunning with questionable motives. I was biding my time until Web's emotions weren't stretched so impossibly thin. The idea of his brother being as much of a target as he was might send him spiraling out of control, and as much as I normally liked his unpredictability, now wasn't the time for him to go off half-cocked.

The older woman made a face which made me stifle a laugh. "Wyatt went into law enforcement?" Her opinion of his career choice was evident in the twist of her lips and the tone of her voice.

Webb laughed. "He had to. It was the only way to keep me out of jail."

The woman's eyes shifted to me and one of her white eyebrows lifted. "So, this is your lady friend? I take it you're not married. How about Wyatt? What about kids? Did either of you boys have little ones?" She sounded so hopeful that it pulled at my heartstrings.

Webb threw his arm around my shoulders and tugged me to his side. His lips brushed my temple. Suddenly the deep, dark swamp was the most special place on Earth.

"Well, I'm mostly still trying to figure things out, how to live a life not on the run. Ten has been awesome enough to agree to help me out with that for a little bit." Belatedly, Webb introduced me to his aunt. His smile was sharp when he gleefully informed her I was also in law enforcement. The older woman looked like she was sucking on a lemon when she shook my hand. "No kids for either of us. Wyatt works too hard, but eventually, he's gonna find the right person and settle down. He's wanted a family of his own for a long time."

Clara wrung her hands together and gave Webb a pointed look. "You mean he's going to meet the right *man* and settle down, don't you, boy?"

I felt Webb stiffen in shock next to me. "What? How did you . . . ?" He trailed off as the older woman waved her hand in front of him.

"He was always a good boy. Quiet, too serious, even when he was little. I remember how keen he was on the neighbor boy.

Always wondered if that kind of interest was going to turn into something more serious as he got older."

Webb huffed out a breath and lifted a hand to rake his hair back from his forehead. "Jolene wasn't as observant as you. She didn't take the news well. I overheard her once, screaming at Wyatt that the reason we didn't have a home anymore was because of him. She told him you wouldn't let a pervert around the rest of the kids on the property. I'm sure he knew it wasn't true, but I think that a tiny part of him always wondered."

His aunt made a pained noise low in her throat. "Oh no. We don't care who you love around here. Lord knows we all tried to love that mother of yours through thick and thin. All we've ever cared about is you boys being happy." Clara gave me a pointed look which made me smile at her. I liked she was protective of both the man and the boy. Webb needed all the belated mothering he could get. I hated Jolene even more than I already did for taking him away from this woman who obviously cared about him deeply.

Webb cleared his throat and shifted his weight. "I'll be sure to pass the message along. I'm sure Wyatt will be happy to hear things aren't always as they seemed. He won't be surprised. Nothing with Jolene was ever cut and dry, much less shocking. I can't believe you looked for us. I didn't even know I needed to hear that."

She reached up and grabbed his face between her hands. "I wouldn't have let you go. I regret letting Jolene push me out of your life when you were little. I was always trying to keep a balance between making sure you boys were all right and letting Jolene live her own life. That girl, always such a mess. I'm glad our parents weren't around to watch her ruin the lives of their grandchildren. Now you're here, can you stay a while? Ana would love to see you; so would your uncle."

Webb was shaking his head before she finished speaking. "I can't stay right now, Aunt Clara. I have to find my twin before he does something else with my face to land me in more trouble. You need to be careful. If he comes around looking for family, remember, you don't know anything about him. Growing up with Jolene was bad, but something tells me this guy had it even worse than we did. He looks just like me. You have to ask smart questions if he comes around."

The older woman nodded solemnly. "I understand. I hate to see you go after all this time, but as long as you swear you'll come back, I won't fuss." She gave me a narrow-eyed look. "You can even bring her with you if she leaves the badge behind."

It was on the tip of my tongue to tell her I mostly found lost hikers and responded to wildlife reports, but it was too fun to watch her turn her nose up at the fact I was law abiding. Webb was totally a chip off her hardened block.

Webb squeezed the older woman one last time with a softly spoken promise to return with Wyatt in tow.

We stood in silence as she grabbed her weapon and climbed back into the rusted truck. We waved as she reversed out of the swamp, leaving us alone with nothing but the cicadas chirping.

I wound an arm around Webb's waist, not bothering to ask if he was okay, because I could tell he was still reeling from everything that happened. When some of his weight leaned on me, I realized holding him up was hardly a chore at all. I didn't feel like I was going to collapse or fold under the heaviness at all. It was illuminating. Somewhere along the way, playing this game of chase with Webb had given me back the inner strength that the professional and personal failures in my life had stolen away. Following Webb had led me to the woman I always wanted to be.

Now, I just had to figure out how to keep her around permanently, because Webb wasn't the only person who liked her.

CHAPTER 14

WEBB

I WAS TORN BETWEEN ASKING Ten to spend the night with me, and needing some space to sort myself out. It would've been very simple to let myself get buried under all the revelations from the past. Everything I'd learned today, from facing my father for the first time to learning my family hadn't wanted to let either Wyatt or me go, was enough to choke on. I was pushing back all the what-ifs and what-might've-beens with sheer determination. Being able to focus on Ten and all the ways our relationship was changing helped. Thinking about the future didn't have the same hollow, airless quality that pondering the past did. When I pictured all the good things I could have standing right in front of me, it made it much easier to push forward instead of stumbling back.

When we got back to the hotel, Ten gave me a quick kiss and whispered, "Call your brother. Come find me when you're done, if you need me. Text me if you don't." She silently slipped away, taking most of my heart and a huge chunk of my soul with her. I'd never met anyone who understood what I needed and went out of their way to give it without question. The unvarnished acceptance she gave me, even if it came reluctantly and sometimes with a bit of hesitation, was precious. I'd grown up feeling like I was cast off and thrown away. Instead of trying to find a place to belong like Wyatt did, I went out of my way never to stick around long enough for anyone or any place to feel familiar. Nobody could get sick of me or take issue with the man I was if I kept my bags packed and one foot out the door at all times. The way Ten fit me into her life, into her time, finally made me feel like I found my place. It was a spot she saved especially for me. It was mine, and I was pretty sure I would fight to the death to keep it.

I watched her hips sway and her hair swish across her back until she disappeared into her room. I'd been alone and dealing with my shit for a long time. I knew I could unscrew the cap off the bottle of poison that was my past, take a huge gulp and lay it all out for Wyatt, and still survive the way it burned. Knowing this time I didn't have to suffer through the pain alone was a nice development. I'd never had anyone besides my brother to lean on, and Ten sure was a pretty pillar of strength. She was like the Parthenon: a strong, beautiful, precious thing that managed to stay standing, no matter the chaos and turmoil that surrounded it. A place where men once worshiped, but had been battered and worn with time.

Entering my room, I played with my phone for a few minutes before doing as Ten instructed and called my brother. It was late on the East Coast and I wasn't even sure if Wyatt had been assigned a new case recently or not. He always worked weird hours, but when he was on a case, it was impossible to tell if he was awake when he should be sleeping or vice-versa.

"What's wrong?" My brother's voice was raspy with sleep, and I could hear the exhaustion wrapped around each word.

"Nothing. I wanted to talk to you about a few things, but you sound beat. I can just call you tomorrow." I plopped down on the edge of the bed so I could pull my boots off. I suddenly felt a whole lot older than my thirty-two years, and weariness pulled hard at every muscle in my body. I rolled my shoulders and cracked my neck, but neither helped the tension coiling up and down the line of my spine.

"No. I'm up. I was going to text you, but I fell asleep watching the news, which has my baby brother's damn face plastered all over it. I flagged the accounts you told me about. If anyone tries to access the money, an alert will go out, and we can track down our missing sibling. It's not much, but if money is his primary motivation for getting you out of the way, he might go for it even without you being locked up." I heard him moving around. There was a *thunk* and then a loud string of dirty words as something rattled and fell to the floor. "Fuck me. I kicked the edge of my coffee table. Hurts like a son of a bitch."

I laughed and threw myself back onto the bed. "Ten still thinks you need to be careful. She thinks you're a target as well."

"Tell Ranger McKenna I am perfectly capable of handling whatever comes my way. She's got her hands full with you." I could hear the smile in his voice.

"She does. Very full. But she's smart, and she's worried about both of us. It's kind of nice to have that for once." I tapped my fingers on my abs and stared up at the ceiling. "I need you, Wyatt. If something happens to you, my entire world will fall apart."

My older brother grunted. "You needed me then, Webb, you don't need me now. You aren't a wild, aimless kid anymore. Without even trying, you grew into a competent, reliable man. I know you don't see those things in yourself, but they're there."

I blinked in the darkness, slightly taken aback. Wyatt always told me he loved me and believed in me. This was the first time he's ever mentioned trusting me enough to take care of myself. "I went to the family compound in the swamp tonight. I wanted Ten to see how little we had growing up. I wanted her to understand why I did so many of the things I regret in my past. While we were there, I saw Aunt Clara."

I heard Wyatt suck in a sharp breath. He exhaled it a moment later, and I swore I could feel his emotions vibrating through the phone line. "Are you okay?"

Of course, he thought of me first. It's what he always did.

"It was actually good. She looks so old, but still the same. She rolled up with a loaded shotgun." A chuckle escaped when I recalled the bizarre scene. "If she'd been a few minutes earlier she would've got quite a show. Ten helped me exorcise a lot of old ghosts tonight."

Wyatt groaned. "Not as wild, but you're still impulsive as hell."

"I know." I sighed. "Aunt Clara swears up and down she looked for us. She didn't think Jolene was going to take us and disappear. She made her leave the property because she found out that Jolene gave away the other baby. She was pissed. She cried for us, Wyatt."

My brother was quiet for a long time and when he finally spoke his voice held quiet fury in it. "She could've done more. I know she tried to help, but before you came along, it was just me and Jolene. I was alone so much . . ." He trailed off, and I heard him swear under his breath. "Besides, I can only imagine if she found out I was not only a federal agent, but a gay federal agent. She would have a heart attack."

I shook my head even though he couldn't see me. "She asked about you. I told her you went into law enforcement and she already seemed to know about you liking dick. She wasn't even slightly fazed by it. Though she was properly disappointed you decided to become a civil servant. She's nothing like Jolene. I've been trying to stop myself from wondering how things might've been for us back then if she'd gotten her hands on us before Jolene bolted, what it would be like if she'd managed to find our brother and bring him home?"

"We don't get a redo. All we can do is make the most of what we've got now. We've always had each other, and it was enough.

Now you have Ten, which is even better. You've always needed someone strong enough to hold you in place. I was terrified if I tried to hold you still, you'd resent me, accuse me of trying to control your life, so I always let you go." Wyatt sounded slightly guilty about the fact he'd never been the one to put a leash on me, when in reality, it was the best decision he ever made. I would've chewed my own arm off back then to get away when the walls started closing in on me.

"We deserve a redo though. I'm okay with where we ended up, but it's okay to want more than what we were given. I told Aunt Clara we turned out all right despite Jolene's best attempts to ruin us, and it's true. I told her I would try and get you to visit when I have time to come back. You need to consider it. I think you need some kind of closure. I think you need to see we have a family, something you've always wanted."

Wyatt made a rude noise, and I heard sheets rustling and the sound of something heavy hitting glass. I would almost bet he was putting his gun and badge on the glass nightstand next to his bed. "I want a family, but I never said it needed to be our family."

"Making peace with our family might help you get some much-needed perspective on what you need to start your own." Wyatt wasn't as open with the details of his love life as I was, but I knew he had issues with commitment and found every man he was with lacking in some fundamental way. He was searching for perfect, a recreation of that teenaged boy who vanished when Jolene shattered his world. His plan was bound to fail because perfect didn't exist. I'd asked him once if he set his standards so high because he knew no normal person could reach them, assuring that he remained alone. He told me he wasn't going to waste his time on a man not willing to reach for the stars.

"I'm too tired to fight with you about this. I'll think about it, which is more than I ever thought I'd be willing to do. I need to catch a few Zs. I have a briefing for a new case in the morning. Where are you off to next?" He let out a jaw-popping yawn, which made me respond in kind.

"We're headed back to Wyoming. I'm sick of chasing my tail. I have no idea where to look for this guy, no one even knows his damn name. Jolene is MIA. Bernard is useless even if his statement about knowing there were twins will get the FBI off my ass for now. If my twin wants me, he knows where to find me, which is why we think he targeted banks in that region in the first place. I'm gonna stay in town for a few weeks and see what happens. I don't want to bring any more drama to Cy's doorstep. He'd shit a brick if I put Leo in danger on purpose." Plus, I was ready to go home. I'd never had one before, so I had no idea I would miss it as much as I did.

"Be careful. When you get back to Sheridan, talk to that sheriff and let him know trouble might be headed his way." The command was heavy handed, but there was something else in my brother's voice I couldn't quite put my finger on.

"That sheriff has a name. I thought all you guys with badges respected each other without question." I was teasing him, but I was starting to wonder if there was more to Wyatt's animosity than he let on.

"Goodnight, Webb." The terse farewell was followed by silence, letting me know he'd ended the call.

I laid in the dark for a while, thoughts swirling, nerves stretched taut. Eventually, I hauled my ass up and made my way into the shower. Messy sex in the swamp, and stress sweat on top of the natural mugginess of the South, had left me feeling grungy and sticky. It wasn't until I was washing the day away that I realized I needed to be clean because I didn't want to crawl in bed with Ten smelling like something that escaped out of a sewer. I didn't want to be alone. Not just for tonight, but for all the nights in the foreseeable future.

I wanted someone to hold me in the dark and tell me the monsters didn't matter. I wanted a warm body pressed against mine, and the sound of someone else's heart beating in my ears.

I wanted Ten.

When I was clean, I wrapped a towel around my waist and padded over to the adjoining door. I knocked and waited for a response from the other side. When a soft, "Come in," hit my ears, I slipped into Ten's room, zeroing in on the bed and the woman in the center of it. She had the lights off, and she was under the covers, but I could see she had her eyes open, and my gaze lingered where she had one bare leg sticking out of the fabric. The phone in her hands cast her face in a pale blue glow.

Without saying anything, I walked to the other side of the bed, dropped the towel, and crawled in next to her. Naked skin pressed against naked skin as I pulled her into my body. One of her arms went around my neck as I nuzzled down into the curve of her shoulder.

"How did it go?" Her lips touched my temple as I traced random patterns on her flat stomach with my index finger.

"It went. He's stubborn, and he had to deal with a lot worse from Jolene than I did. I hate that he carries so much hurt around with him." I let myself sink into her warmth and sighed in contentment when I felt her knee press between my legs. "I told him we were on the way back to Wyoming tomorrow. I've missed it, and I want to know what happens once we get back."

She hummed a little and rubbed her nose along the outside of my ear. The light contact sent shivers throughout my body. "I thought we agreed to let your brother make the next move. This is his game, and we don't have a rulebook."

I grunted. "No, what happens with *us* when we get back. Are you going to go back to avoiding me even though it's obvious you can't stay away? Are you going to pretend none of this ever happened?" I released a pent-up breath and asked what I really wanted to know. "Are you going to compare me to Cy and realize, once we're standing next to each other, I come up short just like all the other men in your life have?"

She gasped, and I felt her shake her head. "No. I'm not going to pretend this never happened and I'm not going to compare you to Cyrus. There is no comparison."

I jerked my head back reflexively. I'd forgotten how much it could hurt to be told you came up short by someone you cared so deeply about. Every instinct I had was telling me to run, and apparently Ten could sense my violent, visceral reaction, because she threw herself at me. Her hands landed on my chest as she climbed on top of me and pinned me to the bed beneath her.

"There's no comparison because I've never felt the things you make me feel when we're together. I already told you, things with Cy were familiar. I know what it feels like to be convenient and forgotten. Until you came along, I had no clue what it was like to feel . . . necessary. I've never been with anyone or had someone in my life who makes me feel like they need me to survive the way you do. Not just a warm body to be used for a quick release, but *me*. No one gave me the words you have, Webb. You come out on top each and every time." I growled in the dark because I couldn't see her face clearly. We were going to have to do this in the middle of the afternoon one of these days so I could memorize her expression and the look in her eyes when she got all commanding and serious with me. I also wanted her to see how much I liked it.

I put my hands on her waist and rolled her until I was stretched out over the length of her long, lean body. Relief at her words made me lightheaded.

Needing a break from the onslaught of emotions, I tried to turn the mood toward something more playful. "You know, I come when you're on top, too."

I hoped she could see my grin in the dim light. It was on the tip of my tongue to tell her she felt as vital as air, as important as food and water, but I wasn't sure she was ready to hear that I couldn't survive without her. It was ingrained in me to keep on going no matter what shape my heart was in, but I had no idea how to keep going when I handed it over to someone else.

CHAPTER 15

TEN

WHEN I WOKE UP THE next morning, I was immediately struck by the fact I wasn't trying to scratch and claw my way free from Webb's hold. I also wasn't holding onto him with everything I had inside me. It was the one and only time I'd opened my eyes to another person sharing my bed, completely content to simply be. I wasn't worried about the man next to me trying to smother me with unrealistic expectations and outrageous demands. There was still a niggling doubt in the back of my mind he wouldn't stick around, regardless of how things played out with his crazy family. But rather than focus on the fear, I allowed myself the pleasure of appreciating how good it felt to be pressed up against him for now. I was fully present in the moment, not trying to plan twenty steps ahead or obsessing over the faltering steps I'd taken to reach this place. It was liberating and settled an uneasy piece of my soul I hadn't realized was jagged to begin with. No wonder my heart always felt like it was bleeding. It was repeatedly getting stabbed by those pointed shards.

I squinted at the clock, noticing it was well into the morning, fast approaching the noon hour. I wasn't one who slept in on a regular basis, so the late hour surprised me. I figured all the emotional upheaval on top of all the sexual acrobatics with Webb the last day or so had caught up with me. And him, too, judging by the look of things.

Webb was on his side, one long arm stretched out so it rested across my hip. His other was bent up under his head, his cheek on his palm. His long, golden eyelashes cast shadows on the sharp curve of his cheekbone, and his typically smirking mouth was open in a slight part, his breath coming in low, soft puffs as he slept deeply. He wasn't the kind of man who looked young and carefree in his sleep. No, Webb saved the careful mask of indifference and artful disinterest for when he was awake so he could fool the rest of the world. With his eyes closed and his shields dropped, the real Webb Bryant shone through.

There were lines of tension between his eyebrows, and I could see his eyes twitching behind his eyelids. Occasionally, his fingers twitched and flexed against my skin, and I could tell he was running away from something or someone, even in his dreams. The man didn't know how to stay still.

I lifted a hand and rubbed my fingers over the furious V arrowing over his nose. I wanted to stand between whatever it was that always seemed to be chasing him and all his vulnerable places. The man's heart was surprisingly soft considering the beating it'd taken over the years. His armor was much thinner than my own. It was a disconcerting feeling, wanting to protect someone I cared about. I'd gotten so used to forcing myself to function alone, convinced myself I was better off shutting my emotions down, because all they ever did was get me in trouble or land me in a puddle of heartache. I wasn't ready for Webb to blast his way into the guarded parts of my heart so easily. I wasn't sure I was ready to let go of my strongly held belief that I simply wasn't meant to share my life with another person. Hanging my future and my happiness on a man who had never called one single place home for very long was quite possibly the riskiest thing I'd ever contemplated doing.

And I'd faced off with bears and mountain lions, not to mention two-legged predators who were armed to the teeth.

I dropped my fingers to his mouth, tracing the shape of his lips. I missed the arrogant smirk, and the soft smile I swore he reserved only for me.

I yelped in surprise when wet heat suddenly surrounded my exploring digits. Webb curled his tongue around my index finger, and his sleepy, cerulean gaze hit mine with the force of a punch to the gut. I vaguely wondered if I would always react so strongly to this man, if he would always have the ability to catch me by surprise and steal the breath from my lungs. I hoped so. It was a nice change of pace to be breathless with anticipation instead of fear.

I stroked my thumb along the curve of his bristly chin and gave him a crooked grin. "Morning, sleepy head."

His eyes darted past my shoulder to the clock. His eyebrows winged up when he caught sight of the time. "Good thing our flight isn't until later." He let out a yawn and rolled over onto his back, using his hold on my wrist to take me with him. I ended up sprawled across his chest, his hard erection prodding insistently at the inside of my thigh. "What time do we have to check out of here?"

He corded his fingers through my hair at my temples, the sleep in his gaze chased away by a burning, sapphire heat I was starting to recognize very well. I let him use his knee to press my legs open wider and settled more fully on top of him. Every time he took a breath, my nipples hardened at the abrasion from the dusting of his tawny chest hair they were pressed against. Webb must've felt them bead up because a wicked grin slipped into place on his too-handsome face. I tried not to arch like a cat when one of his hands skimmed down the length of my spine. I was only partially successful.

"We have to be out by noon, and we still need to turn the rental in." Our flight wasn't until late afternoon, which gave me plenty of time to psych myself up to get on another plane. Even though the flight was short, I was still dreading it. I was ready to be home, though. Well, back in Wyoming. I missed the wide-open sky, the dirt beneath my feet, the relative predictability of my days. I missed the sense of safety I'd found when I returned home. However, the idea of going back to the ranch, returning to my childhood bedroom in my parents' house was even less appealing than it had been for the last few years. "You're still planning on checking into the Lodge in Sheridan when we get back?"

There were a couple of different places in town where he could stay if he was dead set on staying away from the Warner Ranch. It wouldn't take his long-lost brother long to track him down if he set his mind to it. I was worried about Webb making himself such an obvious target, but I was also selfishly irritated he was going to be more than an hour's drive away from the ranch if something went wrong. He was also going to be too far away if I wanted to touch him, to kiss him, to hold him.

Webb nodded, hands landing on my backside as he pulled me closer to all the hard parts of his body practically begging for attention.

"Yeah. It's in the center of town and close to the sheriff's office. Hopefully, there will be enough foot traffic to keep the crazy bastard from doing anything too violent if he does come for me."

I huffed out a breath and pushed up off of his chest so I could sit on top of him. I loved the way his big body rippled with strength underneath me. I put my hands on his tight abs and watched as his eyes zeroed in on the slight bounce to my breasts as I hovered over him. The tip of his tongue darted out to slick across his lower lip. His hungry response to the sight of my body sent a surge of feminine power pulsing through my veins. I loved knowing I wasn't the only one undone by our undeniable connection and chemistry.

"I want to be there if he comes for you. I can't believe I'm saying this, but I want to stay with you in town until your brother is in custody, or until we figure out how to find him. I hate the idea of you hanging your ass out there with no one to watch your back." If things went bad, they were going to go really bad if Webb's penchant for finding trouble held true.

Webb's entire face softened slightly, and his expression went from lecherous to thoughtful in a blink. He gave my waist a squeeze as his brows winged upward. "You don't have to do that, Ten. You have a life to get back to. You don't have to hang out in Oz with me until I drop the house on the Wicked Witch. I appreciate all you've already done, more than I can say."

"I know I don't have to, Webb. I want to." I actually wanted him to want me there, as well. I wanted him to trust me enough to keep him safe because I was starting to believe he might be the only one I'd be willing to hand my heart over to.

His expression switched back to one full of lust and longing. I let out a surprised squeak when I suddenly found myself underneath miles of masculine muscle and impatient hands. "If you want to be where I am, the door is always open. As long as you want to be there for more reasons than to make sure I haven't tripped over another bad decision that's gonna bite me in the ass. I need you to want *me*, Ten, not just want to keep me safe."

If his insecurity didn't mirror my own, it would have been tiresome and annoying. I leaned up and placed a kiss on his chin. "Look where we are right now. The last thing on my mind right now is keeping you safe."

He lowered his head, and I felt the bite of his teeth against the curve of my ear. The tiny sting sent a shockwave of pleasure firing through my body. "What's on your mind right now, Tennyson? I'm dying to hear whatever it is."

He flirted as easily as he breathed, so it shouldn't be the turn on that it was. I couldn't deny that when he cranked on the charm, I fell as easily as everyone else. I doubted anyone was immune to those blue eyes and his wicked grin.

"I'm thinking it should be impossible to want you again this soon." I curled an arm around the back of his neck, as he started to nip his way up and down the side of my neck. I tilted my head to the side to give him more access and let out a small hiss in response to the shift of his hips, which put his steel-hard erection right at the apex of my thighs. I was slightly tender from all the insatiable action last night and the end of a dry spell that was longer than I wanted to admit, but I wasn't about to tell him to stop. "I'm wondering why I convinced myself you were a bad idea when you always made me feel like I was someone special."

His tongue stopped to pay particular attention to the pulse fluttering erratically at the curve of my neck. "I *am* a bad idea, but I'll always be good to you. You gave me a reason to try to be better than I was before. I like the man I am with you."

I used my free hand to push my fingers through his golden hair. "I like the man you are with or without me, Webb. I may not have trusted you from the get-go, but I always liked you."

He lifted his head and smiled at me. "You pretended not to."

I rolled my eyes and shifted my legs impatiently along the outside of his. "I'm not pretending anymore."

His gaze shot down to where we were pressed intimately together. "You're not." It was a statement filled with confidence and pride. "There's no hiding how much you like me anymore."

The lightly taunting words were followed by his hips pressing into mine as his teeth grazed my collarbone. I felt his hardness drag through very sensitive places, but my body didn't seem to mind. My breath hitched, and my legs parted even more of their own accord. I felt my insides pulse in awareness and heard Webb grunt in satisfaction when the sweet spot he was rubbing against started to warm and wet. I wrapped a leg around his lean hips, heel digging into the top of his flexing backside. No, there certainly wasn't any way to hide just how strongly and quickly I responded to his touch and his low growl into the hollow of my throat.

The very tip of his cock found the notch where my clit throbbed between the damp folds. We both gasped as his hips kicked forward, the contact sending pleasure spiraling between us. I rolled my body against his in reaction, and soon we were nothing more than writhing limbs and a tangled, incoherently panting unit. It was hard to say who was working harder to find release first. Both of us were heedlessly seeking any kind of relief from the heat and tension steadily building between our flushed bodies. It shouldn't be so easy, so comfortable to take without giving, but Webb didn't seem to mind. He was working on his own agenda, one we both had to put the brakes on when more than just the tip of his now anxious, leaking cock found its way inside my tight and tender entrance.

In all my years of being single, not once had I gotten so caught up in the moment I forgot to be safe. The horrified and rapid apologies that burst out of Webb told the same story. There was a brief pause where we both took a second to recognize there was something extremely powerful at play when we got together. It was nothing more than a silent look we shared, but it spoke volumes. Somewhere in between slow, bewildered blinks, it was understood we would one day return to this place, nothing between us. Bare. Uncovered in so many ways. It would be a huge step, one which spoke of trust and faith on a level neither of us had ever experienced with another person before.

All of the things rushing at us were overwhelming, so I closed my eyes once Webb had himself covered and situated and let myself sink into both the pleasure and promise I'd only experienced with the man moving above me. There was a touch of pain as Webb's body overtook mine. A reminder I was going to feel him later and be unable to forget what we'd been doing, what we were going to do again. As forceful as his thrusts were, his touch was gentle as a hand skimmed over my face and stroked my skin. It was a heady feeling to finally be enough for someone. Not too much, and not lacking in any way. It was a sweet sensation to finally find a place where I fit, not too big, not too small.

Just call me Goldilocks, because I'd finally found the one who fit me and whom I fit just right.

CHAPTER 16

WEBB

WHEN THERE WAS A KNOCK on the motel room's door not even an hour after I'd checked in, I expected to see the sheriff of Sheridan, Wyoming, standing on the other side. Wyatt had gone radio silent after our late-night chat, which wasn't unusual after he got a new assignment, but I still fully expected him to flex his big brother muscle and send the local law to keep an eye on me. I actually fell back a step in surprise when instead I came face to face with Cyrus Warner. I wasn't aware he'd gotten back from his honeymoon already, but then again, I'd had bigger things than his happy ever after on my mind. I liked to pretend I wasn't intimidated by the stern older man, but it wasn't true. There was something about the oldest Warner, my current boss, which made me want to stand up straighter, speak more clearly, and generally be less of a loser than I'd always been. His eyes were an unusual gray, sharp and cutting. The man appeared to see right through everyone standing in front of him, and I'd yet to see him run up against a challenge he couldn't work his way around. He was a dangerous combination of fierce loyalty and ruthless focus. Lord have mercy on anyone brave enough to get between this man and the people he loved.

I reached out to pull the door open wider in welcome and told myself not to shift nervously under the weight of Cy's probing stare. He made me feel like a little kid who'd just gotten caught with his hand shoved in a cookie jar.

"Cy. It's good to see you, man. I owe you and Leo a huge apology. I should send her flowers or something to make up for the scene at the wedding reception." It was Cy's second wedding, but it was Leo's first. She was an amazing woman and deserved to have the most special of days. I fully expected Cy to punch me in the face for ruining it for her once we were face to face again.

The big man moved quietly into the room, eyes immediately landing on the second pile of clothes. Ten had wanted to check in with her family and with work, not that she seemed particularly excited about either chore.

"Leo knows it wasn't your fault. Lane's kept us updated about what was going on with you while you and Ten were running around the South. We were hoping for a quiet resolution by the time you made it back home." He put his hands on his hips and turned to face me. His expression was unreadable, and I felt pinned in place as he watched me fight not to squirm in front of him. Lane was the youngest brother and the easiest going of the bunch. It didn't surprise me at all that he'd been tasked with keeping tabs on me and Ten while we were out risking our fool necks chasing ghosts from my past.

I scoffed and cranked my neck to the side, sending a popping sound through the room. "I have never in my life been lucky enough to be on the winning side of a quiet resolution. You know me, Cy, I tend to be a hail-of-bullets and blaze-of-glory kind of guy." When trouble was your one true love, those kinds of endings were inevitable. I'd gotten used to the noise and chaos.

"I like you, Webb. I think you're a good guy with a lot to offer and a lot to learn. I like your tenacity and how much you care for your family. You remind me a lot of my middle brother." His eyes narrowed, and his head cocked to the side a little. "I don't like the way danger attaches itself to you like a hungry leech. I don't enjoy the way the people close to you end up getting hurt. I'm here to tell you that while I appreciate this mess isn't one you created, I'm not too happy it's spreading to the people who matter the most to me. I don't like Ten being in the middle of it one bit."

I bit back a sharp retort, knowing it wasn't my place to tell him he hadn't exactly treated Ten like she was one of the people who mattered most to him in the past. She could have that conversation with him on her own if she ever felt like they needed a clean slate between them.

"I didn't drag her kicking and screaming into this. She came willingly, walking right by my side. I let her know, more than once, where the door was. She opted not to use it." She'd shown more loyalty, more devotion, than anyone else in my life ever had. "I'm not asking for her to clean things up for me, Cy. All I've asked her to do is patch up the wounds when the truth rips me to shreds. She sees things no one else sees. She keeps everything in perspective for me. If you think you can threaten me or scare me into walking away from her, you don't know me as well as you think you do." And it was insulting. Suddenly, I was the one contemplating throwing a punch.

Cy let his hands fall to his sides, and a heavy sigh escaped from his chest. "I grew up with that woman. You think I don't know there isn't anything in the world that would pry her away from you right now? I've seen the way you two watch each other. I've watched her try and fight her natural instinct to push you away. You had her curious from the start. And while I initially thought you were nothing more than a welcome distraction for her, it didn't take long for me to realize there was something more there. She's careful with you in a way she's never been before. It means she's very aware of the fact she might break you, and she's fighting for it not to end up that way. I still worry. About her, about you. When the things we're trying to outrun catch up with us, it's usually because we're exhausted from trying to keep all that distance between us for so long. I don't want to see either one of you hurt. I don't want to lose any more sleep wondering what kind of pain a member of my family is in."

"Ten's tough. You don't need to worry about her so much. That's my job now." I wanted him to understand that things were different now between me and Ten, that her safety—and her happiness—were now my number-one concern. It was a job I was bound and determined to do better than he ever had. Not simply because my masculine pride demanded it, but because Ten was amazing and deserved my very best. I crossed my arms over my chest defiantly and lifted my eyebrows in a silent challenge.

I couldn't stop a flinch when the big man suddenly moved and dropped a heavy hand on one of my shoulders. His grip was strong, unyielding, but there was no force or punishment behind it. "I wasn't talking about Leo or about Ten . . . I was talking about you, Webb. You think I'd let you on my ranch, trust you with my clients, my entire family's livelihood and future if I, if *we*, didn't consider you part of the family?" His head shook, and I noticed there seemed to be even more of the silver strands mixed with the black. "Not a chance in hell."

There was a thickness in my throat I suddenly had to clear away before I could speak again. "I'm used to families trying to get rid of me, not taking me in."

The hand on my shoulder gave a reassuring squeeze, and then it fell away. "Their loss is our gain. We're here if you need us. You're one of our own. Doesn't mean any of us like the fact we can feel trouble coming from a mile away."

"I don't have any more moves to make, Cy. Gotta wait for the other me to show his hand. Chasing him was nothing but a waste of time, and if I hide, all he's going to do is look for a way to draw me out. He's playing with me, getting off on it, so the quicker he finds me, the quicker it all ends." My shoulders slumped as I finally allowed defeat to pull at the careful act of indifference I'd put in place since this dog and pony show began.

"It's true then? You really have a twin who was out there robbing banks, trying to get you arrested?" He sounded as baffled by the truth as I felt.

I nodded. "It's true. And unbelievably, Wyatt and I somehow ended up being the lucky ones, even though we were stuck with my joke of a mother. Don't know what my other brother's story is, but it has to be pretty fucking twisted if he's putting himself at such risk just to ruin a life that was in no way exemplary to begin with."

Cy rubbed a hand over his salt and pepper beard and narrowed his eyes in concentration. "How is anyone supposed to tell the two of you apart? What if he shows up on the ranch pretending to be you? If he's as dangerous as everyone is making him out to be . . ." He shook his head. "Not good."

I grunted in agreement. "I'm not coming to the ranch. I'm gonna do my damndest to stay away from anyone he could use to hurt me. Aside from Ten." She knew the risks already and was willing to gamble on the two of us besting the unknown. "You need to tell Leo, Lane, and the others to stay away until this is all straightened out. If our paths cross, they need to act like they don't know me because it might not be *me* they're tangling with."

I could see he didn't much care for the simple solution to keep everyone in this town who mattered to me safe, but eventually, he gave a small, grim nod and muttered, "I'll pass the info along, but you know it isn't going to make them happy."

No, I imagined not. Leo was a spitfire and had a true redhead's temper. As soon as Cy told her to stay away, she was going to throw a fit even if she understood the distance really was for her own good. She had a soft spot for me a mile wide. I wasn't sure what I'd done to be taken into the Warner fold with so few questions asked, but I wasn't about to put my good fortune at risk.

Both of our heads jerked in the direction of the door as a loud knock interrupted us. The door was still open, but now a man in a tan sheriff's uniform was filling the empty space. Rodie Collins was another big man who seemed to demand attention and respect as soon as he walked into a room. He was childhood friends with Cy and Ten, but his relationship with the Warners was beyond strained after he'd arrested the middle brother, Sutton, for the murder of his ex-wife. The former Marine was simply doing the job he'd been elected by the people of Sheridan to do, but the protective brothers hadn't seen things so black and white. There was still obvious tension between my uninvited guests as Cy caught sight of the other man.

The sheriff walked into the room, taking us both in with a quick look. He was the same age as Cyrus but looked younger since there was no silver or gray in his reddish-brown hair. He had green eyes, which were both hard and cold as jade. There was no mistaking the man had seen some shit. It was the same look I often saw in my brother's gaze when he didn't realize I was watching him. Once again, I wondered what it was about the sheriff that put my brother's hackles up so quickly.

While I was thinking of Wyatt, I asked, "Did my brother send you to check up on me?"

Rodie shifted his gaze away from a glowering Cy and gave me a little nod. "He left a message with dispatch late last night. Tried to call him back this morning but didn't get a response. Ten texted that you were in town and that she wanted to brief me, so I figured I'd stop by before I started my patrol shift."

"Wyatt was put on a new assignment today. He's probably going to be out of pocket for a while."

The sheriff snorted and adopted Cy's original pose with his arms crossed over his chest. While the hotel room was plenty spacious, it was starting to feel a little cramped with all three of us facing off and the two older men silently scowling at one another.

"Your brother is bossy." Rodie made the statement, leaving no room to argue. "Most feds are."

"He's worried about his kid brother. Give the guy a break." Cy's tone bordered on rude, but the sheriff didn't react with similar animosity.

"Didn't say it was a bad thing. Guy's got one hell of a dangerous job, and his little brother is up to his neck in a shitstorm. All I'm saying is, I woulda stopped by with or without Bryant issuing demands from Washington." He pulled his attention away from Cy and settled it all on me. "You got a plan if this guy comes at you hard in my town, kid?"

I sighed and moved my hands so I could push them through my hair. "No. I have no clue what I'm doing. But I know I feel better doing it here on my home turf than somewhere out there." I pointed out the open doorway indicating the rest of the world.

He arched a mahogany brow in my direction. "Does Ten have a plan? She doesn't usually jump into anything blind."

I felt the hair on my arms lift up and my spine straightened involuntarily. I didn't like it when either of them talked about Ten like they knew her better than I did. Sure, they had history with her, but neither of them understood the woman she'd become after handing her heart over to reckless lovers and unworthy suitors.

"She's mostly along for the ride right now. Her main concern has been keeping my ass out of jail up to this point. If she's figured out a way to pin my twin down, she hasn't mentioned it." But she had brought up the fact the FBI should be doing more to find the man responsible for the robberies. She sounded pissed her ex wasn't doing his job to her exacting standards yet again.

The sheriff tilted his head to the side a tiny bit and did the same thing Cy did: took in Ten's things scattered around with mine, then frowned at me. "She likes you. Don't fuck up."

I barked out a laugh. "Do you guys have any idea how pissed she'd be if she knew you were both here checking up on me and my intentions on her behalf? She'd kick both your asses and then she'd kick mine for saying anything about our personal lives to you."

Rodie shrugged with zero shame. "She's special. She's worth protecting."

I rolled my eyes and then my shoulders. "Is every guy in this town halfway in love with her?"

Cy snorted and Rodie returned my eye roll. "She's one of my best friends. We've been through a lot together, but she is not my type, so relax, kid."

I scoffed. "She's everyone's type." Who could resist those long-ass legs, all that white-blonde hair, and those emerald eyes? Not to mention her quick mind, unwavering inner strength, and sassy mouth. Then there was her huge heart. So big and soft, all I wanted to do was protect it forever. I had to start counting backward from a hundred to keep myself from getting hard thinking about all the things Tennyson McKenna did that made her so special.

"What about your brother? Is Ten his type?" Rodie's rumbled question stiffened my shoulders and had me narrowing my eyes. Wyatt wasn't secretive about his sexuality, but he didn't wave a rainbow flag around behind him everywhere he went either. Considering his animosity toward the sheriff, I highly doubted he'd spilled his orientation during one of their few, stilted conversations.

"No. Ten is definitely not Wyatt's type." I couldn't hide the automatic defense of my brother, which found its way into my tone.

Rodie gave me a hard look, then lifted his chin in a sharp jerk. "Exactly. Ten is wonderful, beautiful, and a force to be reckoned with, but she isn't everyone's idea of the perfect partner. Have her give me a call when she gets back into town. Tell your brother I did as he requested, so he doesn't keep annoying my staff. If you get into trouble, you know where to find me." He turned before I could ask questions or put together what he was saying between the lines of his actual words. He paused on his way out the door and looked at Cyrus over his shoulder. "We have a better chance of keeping the kid safe if you realize I'm not, and never was, the enemy, Cy."

Once Cyrus and I were alone again in the room, I threw my hands up in the air and let myself flop down on the side of the bed. "What was that?"

Cy sighed, something he was very good at, and told me he was heading back to the ranch. He also left with the warning, "Rodie's a good cop. He really is. But he can be blinded by duty. Don't trust him to put your safety before his job. Remember, if you need anything, let us know."

Once I was alone in the quiet room, I tried to grasp all the things changing around me.

Somehow, I'd ended up with a woman willing to stand by my side no matter what. An adoptive family who not only wanted to take care of me for once, but also worried about me. Ties to my old family I never realized were there. And my older brother was finally trusting me not to screw things up when left to my own devices.

Without realizing it, my old friend trouble suddenly had a lot of competition for my time and attention. Falling into the comfort of the disorder and dysfunction I'd always embraced no longer seemed like the best idea. I finally had people who wanted to keep me around, and letting trouble come between me and their acceptance wasn't an option.

It looked like I was going to have to call it quits, finally break up with the familiar bad following me around once and for all.

CHAPTER 17

TEN

WHEN WE GOT BACK TO Wyoming, I thought the unknown between Webb and me would lead to tension and unease. But rather than getting a moment to acclimate to my new normal, which prominently featured the handsome blond drifter, I was immediately thrust back into my old normal when I checked in with work. A family vacationing from Florida lost track of their five-year-old where they were camping, and it was an all-hands-on-deck kind of situation because they'd waited for over twelve hours to report the child missing. They thought they could find him themselves, not considering the sheer vastness of the wilderness, the way it all blended together, and the dangers involved. It was still warm enough during the day, but the temperatures dropped quickly when the sun went down, which was hard on adults but would be nearly impossible for a child to survive without the proper gear. The parents were a mess, and there was really no way I could say no when my boss asked me to join the search. I was still queasy from the flight home, and on edge about Webb's precarious situation, but I jumped into the search-and-rescue mission without a second thought.

When I called Webb to hastily fill him in on the situation, he promised to keep himself under lock and key so I wouldn't have to worry about him on top of the stress of trying to find the little boy before something with sharper teeth and claws did. I appreciated his instant understanding more than I could say. And when he told me not to come back until I had found the little boy, it took everything inside of me not to blurt out how much he meant to me.

Webb didn't tell me to be careful or make me promise to be safe. He trusted me to get out there, face the hostile terrain and unknown predators, and do my damn job. The fact he didn't coddle me or try and save me from what I was meant to be doing did more to pull me closer to openly admitting how I felt about him than almost anything else could have. Webb's belief that I was capable of taking care of myself, as well as him, was something special, something I'd never experienced before. I was glad I had several long, quiet hours in the woods to wrap my head and heart around the tectonic shift in my emotions that was taking place.

I thought I knew what love felt like.

It was tumultuous. It was treacherous. It left me in shreds and feeling empty inside like I'd given too much of myself away. Love put holes through my soul and dragged my heart over the coals. It was never something I believed to be effortless.

But then Webb came along and with a single crooked smile changed all of that.

I had worked so much harder convincing myself he wasn't right for me. I put so much effort into convincing myself he was nothing but trouble, I almost missed how painless caring about him was. There was no sting. There was no scalding burn as love torched my insides and left my emotions in ash. If it didn't hurt, how could it be something as powerful as love?

I got it now. When I finally got it right, love felt like a warm blanket wrapped around all the places inside of me others had left cold and barren. When I let myself love the right person, it didn't hurt at all, and that was the feeling I was missing. I'd gotten so used to the ache deep in my chest, I'd completely forgotten what it was like to wake up in the morning and go to sleep at night without it pushing down on me. I felt lighter than I had in years, and that was saying a lot with a missing child I was focused on finding and the man I was starting to realize I could love wholeheartedly caught in the crosshairs of a very dangerous man.

When I got to the campsite, Rodie already had several of his guys speaking to the other campers, and one of the deputies quietly mentioned there was an entire water rescue team scouting the river. It wouldn't be the first time they had to pull a body out of the fast-moving water, but my heart broke at the thought of it being one so young with his entire life ahead of him. The rest of the guys from the Ranger's office had already taken off in a bunch of different directions, checking out the usual places scared and disoriented hikers ended up when they got lost in this area. So far everyone had radioed in with bad news. There was no sign of the child anywhere, and none of the other campers had seen him. When I asked if I could talk to the family, the deputy in charge of the scene shook his head at me and pointed farther away to where a distraught woman was wailing uncontrollably as a man held her in his arms.

"The paramedics gave her a sedative a few minutes ago. She's probably going to be an incoherent mess. Blaming herself. The guy's her boyfriend. Doesn't seem all that interested in the fact the kid is missing. He actually talked her into waiting to contact search and rescue." The cop's eyebrows winged up. "Rodie's coming up to have a chat with him."

I nodded. If I were involved in the investigation beyond finding the boy, I'd want to have a talk with the guy, as well. I let my gaze drift away from the couple and noticed a little girl standing off to the side looking a little bit lost and afraid. I cocked my head as she watched the crying woman slowly start to quiet, the wails turning to whimpers.

"Who's the little girl?" I pointed to the child with the long, red ponytail and narrowed my eyes as she shifted on her feet. Her sneakers were untied, and she had an ugly red gash on her cheek. It looked like someone hadn't done a very good job of keeping an eye on her either.

The deputy glanced over at the little girl and pushed up the front of his tan hat with the tip of his index finger. "She's the older sister. She was the one who noticed the kid was gone early this morning. We've asked her a couple of times if she has any idea where he might have gone, but she isn't saying anything. She's scared."

I narrowed my eyes at the boyfriend who was now yelling at the people coming through the scene about their incompetence. He kept saying if this had happened back home in Florida, the little boy would've been found already. His whole demeanor was off, and the little girl flinched every time his voice rose an octave.

Growling under my breath, I tugged on the black baseball hat with the Forest Ranger logo on the front and situated my ponytail through the back. Keeping my eyes on the girl, I moved away from the deputy and headed in her direction. I was a few feet away when the boyfriend was suddenly standing in front of me. I lifted my eyebrows when one of his fingers shot out and poked me in the center of my chest. I stopped moving and slowly sidestepped him, intent on getting to the little girl.

I stopped short when a hand wrapped around my upper arm and jerked me back a step. The idiot was bold, putting his hands on me in front of so many witnesses, most of whom had uniforms and badges in plain sight.

"What do you think you're doing, lady? You can't talk to her without permission." The guy had small, beady eyes and a twitchy, aggressive demeanor. I disliked him on sight.

"I need her legal guardian's permission. Not yours." I glanced at the now limp and hazy woman who was all but hanging in the arms of a female deputy. "Ma'am, do you mind if I talk to your daughter for a few minutes? You do want us to utilize every resource we have to locate your son, don't you?"

Yes, the woman was distraught, and not altogether in control of her faculties, but all I needed was the slight dip of her chin in agreement before I blatantly stepped around the boyfriend and crouched down in front of the obviously terrified little girl. She was able to give me permission without a word by nodding quickly. The agreement would stand up in court if it came to that, and there was no way I was leaving this campsite without speaking to this child.

I tipped the brim of my hat back and gave her a grin. "Hi, sweetheart. You've got a nasty cut on your cheek. Did you let someone look at it?" The little girl shook her head violently and took a stumbling step away from me.

"You're scaring her. Leave her alone." The boyfriend barked the command from behind me, but we both ignored his bluster. "Diane, tell the cops to leave Emily alone. We can find Christian without them. He's just screwing around. Stupid kids."

Man, I couldn't wait for Rodie to show up and rake this guy over the coals. Hopefully, he would find a reason to lock up the asshole overnight. His intentions were obviously not good, and he seemed indifferent to the care and well-being of the children.

I cocked my head at the little girl. She was staring intently at the logo on my hat. I pulled it off and handed it to her. "You can have it if you talk to me just a little bit and let me fix up your scrape for you."

Tentatively, she reached out a hand and took the hat. She also reached for my hand when I stuck it out in her direction. "You don't have to worry about getting in trouble if you talk to me. I promise no one will be mad at you, and no one will hurt you. All we want to do is get your brother back safe and sound. He called you Emily. That's a very pretty name. My name is Ten."

The little girl gasped, and her eyes opened wide. "Like the number?"

I smiled at her and rose to my feet. "Just like the number. How old are you?" My guess was not much older than her missing brother.

"I'm seven. I'm older than Christian, so it's my job to watch him. Kenny said it's all my fault he's gone." She sniffled as I led her to the back of one of the ambulances still parked onsite.

"Kenny is wrong. Sure, big sisters should keep an eye out on their little brothers, but it's his job and your mom's responsibility to keep you both safe. You didn't do anything wrong."

I hefted her up onto the ledge formed by the open doorway in the back of the big vehicle, and helped her situate the too-big hat on her head. She wiped dirty hands over her face and looked down at her feet. I used a finger under her chin to tilt her head back so I could look at her scratch. It was a superficial wound, but it'd been left untreated long enough it was starting to scab on the sides. "Did you get this running through the woods playing with your brother?"

She bit down on her lower lip and shook her head. "No."

I lifted my eyebrows and moved to the side as a female paramedic popped up seemingly out of nowhere to fuss over the little girl.

"Do you want to tell me how you got hurt?" I saw her gaze dart over my shoulder to where her mother's boyfriend was raising hell. Rodie had shown up sometime in the last ten minutes. His patience for the hostile man's antics was even less than mine had been. All the yelling and blustering was going to come to a stop real quick if the big sheriff had anything to say. If there was anything bound to set Rodie off, it was someone questioning his ability to do his job. He took a lot of pride in being an elected official and the only man in charge of law and order for such a huge, untamed part of the state.

The little girl winced as the paramedic wiped something across her cut. She looked back down at her dirty shoes, and the too-big hat on her head slid so I couldn't see her face.

"Christian and I were bored. Mommy promised we could go fishing and swimming. Kenny didn't want to, though. He wanted to stay by the tent and smoke his funny cigarettes." The paramedic straightened and gave me a look. I inclined my head in Rodie's direction, indicating she should go tell him about the 'funny cigarettes.' If nothing else, if he had weed on him, it would give Rodie a reason to throw the loudmouth in the slammer for possession. People tended to forget marijuana was still illegal once they crossed the border between Colorado and Wyoming.

"So, you wanted to go have fun, and Kenny didn't let you?" The bigger story was starting to make more sense to me. The little boy hadn't run off for no reason, and the adults hadn't called it in because they had something to hide.

"Yeah. He yelled and told us to be quiet. Christian got upset and started crying. One of the other dads at the campsite next to ours came over to see if everything was all right. Kenny got really mad about it. After the guy left, he knocked Christian down, and he smacked me across the face."

Of course he fucking did. "Where was your mom, sweetheart?"

If the woman put that loser ahead of her own kids, I was going to make it my mission in life to ruin her.

"Mommy wasn't there. She went to the store. Kenny is nice when she's around. Not so nice when she isn't. Christian got really upset and ran off. I tried to go after him because it's my job to watch him, but Kenny caught me. I wasn't fast enough." I heard her sniff again. "Kenny told Mommy that Christian was playing a game. At first, she thought he was just hiding and being a brat. She didn't get nervous until later."

I nodded and reached out to squeeze the little girl's shoulder. "Where do you think your brother went? Is there a reason you didn't you tell the nice deputies what happened when they showed up?"

She finally looked up at me with watery eyes. "Kenny told me not to say anything. He told me he would punish me if I said he was the reason Christian ran off." She shrugged a shoulder. "I don't know where he went, but I don't think he'd go hide in the woods. He's scared of bears."

I gave her a reassuring grin. "That's good to know. What about down by the river? You said he wanted to go fishing."

She shook her head again. "No. He can't swim, and he's kinda afraid of water."

Running her story back through my head, I pinpointed an obvious answer as to where the little boy may have gone. "What about the other dad who stopped by to check on you guys? Maybe he tried to go get help after Kenny hit you? I think that sounds like something a good brother might do."

Emily tilted her head to the side, and I reached out to catch my hat before it fell off her head. She blinked up at me and slowly gave a small nod. "Maybe. He didn't want the dad to leave. He wanted to tell him how mean Kenny was to both of us."

I let out a slow breath. "Can you tell me where the dad is in the campsite? Do you remember what he looked like, what his family looked like?"

Emily let her eyes dart around the busy campsite, her teeth working her bottom lip so hard I was worried she was going to make herself bleed. Finally, her small shoulders fell, and her entire body seemed to wilt in defeat.

"I don't see them anywhere. Maybe they left." She fell quiet again, so I reached out and gave her shoulder a reassuring squeeze.

"I'm going to talk to your mom, Emily. I'm going to make sure she knows that Kenny isn't so nice to you and Christian when she's not around. Thank you for talking to me, for trusting me." The little girl moved to hand me the hat back, but I told her to keep it.

I left Emily with the paramedic to do a more thorough exam. I made my way over to where Rodie now had the boyfriend cuffed and sitting in the back of his rugged blazer. Normal patrol cars didn't cut it in this kind of terrain.

"I need you to track down the family who was renting the campsite next to theirs. I think they might have a stowaway onboard and not realize it. The sister says the little boy wouldn't run to the woods or the water because he's scared of both. But a concerned citizen interfered earlier when he heard this dirtbag getting rough with the kids when the mom stepped away. The little boy might have been looking for another adult to intervene; both the kids are terrified of him," I pointed at the boyfriend with a sneer. "Christian may have hidden away thinking he could get help and not get hurt if he had distance between him and this bully."

The man opened his mouth to say something, but twin looks of disgust from Rodie and me made him snap his mouth shut before he uttered a sound.

"How'd you get the girl to talk?" Rodie asked the question and issued orders to get the name of the family and to put out a BOLO alert on the car once they had a make and model.

"I bribed her with my hat and promised her this guy wouldn't ever be able to hurt her again. Once the mom gets her act together, you need to evaluate her response to hearing her boyfriend has been abusing her kids right under her nose. If she doesn't take the threat seriously, I want CPS involved." I wasn't going to let the little girl down. And I wasn't going to stand around waiting to hear if someone found the car or not. I needed to pick my way through the woods on the off chance I hadn't guessed little Christian's motives right. After securing a promise from Rodie that he would vet the mother thoroughly, I asked where they needed boots on the ground for the grid search.

Many cold and dark hours later, the radio attached to my hip crackled to life. I was tired, frustrated, and worried I'd gotten everything wrong. Rodie's deep voice was full of relief and rough praise when he let everyone know the boy was found hiding in the fifth-wheel the other family was towing behind their truck. They'd been stopped at the New Mexico border. The boy was hungry and exhausted, and terrified, but otherwise unharmed. A collective cheer went up from the search party, and I felt like I was going to collapse with relief.

Rodie asked me to switch the radio over to a private channel. There he told me the mother was horrified when he told her the reason her son had taken off was because of the abuse at her boyfriend's hands. According to Rodie, she was snowed by the guy. A classic case of him being too good to be true. She demanded charges be pressed against him for injuring her daughter, and the woman was visibly relieved when she was told her son was none the worse for wear. He also complimented me on my uncanny ability to always see between the lines everyone else missed.

I was so happy the kid was going home and the mother was going to do right by her children. It brought to mind how crappy Webb's upbringing had been, and how none of the adults in his life were there to do right by him when he was little. And, for the first time in forever, instead of wanting another case to distract me, or another circumstance to get lost in so I didn't have to focus on my failures and faults, I was ready to go home.

Not back to my family's ranch. Not even to Sheridan, even though that's where I'd always considered home. Nope, I was ready to get back to the man who'd both tied me down and set me free at the same time. I had somewhere I wanted to be, someone I wanted to be with, and there was no arguing against the warmth sizzling under my skin when I realized Webb would actually be there waiting for me.

I might not have fallen in love with Webb Bryant hard and fast. But I was pretty sure I was drifting my way there, nice and slow. When I reached the final destination, I wouldn't be beat up and bruised from a crash landing. I'd still be in one piece, which meant there would be so much more of myself for the man who was starting to mean everything to me.

CHAPTER 18

WEBB

TEN WAS FILTHY AND OBVIOUSLY dead on her feet when she finally found her way back to the hotel room in the early hours of the morning. I'd been restless and worried, trapped in the room, unable to do anything but wait for her return. I was determined to keep my promise and stay put so she didn't have more to worry about when she was out on the job. Finding the little boy needed to be her priority, and I understood that without her having to say a word. She had a calling, one I was insanely impressed by. There wasn't a single scenario in which I could imagine standing in her way while she did what she had to do. I always wanted to be someone in her life who helped her, not hindered her.

I took one look at her and practically carried her to the bathroom. It wasn't as swanky or atmospheric as the one in New Orleans, but there was plenty of hot water and enough room for me to wrap my arms around her and hold her up as she practically collapsed from exhaustion. I quickly washed her long hair, picking bits and pieces of bark and pine needles out of the pale strands. She had a scratch on the side of her neck I made sure to clean, and rubbed the rest of her down with efficient movements so I could get her from shower to bed in the shortest time possible.

She tried to ask about the visit from Cy and Rodie. Apparently, the sheriff mentioned he'd already spoken to me, and Ten wanted to know if the other protective men in her life had tried to warn me away. Not wanting to get her worked up when what she needed was rest, I distracted her with a kiss and wandering hands. She went pliant under the gentle stroke of my hands and let me maneuver her to the bed. She returned the kiss automatically, but I could tell it was taking the last of her reserves to respond. I appreciated the effort but was determined to take care of her the way I'd been trying to from the get-go. It was the first time I'd ever actively put someone's needs in front of my own, and I was surprised how good it made me feel. She gave a soft sigh of contentment as soon as her head hit the pillow and her eyes immediately slid shut. Her naked body disappeared under the white sheets, and her breathing went deep and even in about a second.

I sat on the edge of the bed, and watched her long enough that it passed being romantic and probably bordered on the edge of creepy. I couldn't look away from her. I still had trouble believing she was here. I was in disbelief she came back to me when she made it a point to remind everyone on a regular basis she was fine on her own and didn't need help. The fact she relied on me and trusted me to hold her up when she was ready to fall meant everything. I was finally starting to see the man my brother tried to convince me I'd grown into.

It took effort to pull myself away from her side, and from the daydream I was weaving where things would always be this way between us. I knew she wasn't always going to be soft, and I knew I wasn't always going to be settled. I usually left before I found myself having to compromise, so sticking things out for the long haul meant learning how to give as well as take really damn fast. It was a good thing I was a quick study.

I ditched the towel I'd wrapped around my waist after our shower and climbed into bed on the opposite side of Ten. The sun was going to be up soon, but I could feel sleep tugging at me in all directions. As soon as I was stretched out, one arm bent over my head, Ten rolled and slotted herself against my side like she'd been filling the empty space there for years rather than a few intense days. I let my arm fall around her shoulders and pulled her closer. Her skin was still slightly damp from the shower, and I loved the way it felt so smooth and soft against mine. She was such an intriguing mix of contradictions. Her demeanor was as hard and cold as stone, but when she let you close enough to touch, she was all velvet and silk. Her mind was razor sharp, but her heart was so tender and unprotected. She acted as if she'd lived a thousand lives and was carrying the weight of too much experience on her shoulders, but there was an innocence and wonder in her eyes, which still made her seem slightly naïve as to how bad the things humans were capable of could be. She might not admit it, but Tennyson McKenna wanted to believe the best in people, even when she'd been let down time and time again. I was determined to finally be the one who rewarded her unwavering faith.

She threw an arm over my waist and hitched her knee up so it was resting on my thighs. Since we were both naked, and having her in my arms felt better than anything ever had, sleep took a little longer to find me than I thought it would. I concentrated really hard on anything but the woman curled up beside me until I finally floated away with the lull of slumber.

I woke up a few hours later with Ten's name on my lips, my hands tangled in her hair, and my very hard dick trapped between her pretty, pink lips. The sheets were wrapped in a tangled mess around our legs, and the only light in the room was coming from the early morning sun peeking through a small crack in the closed curtains. It was enough I could see the mischievous gleam in Ten's eyes as her head lazily bobbed up and down the length of my cock. She did a swirly thing with her tongue, licking across the swollen head and flicking the tip of it along the length of the dripping slit. I had no idea how long she'd been awake, or how long she'd been working me over, but I felt pleasure pooling in my gut and the start of an impending orgasm at the base of my spine. I was impressed she worked me up so fast, and kind of pissed I missed any of this moment to sleep.

Her tongue flattened along the underside, the tip leaving a wet trail up and down the thick vein I could feel throbbing in time with my rapid heartbeat. She took me so deeply I felt the tip of my cock brush against the back of her throat. Her emerald eyes teared up briefly, and I pulled on her head where it was trapped between my hands to get her to let up. I didn't want to hurt her. I didn't need her pain to get off. I just needed her.

She let me pull her off the rigid pole of flesh in her mouth, and watched me with curious eyes as I struggled to catch my breath and regain some control after her surprise attack. I used my thumbs to caress the delicate skin of her temples and gave her a smile that was tied to the strings of my heart.

"You don't need to swallow it for me to get there. I'm already close." So close. I was leaking precum, the whole shaft twitching every time she exhaled and her warm breath hit the wet skin she'd left behind.

She quirked a challenging eyebrow at me and gently scratched her fingernails up the line of my inner thigh. The small burn that followed almost brought me up and off the bed. "How many times am I going to have to tell you? I never do anything I don't want to do. Especially in bed. If I want you so far down my throat I can't breathe, if I want to feel every single inch of you vibrate against my tongue as you come, I'm going to do whatever I have to do to make it happen."

I chuckled and loosened my hold on her head. "Like a sneak attack."

She laughed softly and when her head lowered, the long length of my shaft brushed against the side of her cheek. "This thing was poking me in the stomach for an hour before I decided to teach it a lesson. It's not very well behaved when you're asleep."

Surrendering myself to her skilled hands, I withdrew my hands altogether and placed them behind my head like a sultan waiting to be serviced. I cocked an eyebrow back at her and lifted my chin in challenge. "Do your worst then."

She let out a low laugh and wrapped her hand around the wide base of my erection. "Nope. You only get my very best, Webb. You and only you."

She'd saved her best for only me, just like I'd saved the words that meant something just for her.

My response was stolen when she dropped her head once again and warm heat encased my cock. She hollowed out her cheeks with a long suck that filled the room with undeniable sex sounds. I was pretty sure my eyes rolled back in my head, because everything went dark for a second when I felt the tight sleeve of her throat surround my pulsing cock. My hands tightened into fists, and I was reduced to nothing more than grunts and the occasional moan of pleasure. Ten put a hand on my clenched abs to keep me from moving as she worked me down as far as she could. My dick liked the attention. I loved the way she kept her eyes on mine, even as they watered.

She made a pleased sound, a little hum of delight at her complete and utter power over me, and then it was all over. I barely got out a shout of warning, telling her to pull off, before my hands flew to hold her in place at the same time. I forgot myself, forgot her, and lost myself in the powerful sensations sweeping throughout my body. She couldn't keep me still as my hips kicked up and my hands once again found their way into her hair. I bucked into her as a warm rush of satisfaction flooded her sweet mouth. Her eyes widened in surprise, but she took everything I fired at her like a champ. She swallowed every salty drop and lifted her head, but not before pausing to drag her tongue over the super sensitive slit. I almost cringed from the zing on such a sensitive spot, but it turned into a shiver of satisfaction as Ten moved to drop a series of light kisses along the line of my hip bone.

It was a minute or so before I came back down from the high. When I did, she was lying on my lower half, her hands stacked on my stomach as she watched me with confident, sparkling eyes.

"Good morning." The tone of her voice matched the grin on her face, and I was so fucking happy to be the reason for it.

"Good doesn't even begin to touch it." I yawned and reached for her. "Come up here and let me start your day off right."

Both her pale eyebrows winged up, and it took a few more minutes of coaxing before she relented and let me position her, so she was kneeling on the bed, her knees on either side of my head, with one hand braced on the wall and the other on the top of the wooden headboard. She mumbled no one had ever done this for her before, and once again, I wanted to strangle the men who'd come before me. They might be slightly older, and supposedly more experienced, but they didn't know jack about the things this woman needed. I could feel her thighs trembling next to my ears, and I could see the way her body went slick and ready at the first swipe of my fingers through her delicate folds. I heard her suck in a sharp gasp as I lifted one hand and settled it on the top curve of her ass. Her muscles tensed under my hand as soon as she felt the first glide of my tongue through the slippery moisture gathered at her entrance. I used the fingers of my free hand to give my mouth better access to all her sweet, hidden places. She shivered above me and started to roll her hips when I worked my tongue inside of her, flicking it in and out of her opening, twisting it around the tiny bud of her clit, generally driving her insane with my mouth in every way I could think of.

She all but screamed my name, her legs tightening on either side of my head. I loved how uninhibited, how wild she was when we were together like this. She was controlled, so exact in everything else; it was like a little secret only the two of us shared.

I slid a couple of fingers into the clenching channel of her pussy, collecting the moisture from my mouth and her pleasure. When she was stretched by both my tongue and fingers, her head tossed back, and I felt the ends of her hair tickle across my stomach, the small kiss of those silky strands was almost enough to get my dick hard again.

While Ten was blissed out, eyes closed, bottom lip caught between her teeth, I pulled my now-soaked fingers out of her clasping body and slicked them along the soft, hidden crevasse between the perfectly rounded globe of her ass. I waited for a protest, for her body to stop writhing or still above my mouth, but when there was no sign of hesitation, I slipped just the tip of my index finger into the softly quivering pucker between her cheeks. I locked my mouth around her clit at the same time, sucking and using the edge of my teeth to torment the tightly bundled collection of nerve endings.

Ten's entire body tensed. Her legs locked around the sides of my head, and then my name escaped on a long, low wail loud enough to wake the neighbors on either side of us. When she rocked backward, the motion pushed my probing finger deeper inside of her. When she squirmed forward, it pushed more of her wet, willing pussy into my mouth.

Suddenly one of her hands was wrapped in the longer hair on the top of my head. Her breath was coming out in choppy, uneven pants, my name escaping on every other puff of air. Ten was actively riding my mouth, grinding on my face, taking every ounce of pleasure I was giving her and reveling in it. She pulled on my hair, and I used my teeth on her clit. She dropped a string of words that may have made a lesser man blush, and I felt her body quiver and flutter under my mouth. There was a flood of moisture that hit my tongue, and her sweet flavor filled my mouth.

A moment later she rolled to the side and collapsed in a limp heap on the bed next to me. It was my turn to watch her with knowing satisfaction. I wanted to be the one to put the look of bewildered wonder and awe on her face every day from here on out.

I reached out to lace the fingers of our hands together, lifting them and placing a kiss on the back of Ten's. I wasn't ready for our connection to be lost. I would never be ready.

Unfortunately, the real world couldn't be held at bay any longer just because I wanted to bask in the aftermath with Ten. It was too early for her cell phone to start screaming, but it did anyway. It didn't stop until she untangled herself from me and the sheets and went to grab it from the spot I'd left it charging in the bathroom when I stripped her down.

I heard a mumbled greeting and then another long line of dirty words, but these ones weren't thick with sensual heat. They were hard and angry. She came out of the bathroom looking the same way, pushing her hair off of her face.

"Get dressed." She moved toward her suitcase, and I watched her slip back into the skin of the woman who kept everyone, including me, at arm's length.

"Why?" I sounded like a petulant child, and I wasn't going to apologize for it. I resented having our peaceful morning interrupted.

Ten lifted her head and gave me a pointed look. "That was Rodie. The FBI are here, and they want to talk to both of us."

By 'FBI,' I knew she meant her ex. It was my turn to swear, and just as easily as she'd pulled her armor on, I did the same. Hiding behind a grin and untroubled façade. It made the moments we were real with one another even more obvious.

CHAPTER 19

TEN

WHEN RODIE CALLED AND TOLD me Gage was waiting in his office acting like the king of the universe, I automatically slipped into battle mode. Probably too easily for Webb's taste, but every protective instinct I had fired to life and screamed at me to keep him safe. I wasn't going to let Gage sacrifice Webb on the altar of his career like he had so many others.

When we left the hotel, I felt like a paranoid mess. Webb had a straw cowboy hat pulled low over his eyes and an old, tattered flannel shirt that was missing the sleeves over a tank top. I think he was doing his best to blend in, but the look made him stand out even more than he normally did. I felt like he had a giant bullseye painted on the center of his chest. I stayed close to his side, eyes darting around the mostly empty parking lot, snagging on every shadow and flicker of light. The hair on the back of my neck stood on end, and a bolt of unease shot down my spine.

"I swear to God, someone is watching us." I bit the words out between clenched teeth as one of Webb's hands landed between my tense shoulder blades. "Don't you feel it?"

His sapphire eyes flashed at me from under the brim of his hat, and I could see his mouth was pulled into a tight line. "Just keep moving."

Those words were pretty much his answer to everything he'd come up against in his life. When things got tough, when things became complicated, he just kept moving. I wasn't so sure his method was going to work for him this time around. He was going to have to stay still if he wanted to give his twin a chance to catch up to him.

Webb kept his head down and stayed in line with my quick movement toward the truck. It was the one I drove for work, so the distinctive dark green and tan with the Forest Ranger's logo on the sides was hard to miss. I should've left it behind and grabbed my SUV from the ranch, but I'd been so tired and in such a hurry to get to Webb when I finally came out of the forest last night, I wasn't thinking with the cautious part of my brain. I might not have been thinking with my mind at all. Where Webb was concerned, my heart seemed to be leading the way, and the rest of me followed blindly along.

We shared an intense look across the cab, and he wordlessly reached out and wrapped his hand around mine. I returned the squeeze he applied to my fingers and quickly turned over the engine and pulled out of the parking lot. I felt like a sitting duck. My imagination ran wild as I pictured someone with Webb's face, but missing his heart and his soul, staring down the barrel of a rifle with the two of us in the crosshairs.

When we walked into the sheriff's station, it was obvious Gage had thrown his weight around and tried to take over. There were men in suits milling about with the deputies. Several had phones pressed to their ears as they did their best to ignore the side-eye thrown by the local boys. Rodie wasn't so easy to push around and had corralled the pushy fed into an empty meeting room, grumbling about Gage trying to commandeer his office as soon as he showed up. Considering he knew the dark and dirty history between me and my former superior, it didn't surprise me at all that Gage was sitting in a wobbly chair drinking tap water instead of bottled. There was no way Rodie was going out of his way to make my ex comfortable. I kind of loved him for it.

I did not love the way Gage zeroed in on Webb as soon as he followed me into the room.

"What do you want, Gage? What's this production about?" I crossed my arms over my chest and narrowed my eyes at the man who'd always found me lacking.

Rodie shut the door and leaned up against the wood, an irritated scowl stamped on his face. "I asked the same thing the minute he showed up, but all he would say is he needed to speak with both of you."

Gage cleared his throat and tugged the knot of his tie. I fought the urge to roll my eyes at the nervous gesture. He wasn't used to not being in control of the situation, and I doubted he expected the three of us to present a united front against him.

Webb slipped around me and took a seat opposite the other man. He used an index finger to push back the brim of his hat and locked eyes on the man who tried to ruin his life not so long ago.

"I know Ten told you to talk to my old man, Agent Gordon. I know there is irrefutable proof out there that I have a twin brother, and I know you know it. Why am I here?" Webb kept his tone even and his face impassive, but I could see the tension across his shoulders and the impatient way he tapped his fingers on the table in the front of him.

The fed pulled on his tie again and looked away. If I hadn't known Gage as well as I did, I might have missed the fact he flushed under his tan.

"I did speak with Mr. Bernard. He verified he fathered twins with Jolene Bryant as well as one other child. I can confirm the FBI recognizes the possibility that it was your twin who committed the robberies we arrested you for." Gage's gaze shifted from Webb and locked on to where I was hovering behind him. "Once we had the information from Bernard, we started looking into the possibility that the other suspect was involved in armed robberies before the ones that were committed around here. The robberies were too practiced and too well planned to have been the perpetrator's first time."

My eyebrows shot up, and I reached out and put a hand on Webb's shoulder as he leaned expectantly on the table.

"Seems like it should've been something you started with when you couldn't pin the robbery on Webb." Rodie's gravelly voice was thick with censure and accusation. He might not be a federal agent, but the man knew how to run an investigation. Something Gage had never been particularly interested in. He liked the limelight and accolades, not the actual work.

Ignoring the looming sheriff, Gage looked down at the table in front of him and had the good grace to appear properly remiss. "There were several steps I admit were rushed in this case. Both the Federal Bureau of Investigation and the Colorado Bureau of Investigation would like to apologize to Mr. Bryant." Gage huffed out a breath and plowed a hand through his hair. "When we started digging into similar crimes, we found a string of robberies matching the profile throughout the South. Several in Florida and Georgia. The suspect wore a disguise, but he did leave DNA behind at a couple of scenes. It matches yours."

Webb stiffened under my palm. "Are you asking me for an alibi again?"

Gage shook his head. "No." He sheepishly looked back at Webb. "Your brother verified your whereabouts for several of the dates."

I heard Webb growl under his breath. I was forced to let go of my hold on him as he leaned threateningly over the table. "You checked with Wyatt because whatever I said wasn't going to be good enough?"

Gage glanced away again, but he wasn't finding support from any corner of this room. I would be pissed as hell if my integrity was questioned the way Webb's was. In no way did he have to prove himself to Gage. He was three times the man Gage was, without even trying.

Gage chose not to answer the pointed question. "We've started a full-blown manhunt for your twin brother, Mr. Bryant. We're also still trying to track down your mother. We believe you both might be in danger."

Webb snorted and leaned back in his seat. "No shit. Was your first hint the way he tried to frame me for his crime?"

Gage grunted and put his hands flat on the table in front of him. "We also believe anyone closely associated with you may be in danger." He lifted his gaze to mine, and a flash of something that may have been regret flickered in my direction before he blinked. "I'd like you to consider going into protective custody. You too, Tennyson. You're a liability."

I bristled instantly. I took a step back as Webb jumped to his feet, the chair he was sitting on flying backward. "She's not a liability. She's an asset. The only one I've ever had. She's got a better chance of bringing my brother to justice than you ever did because she didn't automatically discount every word out of my mouth as bullshit. She actually listened when I told her I didn't do a damn thing."

Gage made a strangled sounding noise low in his throat. "I don't think she was particularly unbiased in this case, Mr. Bryant."

Webb growled again, but this time it was loud enough to echo throughout the room. Rodie moved fast for such a big man. He had a hand wrapped around Webb's bicep and was pulling him back before the blond man could launch himself across the table separating him from my ex.

"Not today, kid. He's looking for a reaction. Searching for something to hang you up on so he gets his own damn way. Don't give it to him. If you don't want to go into protective custody, you don't have to. We'll keep an eye on you, just like we planned all along." Rodie narrowed his eyes in Gage's direction. "I get that you think we're nothing but a bunch of hicks and hillbillies, but believe it or not, my entire staff is highly trained and invested in keeping Webb in one piece."

"This is a federal investigation." Gage tried to puff his chest up, but the gesture came off as infantile and ridiculous when he was so clearly outmuscled and outmanned by the other two men in the room.

"It's a federal investigation you screwed up." I kept my tone even as I addressed the man who was not going to stash me and Webb away in some dark hole while he tried to save face. I was well past stepping out of anyone's way to make their path easier. "We're aware of the risks involved by staying in Sheridan and using Webb to lure the twin out."

Rodie rubbed a hand over his chin and pointed a finger at Gage. "Do you have a name for this guy? Can we stop calling him 'the twin' or is that against FBI protocol for some reason?" The sarcasm in his tone was so thick it could be cut with a knife.

Gage rose to his feet, realizing he was the only one still sitting. "He has several aliases, but his given name is Weston Jacobs."

Webb looked over his shoulder in my direction, his blond brows dancing upward. It was a strange coincidence the lost brother also ended up with a name starting with a W.

"Where did he end up after Bernard ditched him?" My heart twisted around itself at the sadness in Webb's question. The man he'd never met and who had tried to trap him behind bars was still his brother, and part of his heart hurt for him.

Gage gave a slight shrug. "We're not entirely sure. He was in the system until he was five or so, then he mostly disappeared. There are a few misdemeanor charges under the Jacobs name throughout his early twenties, then nothing. It's like he went out of his way to drop off the radar. A good move if you're planning on robbing banks."

I sighed and rubbed my hand over my forehead. "We think he's going after the trust funds Bernard set up for the boys when they were little. Robbing banks must have lost some of its appeal."

Rodie frowned and cocked his head in my direction. "Why try and blackmail Bernard and go after the trust funds if he's got a stash from the previous robberies? Where did the money go?"

"That's a good question." Gage's interjection was met with angry glares all around.

"Shoulda asked it sooner, Special Agent." Rodie muttered the words as someone pounded loudly on the outside of the door.

He stepped aside and opened the door to one of Gage's minions. The agent in the suit cast a worried glance around the obviously tense room, gaze flicking between Webb and Gage nervously. "Sir, there's been a development. We need to talk to you."

Gage straightened the tie he'd almost completely loosened and easily slipped back into the role of cocky Agent in Charge. "Did you locate the suspect?"

The new arrival shook his head. "No."

Gage frowned. "The mother?"

Again the fed's head shook from side to side. "No, Sir."

Gage tossed his hands up in the air like a petulant child, and I watched as both Rodie and Webb exchanged amused grins. The gesture made me cringe. I was starting to question my sanity. How had I ever been attracted to someone so ridiculous? I couldn't believe I used to find him suave and sophisticated. It showed just how much of the world I still needed to get out and experience.

"What kind of development warrants you interrupting my meeting, Agent Gould?" Gage was posturing, trying to reclaim his status as head asshole. But it was apparent to anyone with eyes that he was the low man in the pecking order out of the three men in the room.

"Uh . . ." the clearly anxious agent again looked from Webb

and then back to Gage. "It involves Agent Bryant, Sir."

Instantly, Webb went still for a split second before going on high alert. His head whipped around, and before either Rodie or I could move to block him, he had the other FBI agent against the wall, hands fisted in his boring navy-blue blazer as he demanded, "What about my brother?"

I quickly slipped to his side and worked to pry his hands off the wild-eyed man. I felt the muscles in his arms trembling, and I watched as a muscle ticked furiously in his cheek.

"Webb. Let him go." He didn't want to. I could see it in his eyes when he turned his head to look at me, but eventually, his fists uncurled, and he took a step back. He was still breathing heavily, and his eyes were blazing with blue fire, so I purposely put myself between him and the agent. "What's wrong with Wyatt? The Bryant brothers are very close, so whatever information you're here to pass along to Agent Gordon, Webb will want to hear, as well. You guys owe him at least that much after screwing up this case so badly from the get-go." A little well-placed guilt went a long way in getting me what I wanted.

Eventually, Gage heaved a sigh and uttered a reluctant, "Go ahead, Gould. Just tell me what happened."

The other agent gulped so loudly it echoed through the room. He deliberately slid along the wall so he could put some space between himself and a silently seething Webb.

"We just got word from the unit director at the DEA. Agent Bryant was supposed to start building his cover for a new assignment today."

Gage tapped the toe of his shoe impatiently. "And?"

The other agent fidgeted nervously with his phone and shifted, so he was looking at Webb instead of his boss. "His cover was blown. Someone at the agency let his location slip to Bryant's former partner. Bryant's old partner called in with an emergency status, stating Bryant's brother had reached out and needed to verify his location ASAP. He realized something was off and alerted us to the situation right away. Unfortunately, before we could contact him, Agent Bryant was shot multiple times by the informant he was supposed to meet. He's in critical condition in a hospital down in San Antonio right now."

The entire room went dead silent. All eyes turned to Webb waiting for the inevitable explosion. I could hear his breathing turn labored and harsh. I could feel the way his big body was almost vibrating next to mine.

Of course, it was exactly then when Gage finally decided to do his job and ask the right questions. "How would Jacobs know to contact Bryant's former partner? I highly doubt a former agent would put your brother at risk by giving classified information to anyone, even you."

I grabbed Webb as he suddenly sagged against me. I wrapped my arms around his chest to keep him upright and felt the way his heart was pounding furiously under my palms.

"My mother. She's the only one who could've told Jacobs about Grady. We have a deal. Wyatt always lets Grady know where his assignment is taking place and if either of us has an emergency, Grady is the go-between." That was strictly against department protocol, but after Wyatt disappeared in the Wyoming woods on his last deep cover assignment, it didn't surprise me they'd come up with a backdoor system to let each other know they were safe. It was also the failsafe so Webb didn't go off half-cocked trying to track down his brother when he was forced to drop off the radar. If Grady said Wyatt was okay, then Webb believed him. As for telling Jolene anything about Wyatt's comings and goings, Webb couldn't let go of the idea his mother might one day care about her son's well-being. He'd given her Grady's info to use just in case, and now he was regretting the misplaced faith he had in the woman who ruined him with every fiber of his being.

His eyes fluttered closed, and I felt his heart break apart under my hands. I swore to myself I was going to do whatever it took to hold the pieces together for him.

CHAPTER 20

WEBB

"YOU CAN'T GO TO SAN Antonio. I know everything inside of you is screaming at you to get to Wyatt's side, but you can't go, Webb."

Ten's voice was calm, her eyes sympathetic. I still wanted to dart around her and run for the door.

She'd taken me back to the hotel while I was still in a daze hearing my brother was injured and clinging to life so far away from me. When he enlisted, my worst fear was that he would get killed in a place I couldn't access. My fear lessened slightly when he joined the DEA, but it was still there. That fear was what had spurred me into action when Wyatt went missing in Wyoming during the case that brought me into Ten's life. Now my worst fear had come to light, and I was having a hard time listening to anything besides the shriek of panic in my head.

"He means everything to me." Normally I'd be embarrassed that my voice cracked, but there was no place to hide from the raw emotion eating me alive on the inside.

"And you mean the world to me. I can't watch you run, be led blindly around by your nose. This guy has it in for you, Webb. Sure, injuring Wyatt helps him get a step closer to the money, but it also serves the greater purpose of making you suffer. He's targeting your weakest points." Her tone indicated she was frustrated and tired of the conversation. We were headed down a one-way road, and we both knew we were about to crash into a dead end. The impact was going to hurt like a son of a bitch.

I was pacing back and forth in front of the bed, hands pulling at my hair as I tried to control my breathing. Every instinct I had was telling me to run. Not only so I could get to my brother's side, but so I could also remove the danger I'd brought directly into Ten's life. Agent Gordon's warning was blaring in my mind behind the fear for my brother. As long I kept Ten close, she was a target. I'd done that to her, and even if she knew the risks and was trained to handle the threat, it made me feel like shit. I was pretty sure I was irrevocably in love with her. But could I really claim that if I was putting her life in danger by selfishly keeping her close because she was the only unwavering ally I had?

"If he dies and I'm not there," I shook my head uselessly. "That isn't something I'll ever come back from, Ten. Wyatt gave up everything for me, sacrificed his entire life. I should be able to put mine on the line when he needs me most." And wasn't that what it all really came down to in the end? Wyatt had always been there for me, no matter what. I needed to be able to say the same.

Suddenly, Ten was standing directly in front of me, causing my jerky pacing to stop. Her hands grabbed either side of my face and held me in place until I met her gaze. "Wyatt isn't going to die. He's not going down without a fight. He deserves to see the man who did this to him punished, and he deserves the chance to finally close the door on Jolene."

My mother. She was another open wound I was steadily bleeding out from. One which was poisoned and had festered for a long time. I'd done my best to protect the rest of the world from Jolene, but she'd done her very best to take everything that mattered to me away. If Wyatt died because of her . . . I hated the dark places my mind went to at the end of that sentence. I hated Jolene, but I'd never wished harm upon her, aside from wanting her to suffer in the same ways she'd hurt Wyatt and me. At the moment, I was certain if my brother didn't make it through this, then neither would she. And those tormented, twisted thoughts had me feeling like the worst brother and son who had ever walked the Earth.

"I hope to God Jacobs did something horrible to her to make her give up Grady's name." The words felt like they were ripped from my chest. The only reason I'd given Jolene a way to contact Wyatt when he was deep undercover was because I was worried about something happening to me, and my brother not knowing about it while he was working. Jolene wasn't a great choice as an emergency contact, but she was the only option I had before coming to Wyoming. I should've changed it to one of the Warner's as soon as I moved to the ranch, but hindsight was always 20/20. Wyatt was going to kick my ass when he woke up and found out Jolene was the one who sold him out. He was going to wake up, I refused to believe otherwise.

Helplessness and hopelessness, I couldn't shake either feeling away.

I was stupid to think Jolene would ever use any information she had on either of us in the way it was intended. I was ultimately the reason Wyatt was lying in a hospital right now, full of holes, and I knew there was no way I could face myself if the same thing happened to the woman standing in front of me.

As gently as I could, I pulled Ten's hands away from my face. I took a step backward and watched her sharp gaze follow my every move like a hawk. We hadn't been together all that long, but she was smart, and she always seemed to know me better than most of the people who filtered in and out of my life. Yes, I needed to be with my brother, but I was also scared. Everything was falling down around me, and she had to know I couldn't stand by and watch her be crushed under the weight of the rubble.

Ten crossed her arms over her chest and tapped the toe of her cowboy boot impatiently on the floor. Her blonde eyebrows pulled together in an angry V over her eyes, and her mouth flattened into a hard line.

I pushed out a breath and dragged a hand over my face. "You can't guarantee Wyatt will pull through. No one can. It's my fault he was ever at risk in the first place. I never should've trusted Jolene with something as important as a way to contact him when he was going undercover. I know where I need to be." As far away from Ten as I could get, before my twin brother tried to take her out and strip me of every person I had allowed myself to love.

Ten shook her head, and her whole body stiffened. "You *want* to be there. You *need* to be here so we can stop Jacobs from hurting more people. You know he's expecting you to run to Wyatt's side. He knows you're going to be distracted and focused on your brother, not your safety. He's setting you up again, and you're going to let him? I get that you're caught between a serious rock and a hard place, but you need to use your head right now, not your heart. You need to stay here, Webb." She sighed. "We came back to Wyoming to have the home-field advantage. You're throwing it all away and asking me to watch you purposely waltz into the fire, unprotected and alone."

The words, "I need you to stay here with me," had gone unsaid, but I could hear it loud and clear. It was like my heart was being pulled apart. Half of it was in Ten's hands, the other half was in San Antonio with my brother.

"I told myself I could stay for you. I wanted to be the guy who never let you down, Ten." I let my head drop. "He's my only family." He wasn't the only person on the planet I loved anymore, and I wasn't sure how to handle it. I had to be there for Wyatt, even though I could see Ten pleading with me to be here by her side to finish things with my twin. "I'm sorry."

She shook her head again and let her arms fall to her side. "I wouldn't ask you to stay if I didn't think it was for the best. The FBI wants you in protective custody. They've launched a full-on manhunt for your twin. This is serious. The danger is very real. I know your head is all over the place right now, but if you run, if you go, it isn't something you can undo. Wyatt would not want you reacting instead of thinking things through. Plus, I will always remember you walking out the door when I begged you not to. I will never forget that you didn't trust me enough to keep us both safe. You're not giving me a chance to prove to you I could be part of your family, and you're not behaving like you want to be part of mine."

Her words sliced through me like a blade, adding to the injuries my heart was already suffering. I was nothing like her asshole ex. I knew she was fully capable. I was the one who was going to come up lacking, no matter how hard I tried to be enough.

"I believe you can keep yourself safe. I'm not so sure safety and security are things I'm meant for. Maybe this is all supposed to come full circle. I did some really ugly things in the past, and facing off with Jacobs is literally coming face-to-face with all the worst parts of myself. I could've ended up just like him, Ten. I was really close." So close the line is pretty blurry. "I've worked harder to be here with you than I've ever worked at anything in my life. You have to know walking away will be the hardest thing I've ever done."

I heard her breath hitch, and her long, bronze eyelashes fluttered as she rapidly blinked her eyes. The glittering green turned bright and luminescent as moisture glazed the surface and slowly started to roll down her cheeks. She lifted an angry hand and swiped at the tears like they had betrayed her, which I guess they had. I was stepping on all her soft spots. I was squeezing her huge heart in my hands after I promised her over and over again I would take care of it.

"You can come with me." If Wyatt didn't pull through, I was going to have no one to lean on. If my brother died, I was going to spiral out of control and come untethered from the few things in this life that kept me grounded. "I want you to come with me." The last words were barely a whisper. We both knew she wasn't going anywhere. She put everything on the line when she asked me to stay. I dropped everything we'd been building when I told her I had to go.

Ten blinked her eyes. It was her turn to take a step back. "I know you want me to go with you, and if the situation were different, I would. But I can't. I'm not going to run off with you, not knowing when we would be back. I'm not standing idly by while the man I might love makes rash, emotional choices. Been there and done that. We know how that all worked out."

It didn't. We were facing what would be the end of us. We both knew it. I had to go, she felt like I should stay. We were never going to agree and she was to scared to lose someone else, she couldn't see she was the one making hasty, emotions choices which could destroy us.

"We should stick together. That was the plan all along." Ten's breath caught again, and she swiped a hand across her eyes in a furious gesture. I was going to be another man in her life who made her stand on her own. I was proving no better at taking care of her heart than Cyrus or the jerk FBI agent had been. She deserved better than all of us.

She said she might love me, which meant she did. And I was going to be stupid enough to walk away from the only thing I'd really wanted in a long-ass time? "I can promise to come back for you." I tried to sound confident, but even I could hear the lie in my voice. If Wyatt died, if my brother was taken from me, I had no clue what I was going to do or where I would end up. I did know I wouldn't be the kind of man Ten could love anymore. There would be absolutely nothing good left inside of me when grief was finished hollowing me out, and she deserved more than an empty shell of a man.

She pushed some of her hair off of her face, which had started to cling to her wet cheek, and took another step away from me. The distance felt insurmountable even though she was still close enough to touch. "I don't want your pretty words right now, not when they don't mean anything. You're going to end up dead, or maybe I will." She sounded scared and confused, but I didn't think it was the fear of dying or of me getting hurt. She was scared I was going to go and never come back.

"It's never been you versus the rest of the world for me, Ten. I am always going to be on your side, even if I'm not standing right next to you." I closed the distance between us, pulling her into my arms. We were both shaking, dread and regret colliding with the same force our bodies did. I hated myself for hurting her, but I would hate myself just as much if I weren't there for Wyatt. It was really an impossible position to be in, because this wasn't the first time, and it wouldn't be the last, that I'd put my brother's well-being first.

I felt all the trouble I thought I'd left behind tighten its claws around my throat, reminding me I was never going to be free.

I smoothed a hand down Ten's soft hair and rested my forehead against hers for a brief moment. She felt so right in my arms, I wasn't sure how I was supposed to let her go.

"Don't let anyone hurt you ever again." Especially not someone like me. I reluctantly let her go, eyes lifting to the door over her shoulder. I could feel the worry for my brother pulling me away from her, and I could feel her concern for me trying to hold me in place.

"I trusted *you* not to. I convinced myself you were different, that I finally got it right." She sounded devastated, which was how I felt as I took the first steps toward the door. "I hate being wrong . . . again. I hope you make it to Wyatt in one piece. I hope the choice you're making is the right one for you, Webb. I hope it's one you can live with." Somehow, I saw the veiled dual meaning behind her words.

I took another step toward the door, stopping to pick up my bag from the floor. I wasn't surprised when I stumbled, but it was the first time Ten wasn't there to set me back to rights. I felt the loss all the way through my body and struggled to breathe through the pain of all the different emotions hitting me at once.

"If I make it back . . ." The words trailed off as she refused to turn around and look at me, yet finished my sentence in her own way.

"Things won't be the same. I won't be the same." She said it with such certainty there was no doubt she believed the words to be true.

And wasn't that a shame? She was perfect before I fucked everything up, just like I always did. Just like I was always going to do.

I listened for my name, for some sign we could be saved if I wanted it badly enough as I walked out the door . . . but she was silent. Once again, I was alone with nothing but bad choices and trouble in front of me.

CHAPTER 21

TEN

WHEN THERE WAS A KNOCK on the door several hours later, I had to pull myself out of the bed I'd collapsed on as soon as the door had shut behind Webb. My head and my heart were at war. One telling me there was no other choice but for him to go; one telling me if he cared enough, if he really felt about me the way I felt about him, he would've stayed. The battle between the two made my head hurt, and I couldn't remember the last time I'd cried so hard. Probably when I was a teenager and realized I didn't know nearly as much as I thought I did about love and life.

At some point, I'd simply let myself go numb and crash out after the emotional outburst. I must've fallen asleep because it was approaching dinnertime when the pounding on the door started. For a brief moment, my heart lurched, hopeful Webb was on the other side, ready to tell me he'd seen the error of his ways and would never walk away from me again. That line of wishful thinking only lasted for a second. I dragged a hand over my face, wincing when I felt how grimy and rough my skin felt. My eyes hurt and my headache was still there, lurking at my temples, but it was manageable, so I kicked the tangled sheets free and stumbled to the door. At the last second, I remembered to look through the peephole to see who was on the other side, because unlike Webb,

I hadn't forgotten there was someone out there trying to bring the rest of his world down around him.

I heaved a sigh when I caught sight of the tall, broad figure through the small opening. I could pick out Cyrus Warner in a pitch-dark room filled with a thousand other men. There was something about him I'd always been drawn to. He had some kind of take-charge charisma that bled so effortlessly from every pore; it was always impossible for me to ignore him. At least it had been until I'd run up against Webb Bryant's chameleon-like charm. Going toe-to-toe with Cy was the last thing I wanted to do while I was still feeling so raw and exposed. It was going to be much harder than normal to pull on the mask of composure and indifference I typically wore around him. But as he lifted a hand and pounded on the door again, making my head bounce and my headache throb twice as hard, I knew I wasn't going to have much of a choice in the matter.

I pulled the door open just as the large man was about to knock again. He stumbled forward a step almost taking me to the ground as we bumped into one another. Not so long ago the feel of his big, muscular frame brushing up against mine would have sent a swarm of butterflies flying in my belly. Now, I was nothing more than annoyed at his intrusion and irritated that he felt he had the right to check up on me.

I pushed him back and used the sleeve of my shirt to scrub across my face. I was sure I looked as bad as I felt inside, but there wasn't a reason to care how messy or miserable I was in front of Cy anymore. He'd slid down the list of men I'd been disappointed by dramatically in the last day.

"What are you doing here?" There was no hint of welcome in my voice, and I couldn't stop myself from throwing my shoulders back and defensively crossing my arms in front of me. Logically, I knew Cy wasn't the person I wanted to fight, but he was the one standing in front of me, so all bets were off. My wrath didn't care who the target was, it only needed a place to land now that it was unleashed and flying free.

Cy carefully and deliberately shut the door behind him. He had on a Harley Davidson T-shirt, perfectly faded jeans, heavy black boots, and a snakeskin belt with a heavy, silver belt buckle. He's always gone against the grain when it came to fitting in the with locals. He'd always been more rock and roll than country. His air of authority dared anyone to challenge whether or not he belonged in charge of the sprawling ranch which had been in the Warner family for generations. Looking at him now, I wondered how I ever thought he was the one and only for me. He was just as different, just as unknown as Gage, yet in a completely different way.

He was all wrong for me, and I should've seen it long before now.

"I was hoping you would enlighten me as to why Webb called me and asked me for a ride to Billings so he could catch a flight. He was tight-lipped the whole drive. But I gather Wyatt is in a bad way." He narrowed his eyes at me as his silvery gaze raked over my face. "I'm guessing he lit out of here without you for a good reason, but looking at you right now I'm having second thoughts."

I sniffed loudly and tossed my head back, wrapping my pride around me like a protective blanket. "Wyatt got shot. Webb left to go be by his side. He was in critical condition when the information came in. His twin leaked his identity to whomever Wyatt was supposed to meet to set up his cover. The bad guys knew he was a federal agent from the jump. He was greeted at his new assignment by a hail of bullets."

Cy dipped his scruffy chin in a slight nod of understanding. "Okay, that explains why Webb could hardly string a sentence together and wasn't making much sense. It doesn't explain why you're still here and not with him when he clearly needs you. What the hell is going on, Ten? Any idiot with eyes can see the two of you are completely gone over each other. Why are you here, if he's going there?"

His broad shoulders stiffened as I suddenly took a step forward, arms dropping so I could poke him in the center of his hard chest.

"You don't get to question why I do anything, Cyrus. You gave up that right a long time ago." He took another step back and held his hands up in front of him.

"Whoa. I'm asking because I'm worried about both of you. You're both kind of a mess, but put the two of you together and you somehow manage to lock into perfect place with one another. Despite what you want people to believe, I know you aren't a cold-hearted, cynical woman. Help me understand what went wrong, Ten. I want to help."

"I didn't ask for your help." I put my hands on my hips and stubbornly jutted out my chin. "I don't want it."

Cy growled under his breath and threw his hands up in the air, frustration wafting off of him in heated waves. "Too bad. You've got it anyway. If Wyatt doesn't make it, Webb is going to go off the deep end. And we both know the only person who can keep him from drowning is you, so why did you send him out into the maelstrom without a life raft?"

I opened my mouth to order him to get out of my room, to tell him to fuck off, to scream at him he should know exactly why I was falling apart in front of him. After all, he'd left me more than once, too. None of those things came out. Instead, all that escaped was a wheezing sound laced with so much pain and disappointment I was amazed I was still standing.

"He left. I asked him to stay, and he left anyway." Suddenly exhausted once again, I let myself fall onto the rumpled bed, throwing my arms out like a starfish and staring blindly at the shadows starting to crawl across the ceiling. "I've never asked anyone to stay,

Cy. Not you, not Gage. No one. Do you have any idea what it's like to watch someone you want to hold onto walk away from you?"

A bitter laugh ripped out of him as he made his way over to where I was sprawled inelegantly. "My first wife left me, if you remember, and so did Leo. Only one of them mattered enough to go after, and now she isn't going anywhere. The difference here is Webb *had* to go, Ten. You asked him to stay when it was impossible for him to do so, and I think you did it on purpose."

I felt the bed dip as he took a seat next to me. I rolled my head in his general direction and lifted my hand so I could press them against my burning eyes. I was fidgety and agitated, having a hard time keeping still as my foot bounced and fingers twitched. "What are you talking about? I asked him to stay because his twin brother is torturing him in unimaginable ways and has had the upper hand for weeks. If he stayed here, he has me, you, and Rodie, not to mention the FBI on his side. It didn't matter. He left anyway."

I flinched as Cy reached out and caught one of my wildly flailing hands in one of his much larger ones. They were softer, less calloused and work-roughened than I remembered, and even though his hold was gentle and friendly, it felt wrong to let him touch me in such a familiar way. I shook him loose and pushed myself upright.

"I love my wife, Ten. She is the person I put first in everything. She is always at the forefront of my heart and mind, but if I got a call saying either Sutton or Lane was lying alone in a hospital clinging to life, I would drop everything to get to them. Even if Leo asked me not to. It would kill me to hurt her that way, but I would do it in a heartbeat. Now, the thing is, Leo would never ask me to stay away from my brothers if they needed me. She understands how important they are to me, and knows it would do irreparable damage to me and our relationship if she tried to make me choose between her and them. You're one of the smartest humans I've ever met, Tennyson McKenna. You can see things more clearly than ninety percent of the population, so why are you acting so blind when it comes to seeing Webb has his back against the damn wall?"

It was on the tip of my tongue to remind Cy that Webb was a grown-ass man, responsible for making his own choices. But, when I stopped for a second and really let Cy's words sink in, I realized *I* was the hard, unmovable place, and his brother was the rock I accused Webb of being caught between. I'd forced him to pick between the two of us exactly like Cyrus said. I told myself I was trying to make Webb pick the right choice, the smart one, which kept him reasonably safe. But any reasonable person not operating out of the fear of rejection would have been able to see he was never going to pick himself, or me, over his injured brother.

Groaning, I plowed my hands through my hair and pulled hard enough it hurt. "You're right. I pushed Webb out the door so he couldn't walk away from me later. I didn't give him a real choice." What the fuck is wrong with me?

"You've been hurt . . . a lot. It can be hard to believe that this time is going to be different, this person is going to be unlike all the others who've come and gone. It's instinct to want to protect yourself. We're all guilty of doing it. And like I said when I walked in, you did give him a choice, but it was an impossible one. Did he ask you to go with him?"

Shamefully I nodded, remembering Webb practically begging me to go with him. "He did. I told him he didn't need me." But really, I was trying to convince myself I didn't need him, because if I admitted I did, things were never going to be the same. I wasn't going to be alone anymore.

"You're the only one he needs, Ten. You're the only person he trusts to hold him together, and I believe he's the only one you trust to be there for you. You wouldn't have fallen for him so fast otherwise. You wouldn't have helped him prove his innocence if you couldn't see the good in him. You wouldn't be here beating yourself up for making a bad decision. There isn't anything in the relationship rule book that says once you let someone go, you can't go and get them back. That boy has been looking for a guide back home since he first showed up. Let yourself be the star he can follow when everything else in his life is dark."

I blinked at the hard man with the incredibly soft words. "Who are you and what have you done with the perpetually grumpy Cyrus Warner? Do you have a twin no one knows about, as well?"

Cy laughed and reached out to give me a hard, one-armed hug. It was quick and totally friendly. I guess the gap between friend and lover had finally closed, and I could see him objectively as one without remembering him as the failed other. I pushed him hard enough he toppled over the side of the bed, landing with a thump on the floor. We both cracked up, and I put a hand on my chest, finally feeling like I could breathe.

"For what it's worth, I'm glad you went after Leo. It's nice to see you happy and all enlightened. She's been good for you. Despite how things ended with us, I always wanted you to be happy." It was a conversation we probably should have had a long time ago, but better late than never.

He knocked his head back against the side of the bed. "I always wanted you to be happy, too, Ten. I've never been proud of the way I handled things between us. I regret ever making you feel like you weren't good enough for me."

"I was good enough, I just wasn't the right one. It took a while, but I get the difference now." I sighed and climbed to my feet. "I've got to go."

Cy lumbered to his feet, as well. "What do you need from me?"

I gave him a slight grin. "Nothing. I've got it from here. I can own up to my mistakes. I can only hope Webb will forgive me for being so shortsighted and afraid."

"There is no love without forgiveness, and that boy loves you. Touch base when you get where you're going and don't forget to watch your back."

That was easy enough to agree to. It was ingrained in me, or so I thought.

Fifteen minutes after Cy left, while I was frantically throwing my things in a suitcase and letting my boss know I was going to be gone for an indefinite amount of time, there was another knock on the hotel room door. Figuring it was Cy forgetting something, or Rodie stopping by to check up on me, I made my way to the door. Diligently, I paused to look through the peephole once again, and immediately recognized the man on the other side, even with the brim of his cowboy hat pulled down.

After the talk with Cy, my emotions were all over the place; my head and my heart were finally on the same page. Without hesitation I threw open the door and practically launched myself into Webb's arms. Any other day I would have been more careful. Any other moment in time I would have known better.

"I can't believe you're here." My words got tangled up, and my heart tried to beat its way out of my chest. "I was coming to you. I needed to come to you."

I tried to pull back so I could look at his face and squeaked in protest when his arms tightened painfully around my waist.

"Webb?"

Slowly his head lifted, and I went stone still. My heart tried to escape again, but for a completely different reason.

The face was the same. Same pretty golden skin. Same devilishly arched brows. Same elegant nose and sharp cheekbones. Same full lips, but these didn't curve with a careless grin. No, these lips twisted into something bleak, stark, ugly. And the eyes were all wrong. Sure, they were the same bright, intense blue, but his were cold, not warm like a summer day. They were glittering with glee and something I could only call evil.

So much for watching my back. If I hadn't watched him walk away from me, I would've seen him coming from a mile away.

"You're not Webb."

"No. I'm not." The voice was all wrong, as well. It was the last thing I remembered before everything went black.

CHAPTER 22

WEBB

I WAS ABOUT TO WALK through the doors of Billings airport when my cell phone rang. For a small, hopeful moment I expected to see Ten's number on the display, but deep inside I knew it was a ridiculous thought. She was done with me. I was nothing more than another person who left her. She flat out told me there would be no forgiveness at the end of this string of impossible choices. Unfortunately, my heart hadn't received the message as loud and clear as the rest of me. The foolish thing refused to let go of the idea that Ten was the one. For some reason, it was fixated on the complicated woman and refused to shake itself loose of her hold.

I didn't recognize the number, and I had a moment of absolute terror shake me to my core. I hesitated a second before answering, as I worked to convince myself it wasn't the hospital in Texas calling with bad news about my brother. On the ride to the airport, Cy had been politely silent while I called the hospital and asked for updates on Wyatt's condition. He was in surgery. That's all anyone would divulge over the phone. The person I spoke to also asked who was Wyatt's next of kin and who was responsible for his medical power of attorney. Neither of those questions boosted my confidence that Wyatt would be fine by the time I showed up in San Antonio.

Cautiously, I swiped to answer the call, my bag feeling like it was full of bricks at my side. I squinted in the direction Cyrus had driven away, wondering if he was the one Ten was going to turn to for comfort. A flare of jealousy, bright and hot, burned in the center of my chest as I reminded myself Cy was in love with Leo, and Ten, even though I'd ruined it, was in love with me.

"Hello." My voice sounded broken, more rasp than words.

"Webb? Is that you?" The voice on the other end of the line was familiar with its slow, Creole drawl, but I was so out of sorts I couldn't immediately place it.

"This is Webb, who's this?" I hated that the distraction of the call was a welcome one. I was having a hell of a time walking through the doors. My throat closed up when I thought about getting on the plane and putting an insurmountable distance between Ten and my heart.

"Boy, don't tell me you forgot about your Aunt Clara already?" There was the click of a tongue and a heavy sigh. "I'd ask who raised you, but we both know the person who was supposed to didn't do it right." I thought I heard her breath catch and maybe a sniffle, as if she was trying to hold back tears. Clara was a tough old broad, so the entire conversation sent an uneasy shiver shooting across my skin.

A surprise bark of laughter shot out of me, and I closed my eyes briefly. "No, I didn't forget. I'm not thinking too clearly at the moment. Wyatt was injured on assignment. He's in surgery right now, and no one will tell me what his odds of pulling through are. He's in Texas, I'm still in Wyoming, and my twin is the one who put him in the hospital."

There was a soft gasp on the other end of the phone, and I could imagine my aunt putting her hand to her chest in an overly dramatic way. "Oh, Webb." She sniffed loudly and let out a heavy sigh. "I would never call and add another burden onto what you're already carrying if I'd known what was going on with your brother." She cleared her throat. "You give me the name of the hospital he's in. I'll meet you there."

I rubbed my wrist across my forehead and felt some of the tightness coiled in the center of my chest loosen. If anything happened to Wyatt, at least I wouldn't be alone. I knew my brother wouldn't appreciate the intrusion after all this time, but I would welcome his complaints if it meant he was awake and well enough to argue.

I rattled off the info she needed to locate Wyatt, grateful I'd reconnected with someone who cared about him as much as I did. I heard a pen scratching over paper and listened as she muttered about foolish boys with dangerous jobs under her breath. When she was done, she said my name in a very somber tone.

"Webb, this isn't a call I ever wanted to make, but deep down, I think I knew it was always going to end this way." I listened as she pulled in a shuddering breath and slowly let it out. "I got a call from the sheriff a little bit ago."

My hand tightened around my phone reflexively. No news coming from the local law was going to be good news. They didn't drive out into the swamp unless something serious came down the pipe.

"Boy, your mama," another deep sigh hit my ears, "She's no longer with us. The NOPD found her body in an alley in the Quarter last night. I'm so sorry, and I'm so angry at her. She couldn't do right by her boys, even at the end."

My bag fell at my feet with a thump. The doors to the entrance of the airport wavered unsteadily in front of me. I heard my heart thunder erratically between my ears, and I could feel my lungs seize up as I forgot how to breathe momentarily.

"Jolene's dead?" It was weird to say the words out loud when I'd been thinking of her demise only hours earlier.

"I don't know if she was trying to make it home and ran into trouble or not, but yes, baby, your mom has passed." Clara sounded surprised by the emotion pouring into her tone. Even though we all knew Jolene was never going to go in an easy way, it was still a shock to hear all her bad choices had finally caught up to her.

I was shocked by how weak in the knees I went, and how empty the center of my chest felt.

"She didn't run into trouble. It came after her." Like it always did. I was conflicted on so many levels as to how I should feel about it all. My voice cracked when I asked, "She was murdered?"

Clara made a strangled sound low in her throat. "She was. The police made it seem like she was doing something she shouldn't have and got caught up in a crime gone wrong. Your mama's reputation precedes her, I'm afraid." She gave a tiny huff. "You don't worry about a thing, boy. Your Aunt Ana is going to handle funeral arrangements, and we'll send her off in a way far better than she deserves." She sniffed dramatically. "We'll lay her to rest next to our parents; you boys can say goodbye in your own time, when you're ready. Right now, let's focus on getting Wyatt home and well." It was clear she'd already drawn lines in her mind. Jolene wasn't hers to worry about any longer, but Wyatt still had a fighting chance. So, she was going to throw everything she had into being there for the boy who'd slipped through her fingers, and she was going to show up for the man who swore he didn't need anyone from his past except me.

I dragged my wrist across my forehead again. It was now covered in cold sweat, and I could see my hand shaking when I lowered it. My vision was still wavering, and my heart felt like it was trying to kick its way out of my chest. I was lucky I managed to stay upright considering the weight of everything going wrong in my life at once. Somehow, I knew in my heart that my twin killed our mother. He'd tried to kill Wyatt. He'd moved beyond making my life difficult to trying to destroy me. Now, he was apparently intent on leaving me all alone in this world. I squeezed my eyes shut, picturing Ten standing alone in that hotel room, her words of warning ringing loudly in my ears. It didn't take a genius to piece together she'd been dead-on in her assessment of the increasingly dangerous situation. My twin wasn't drawing me away to get me alone so he could harm me. He was pulling me away, so Ten was left alone. He planned on completely ripping my heart out of my chest and grinding it to dust in his hands.

"Aunt Clara." I bent and picked up my bag, frantically searching for signs pointing me in the direction of where I could find a rental car. I didn't have time to explain why I needed Cyrus to turn around and come back and get me. "You promise you're going to be by Wyatt's side no matter what happens?"

"I'm headed out the door as soon as I get off the phone with you." She sounded resolute, and I would've kissed her if she'd been standing in front of me.

"Okay. I need you to keep me updated every hour on what's going on with him. There's something I have to take care of in Sheridan before I can get down to Texas. It's important." She was the most important thing in the entire world to me, and if I lost her because of my own indecision, I would be just as wrecked as if I lost Wyatt. My brother had to fight his way back. There was little I could do for him, and he wasn't going to be alone as long as Clara went and stood vigil in my place. I still had time to show up for Ten. There was still a chance I could keep the promises I made to her.

Clara demanded answers I wasn't able to give. I hung up on her in the middle of a rant about me still being a rash, thoughtless boy and how she was going to teach me the manners my mother never thought were necessary. I could tell she was worried, but I needed her to save the concern and belated mothering for Wyatt. All of my focus was on getting back to Sheridan as quickly as possible.

I tried to call Ten, and admitted to myself I was slightly

heartbroken when she didn't answer. I called Cyrus, intent on asking him to go check on her, to make sure she wasn't alone in case my twin brother decided to make a move. There wasn't an answer there either, so I called Rodie. Finally, I got through to someone, but the gruff sheriff informed me he was out on a domestic violence call over an hour away from the city. I pleaded with him to send one of his deputies to the hotel to check on Ten, and my panic must have gotten through, because he promised to send a unit by the hotel. I was desperate enough to suggest he put a call into Ten's ex. The guy was garbage, but there was no question he wanted to put my twin behind bars. If it meant getting him involved to keep Ten safe, I would do whatever was necessary.

Unfortunately, Rodie stated there was another robbery in a small town on the Wyoming-Colorado border. It was too close for comfort in the fed's eyes, too similar to the crimes which brought them into our world in the first place, so the entire team had hit the road shortly after Ten and I walked out of his office this morning. It was frustrating enough that I swore up a storm under my breath as I squared away a rental and once again called Cyrus. I was itching to call the ranch and have one of the other Warners on the property drive into town and check on Ten, but the drive time between where I was and where they were was almost the same, and I was ultimately closer if Lane was out riding the property with a tour. I left Cyrus a frustrated voicemail, explaining I was on my way back, then proceeded to make the nearly two-hour drive in under an hour and a half.

I was just pulling into the parking lot of the hotel when my phone rang once again. I answered it as I ran across the asphalt.

"What?" There was no time for pleasantries.

"How did you get back to Sheridan so fast?" Rodie barked the question in my ear as I closed the distance between me and my woman.

"I drove like there was no speed limit. I don't have time to talk right now, Rodie. I need to get to Ten." I was breathing hard, and it wasn't from running.

"What do you mean you need to 'get to Ten'?" Rodie's voice went hard. "My deputy told me you just answered the door to her hotel room and assured him Ten was fine."

We both went silent and then started swearing at the same time. "That wasn't you who answered the door, was it?"

"Fuck no!" Fear had ice crystals forming in my blood as I dashed through the hallway like a madman.

"Don't do anything stupid, Webb. I'm sending a couple of guys back to the hotel. Wait for them." Rodie's voice held a hard order, but we both knew it was one I was going to ignore.

I shoved my phone in one pocket and searched for the room key in another, all while running faster than I'd ever run before.

When I pushed open the door, I wasn't sure what or whom I expected to come face to face with. But staring at my exact double was so disconcerting I almost fell to my knees. It was almost as if my reflection had walked out of a mirror and was standing directly in front of me. He was even dressed the same. Matching flannel shirt and worn jeans. Identical boots and even the same leather belt. It was so much it made my head spin, but I kept it together when I caught sight of Ten sprawled oh so still and pale on the floor between us. Her blonde hair was streaked with blood, and there was an ugly purple and blue bruise decorating the side of her face closest to me.

I met the blue eyes that were an exact match to mine and asked, "What happens now?"

A laugh which sounded so eerily like my own filled the space between us. "Now *you* get to know what it feels like to be left all alone."

It was then I noticed the gun in his hand. A gun he pointed directly at the unmoving woman on the floor.

CHAPTER 23

TEN

I WAS GROGGY. I FELT like my head was stuffed with cotton candy. One whole side of my face was throbbing. My jaw ached something fierce, and the headache I'd struggled with earlier was a full-blown situation now, pounding behind my closed eyes and shooting bolts of fiery pain across my skull. A moan of agony was trapped in my throat, and I squeezed my eyes shut to hold the tears at bay. My thoughts weren't exactly crystal clear, but I knew I could only be in this much pain if something had gone horribly wrong. I vaguely recalled a feeling of soaring elation, quickly followed by the crash of all-consuming fear. Even out of it, my subconscious was doing its best to keep me still and relatively safe. If I wasn't moving, I wasn't a threat, even if I couldn't kick my brain into gear and recall the danger was I was so scared of.

"You think I don't know what it's like to be alone?" A familiar voice barked the question indignantly. "You've sorely overestimated Jolene's ability to parent. Wyatt and I grew up completely alone. All we had was each other."

A laugh barked out, which made my ears ring and had me fighting to hold back a flinch. I tried to peel an eyelid open to gain my bearings, but even that tiny motion made my head spin and nausea rise up hard and fast in the back of my throat. I stifled a groan and slowly tried to even out my breathing. Someone in this room needed my help, and I refused to be a helpless heap on the floor.

"Now, you don't even have that." There was a smug superiority in the voice I didn't immediately recognize. Both were a deep, rough rumble, shaking with thinly veiled anger and resentment, but one had a different flavor to it, a trace of something soft and deeply southern that tugged at my tired, aching mind.

Someone released a gusty sigh and I heard the sound of rustling fabric. "Why go after Wyatt? Jolene, even Bernard, I understand. Even being pissed off at me for whatever reason makes some sense, but what did Wyatt ever do to you? We didn't even know you existed up until a couple of weeks ago." The south in that voice became even more pronounced as the man speaking with it got more and more agitated. It felt familiar and important. "If it's just about the money, you can have it. I don't want anything that comes with ties to Bernard. He can burn in hell for all I care. I don't want anything Jolene schemed and manipulated to get. I made it this far without taking anything from her."

There was another laugh, and I tried to peel an eye open once again. Everything was hazy, shadows against darkness. All I could make out were two big, indistinct shapes standing a few feet away from me. One was close enough I could touch with the toe of my boot, the other was lurking blurrily off to one side. They were the same size, both bigger and broader than I was comfortable with in my current condition.

"Who cares about money? I have money." The figure closest to me shifted a bit, and I quickly closed my eyes and went back to playing unconscious. "The money makes for a good excuse, a convenient explanation. I didn't really care if dear old Dad paid up or not, I just wanted to see what happened when I rattled his tree. Look what fell out: a twin brother who didn't get tossed out like he was garbage and an older brother who's a goddamn hero."

There was more rustling, and the soft voice grew hard and cold. "We didn't get tossed out; we got dragged around like luggage."

"But you didn't end up in the home of a pervert, did you? And you had big bro there in the middle of the night to keep you safe when the monsters came out to play. You didn't have to fight them all on your own, did you, Webb?" There was so much cold rage in the second voice, I had to use every ounce of willpower I had not to shiver violently where I was sprawled out on the floor. "You didn't have to steal so you wouldn't starve. You didn't have to risk everything so you could escape a house of horrors."

Both of the dark shadows moved, drifting closer to one another until it was impossible to tell them apart through slitted eyes. I sank my teeth into my lower lip to hold back any sound that would escape and slowly tried to move my head. Immediately fireworks colored by bright bursts of agony exploded behind my eyelids, and my efforts to remain noiseless must've failed because suddenly there was a scuffle, lots and lots of swearing, and my legs were jostled as the large, blurry mass of men moved in my direction.

"I called the sheriff before I barged in here. You aren't walking away from this. If you hurt her . . ." The voice that made my heartbeat double in speed went low and deadly.

The voice that was ice cold and made me shiver replied, "I already hurt her. Now, I'm going to kill her, and you're going to stand there and watch, knowing there was nothing you could do to stop me. Your brother is as good as dead. Your mother is dead. Your father is next on the list. Your lover is going to die. And I'm going to rot behind bars. You'll have no one and nothing . . . just like I did my entire life." Insanity. I was hearing pure, unfiltered insanity coming from one of the men in the room.

Oh, right. There was a man with a gun. One I opened the door for. One who looked just like Webb but didn't act anything like him. The void in the blackness of my memory was starting to fill.

I remembered running to the man I believed to be Webb, only to realize my mistake a second later. He pushed me back into the hotel room and pistol whipped me with the very ugly, very dangerous gun he had in his hand. No wonder my face felt like it had been run over by the high school marching band. He'd clocked me with enough force there was a good chance my cheekbone was broken, and I would guess the eye on that side of my face was swollen shut and useless, adding to the confusion as I tried to make out what was going on in the room around me.

"Listen to me . . ." Webb's voice was pleading and softly aching. "I didn't end up in a home with someone who did me wrong, but both Wyatt and I spent several years living on the streets. I didn't steal so I could survive, but I sold the only thing of value I had . . . my body. You can't tell me you don't know for a fact there are all kinds of heartless, ruthless people out there looking for a desperate kid to manipulate and abuse. If you don't think I suffered, that I struggled, you're wrong. Staying with Jolene was no better than being tossed aside by Bernard. But at the end of the day, we survived. We made it, regardless of what they did to us, of who they handed us off to. Doesn't that mean we won?" Webb's voice cracked on the last words, and I could picture him in my foggy mind, doing his best to keep his expression neutral as he pleaded for my life.

He came back.

I knew that was important, but there were so many more pressing issues at hand. I was injured and couldn't latch onto the significance of it at the moment.

"I didn't win shit. I've spent my life on the run. I knew after the first robbery I could never stay in one place too long, but it was the only thing I was good at. I didn't get a chance at normal. I never had a shot at finding a woman who looks at me the way she looks at you." My foot was roughly nudged. I dug my fingernails into my palms and ordered myself to stay still. I could smell the metallic tinge of blood in the air and had a moment of panic wondering if Webb was hurt. "She's a former fed, for fuck's sake. I thought for sure she was going to let the FBI take you. I couldn't believe it when she rode to your rescue. It made me wonder what was so good about Webb Bryant? What made you so special that people are willing to risk everything for you? What did our mother see in you, and not me? Could she tell you were worth keeping and I was going to be someone who always got thrown away? Want to know what her last words were?"

I swore the temperature in the room dropped twenty degrees.

"She told you how to locate Wyatt." Now both voices were Arctic cold and I couldn't suppress a shiver.

"Oh, she gave me the partner's contact info without much hassle when I asked for it. She thought I was you. I just told her I got a new phone and lost all my contacts. She didn't hesitate to hand over everything. Couldn't tell us apart even though we were face to face. She didn't guess who I was until I wrapped my hands around her neck and started to squeeze. She looked heartbroken that her darling Webb would dare raise a hand to her until she figured it out." A bitter, broken laugh echoed around the room and somewhere in the distance, sirens wailed. "Before she took her last breath, she begged, pleaded, implored me to tell you that you were a good boy for always looking out for her. She might not have known how to say it or to show it, but apparently that bitch loved you. You and only you, brother. I regret not letting her believe it was you taking her life. Sometimes my ego gets the better of me. I wanted her to know it was the son she didn't want who was sending her straight to hell."

A roar thundered through the room, and I could no longer play possum. The entire bed I was lying next to shifted, and I would've been crushed under the weight of two bodies and a mattress as the whole thing collapsed on the floor when Webb launched himself at his twin. I scrambled out of the way, choking back bile and lifting my hands to hold my throbbing head as I did so. I barely missed a flying fist as the two men tore into each other like they were trying to reach each other's very souls and pull them from the other's body. Out of the corner of my eye, I watched as a cowboy hat went flying in one direction and the black pistol in another. The meaty sounds of fists pounding into flesh filled the small space as I quickly crawled on my hands and knees to where the gun landed. I picked the weapon up in a shaky hand, pressing the palm of my free hand to my forehead. It really felt like my skull was cracked wide open and the insides were trying to escape however they could.

The distinctive sound of bone breaking, followed by a howl of outrage made my ears ring as I lifted the gun and shakily ordered, "Stop it!"

I was ignored.

Both men were intent on tearing the other to shreds. Both were bloody and vicious in their attacks. Unfortunately, without Jacobs wearing the cowboy hat any longer, they were an exact match, including the way they fought. Dirty, rough, no holds barred. I had no clue which one was winning, which meant Webb could be seriously injured. I cringed as two big bodies slammed up against the wall of the hotel room sending a picture and mirror to the floor. One handsome face had an obviously crooked nose steadily leaking blood. The other identical handsome face had both the top and bottom lip split open. Both faces were flushed red with anger and assertion. Both sets of blue eyes glowed with hot fury, and neither showed any signs of backing down. It was unnerving that I couldn't tell them apart when Webb was so angry and cold.

My frown dug into my face and I raised my voice as loudly as my screaming head would allow. "Knock it off, or I'm putting a bullet in both of you and sorting it out later."

They both seemed to realize I was awake and armed at the same time. Twin blond heads snapped in my direction, and identical sapphire eyes popped wide.

"You're awake." The obvious statement came from the man pressed up against the wall. There was no relief in his tone, so I assumed he was Weston, and the man holding him in a punishing grip was Webb.

But then the other man flicked his eyes to the gun. "How did you end up with that?" Again, the tone was flat, and I was left staring at both the men trying to figure out who was the one I'd handed my heart to.

I waved the gun and leaned back against the wall behind me, so I didn't end up on the floor. I wasn't sure how much longer I was going to be able to stay vertical or conscious. "Let him go and stand over there." I needed space between them since I couldn't see straight. I needed to watch them move for a hint as to which one was Webb.

The men reluctantly separated and moved a few feet apart from one another. The one with the broken nose wiped his arm across the blood dripping down over the lower half of his face, and the one with the busted mouth grabbed for the discarded comforter to clean up his face.

"You can't tell us apart, can you?" The question came from the twin against the wall, his voice now nasally and thin as blood still trickled from the crooked bend in his nose.

I shifted my gaze between them, squinting to try and pull them into focus. I was looking for a sign, a tell from Webb, but neither one of their faces was exactly clear.

"Our own mother couldn't, how could she?" The conversation was biting and sarcastic. Both men looked angry and ready to keep fighting. My head hurt too much to wrestle with the implications of trying to figure out who was who, but I knew if I got it wrong, I would never have the opportunity to make things up to Webb.

Carefully, I cranked my head to the side and braced my wavering arm with my free hand.

"Can't you see it in my eyes?" Those baby blues went from furious to soulful and sincere in the span of a blink. I wanted to believe I would know Webb blindfolded, but the risk was too high if I picked wrong.

"Why did you walk out on me?" I asked the question knowing the real Webb would give me the truth and his twin would simply tell me what I wanted to hear. Webb had handed me the truth over and over again, even when I didn't want to hear it. Even when it made me look like the frightened, neurotic mess I actually was.

The man leaning up against the wall shifted and gave me a slow grin. The smile was Webb through and through . . . or was it? My Webb only smiled like that when he was trying to play someone. "I shouldn't have gone. I'm sorry. I don't know what I was thinking. Bring me the gun. The sheriff is on his way."

The man near the bed spat out a mouthful of blood and rolled his eyes. "I left because I didn't have a choice. I came back for the same reason. The idea of losing you hit me just as hard as the thought of losing Wyatt. I didn't want to choose, but when I had to, I did. I chose you, Ten, and I always will. You come first."

Of course the guy by the bed was Webb. Challenging me and charming me at the same time. Never making anything but loving him easy. Him and his pretty words he saved just for me.

I turned to face Weston Jacobs, but my coordination was still off, and my limbs weren't exactly responsive. The hand holding the gun dropped dramatically, and I started to list wildly to the side. Jacobs let out a battle cry and flung himself away from the wall. He was closer to where I was falling than Webb was, and I knew if he got his hands on the gun it was over for all of us. I tightened my hand on the pistol and forced myself to lift my hand back up as the rest of my body moved backward.

My finger flexed on the trigger, and suddenly I couldn't hear or smell anything beyond the acrid burn of gunpowder. I heard a belated crack as the hotel room door was kicked open, and I blinked away drops of blood that clung to my eyelashes as I went down under the weight of the body still barreling toward mine. Vaguely I heard someone shout my name, then the word 'POLICE.' I thought I heard Cyrus yell Webb's name, then it all turned into another blur I couldn't track as my poor head gave up the fight and shut down completely. This time before everything faded to black, I caught sight of a familiar pair of blue eyes. They were bright with worry and shiny with so many different layers of love. They were the eyes I would gladly follow into all kinds of trouble. They were the eyes I wanted to see every morning when I woke up, and the eyes I wanted to look into every night before I closed mine.

"I won't make you choose again." I was pretty sure I got the words out before I passed out, but if not, I knew he was going to be there when I woke up and I would tell him again.

I was going to get it right this time.

CHAPTER 24

WEBB

"SOME FOLKS ARE JUST BORN bad. Ain't nothing that can be done to help them."

Aunt Clara's words were soft as she sniffed into the handkerchief she had clutched in her hand. My uncle wrapped a bulky arm across her shoulders and gave her a squeeze. My other aunt, my mom's younger sister, had been openly weeping nonstop since the moment the marble headstone went up.

It was an overcast day, so the weather was muggy and stifling. The gray sky fit the somber events of the day and matched the darker colors swirling within the light-colored grave marker. Every time my eyes caught on the dates, I shivered. Ten would run her hand up and down my back in a soothing gesture, but nothing chased away the weirdness of seeing my birthdate on a headstone. It so easily could have been me or Wyatt under the bed of wildflowers, which had sprouted up not long after my brother and mother were laid to rest.

At first, the family fought me when I asked that my twin be laid to rest next to Jolene. They said it was disrespectful and would further taint Jolene's already tarnished memory. In my head, it was fitting that my mother spend eternity facing the son she'd given away. My mother was always running from monsters, always fighting against facing her responsibilities and the consequences of her actions. In the end, there would be no escaping the ramifications of her lifelong string of selfish, manipulative choices. Both mother and son ended up where they were because of Jolene's selfishness.

Besides, he was family. As fucked up as it was, someone finally needed to claim him as one of their own. It was the least we could do, and it gave me an odd sense of peace.

"No." Wyatt's voice was sharp and cracked like a dry tree limb as it snapped across the gravesite. It was so harsh Clara stopped sniffing and Aunt Ana finally put an end to the waterworks. "No one is born bad, but some of us come into this world at the mercy of people who have turned bad, embraced it even, and the cycle just continues until someone dies. There is always a choice between right and wrong; it's up to us to decide how many of each we're going to make."

My older brother looked like hell. He lost a ton of weight the last month while he was in the hospital. His face was gaunt, skin pulled too tightly over his cheekbones and jawline. The doctors shaved his head when they drilled into his skull to reduce the swelling he suffered from the gunshot that nearly killed him. Luckily, he turned his head with millimeters to spare and only ended up with a wicked scar that cut across his temple and halfway around the side of his head. The impact put him in a coma for nearly a week, and he was struggling with some basic motor functions and memory loss, but he was alive. That was all I cared about. He also took a shot to the thigh and one through his hand, so he was using a cane and had his left-hand in a cast and strapped to his chest in a sling. Wyatt had been grumpy and short-tempered since getting out of the hospital. Having the agency you'd given your formative years to drop you on your ass—after stating you were a security risk because of what happened to you on assignment—was bound to put anyone in a mood. However, Wyatt's perpetual glower and increasing dissonance screamed of something else going on.

But today wasn't about whatever was wrong with Wyatt. It was about saying goodbye to the bad parts of our past so we could move forward, toward a bright, unencumbered future. It was time to let go of the anchor we'd both let drag us down for so long. We'd both been cut free from the ties that had bound me to endless amounts of trouble and held Wyatt to the unbearable burden of responsibility. There was no longer anything left to hold either of us back. I didn't have to run anymore, and Wyatt . . . well, my brother finally had a chance to know what it was like to live his life for himself, to pursue his own dreams . . . even if he looked like he was ready to keel over at the idea of having not one single responsibility.

"I think you can make plenty of the wrong choices and still end up all right. As long as you make the right ones when it counts, you'll end up exactly where you're supposed to be, with the person you're supposed to be with. And if you're really lucky, that person will get that your wrong choices were just as important as the right ones were at the time you made them." I caught Ten's hand and brought the back of it to my lips. I gave her fingers a squeeze and sighed when she squeezed back.

It was hard for her, looking at the headstone of a man who not only looked just like me, but one whom she put the fatal bullet in. She didn't remember much beyond Jacobs lunging at her. She told Rodie she meant to pull the trigger but couldn't recall if she did or not.

She did, at the exact same time the deputy whom Rodie sent over and Cyrus broke through the door. My twin took Ten's bullet through the heart. It was obviously a case of self-defense when they heard her story and got a good look at her face. Ten also ended up in the hospital with a severe concussion and a broken eye socket. She'd been forced to take an extended leave from the Rangers while everything healed. She let me baby her while we took up temporary residence in San Antonio, waiting for Wyatt to be discharged from the hospital. It was easy to see she was getting fed up with taking it easy, and even though she had two weeks left of medical leave, I doubted she would be using them. She'd been none-too-subtly hinting that she might be looking at a change in careers when we get back to Wyoming. She loved working for the Forest Rangers, but her mind was wired to solve puzzles and put criminals behind bars. She was ready to do more than find lost people. She wanted to prevent them from being lost and forgotten in the first place. Her true calling could no longer be ignored. There had been more than one hushed conversation with Rodie I'd walked in on over the last few days.

"I think we'll skip the part where we ask if anyone has anything nice to say in memory of the deceased." Clara cleared her throat and used the silk cloth in her hand to wipe at her cheeks. "I think we all wish we could've done better by this poor boy. Maybe things would have had a different outcome, maybe they wouldn't. All I know is we have to focus on what we have right in front of us and never forget how quickly it can be taken away. Let's head back up to the house and have a little something to eat. We need to work on fattening you back up, Wyatt."

My brother swore softly under his breath. He acted as if Clara's concern and care were bothersome, but I could see the way the grooves around his mouth lightened slightly and the way his locked shoulders shifted. Wyatt had waited his entire life for someone to mother him. He still hadn't fully embraced the idea of letting Clara and Ana back into the fold. His trust was too fractured, and his expectations were simply too low, but slowly and surely our aunts were wearing him down. Clara even asked him to stay in the swamp until he was fully healed. The doctors told him he was more than likely going to walk with a slight limp for the rest of his life, and no one knew the full extent of the damage to his hand. He was going to need another surgery once the cast came off and extensive rehab on the injured extremity. Wyatt semi-politely turned her down, insisting he would be fine on his own in DC.

No one was buying his assertions, but I knew my brother well enough to know there would be no pushing him. He would ask for help when he was ready, after he ran himself into the ground trying to handle everything on his own. I was planning on keeping a close eye on him and had already asked Grady to pop in unannounced to do spot checks. The older man still felt guilty for his hand in leaking Wyatt's whereabouts to Jacobs, so I had no doubt he would be all over my brother until he was back on his feet.

I knew better than to offer Wyatt a hand. He was touchy and sensitive about getting around with the cane, and I'd already gotten my head bitten off more times than I could count. Ten didn't have the same reservations. She slipped out of my hold and put a secure arm around my brother as he took the first wobbly steps to the collection of pickups needed to drive to this remote part of the property to finally say goodbye. My brother took her helping hand without complaint, partly because he knew I wouldn't tolerate him being anything but grateful to Ten, and also because he genuinely loved her. She was a wreck when Wyatt finally came to in the hospital. She sobbed over asking me to choose between her and my brother. She admitted she forced me into a corner because she was scared I was going to be someone else who claimed to love her and then left. She was inconsolable until we got to Texas and she saw Wyatt for herself. When he woke up and heard everything that happened with my twin, he was convinced she saved my life, and not only because she killed Jacobs before he could kill me. Ten was the person who came along and finally was tough and persistent enough to give trouble a run for its money. My brother treated her like she was made of magic, and she was the only person he forced himself to smile for anymore.

She wasn't fooled by the flash of teeth.

When she walked back to where I was waiting by the truck we'd rented a few days ago, she sighed heavily and wrapped her arms around my waist, leaning forward to rest her forehead against the center of my chest. "What do we have to do to get him to agree to come back to the ranch with us?"

When we left New Orleans, we were going to take up temporary residence at the Warner Ranch. Cy agreed to let both of us crash in one of the plush, designer bunkhouses he used for his guests until we figured out what we were doing. I told Ten she was worth staying for, she told me I was worth leaving for. We were at an impasse, neither knowing the right answer. I kind of hoped Rodie offered her a job like I suspected, because that would take the choice out of our hands. I was happy wherever, as long as she was happy and doing what she was meant to do. I could survive anywhere. What I couldn't deal with was watching her walk away from her dreams again.

"I don't think there's anything we can do. We have to wait him out. He's spent his whole life relying on only himself. Not an easy habit to break." I slid a hand up her back and cupped my hand around the back of her neck, under her long ponytail. I rubbed my thumb up behind her ear and pulled her closer when her body immediately reacted. I loved the way she shivered against me and the way her hands tightened in the fabric of my shirt at the small of my back.

"Today was harder than I thought it was going to be." Her voice was muffled against my chest.

"Yeah. But it needed to happen." I literally laid my demons to rest.

"He was your brother." She breathed out the words, and her shiver turned to a shudder. I'd told her she had no choice until I lost my voice, but the words were useless. I found her crying in the shower a few times. When I asked her what was wrong, she cried harder and asked what would have happened if she hadn't been able to tell the two of us apart. She had nightmares about putting a bullet through my heart, and all I could do was hold her while she cried and assure her I wouldn't let go.

"He was, but he wasn't. Regardless of our looks, the only thing we shared was DNA. Let's get out of here." One door was closed, and I was ready to open another one.

Once we were in the truck, instead of heading to Clara's, I took us back to the shack on the edge of the swamp where Ten and I first connected, when I was trying to find my way home and to the man I was always meant to be. Once this place had held nothing but bad memories and even worse realities. Now, it felt like the place where my life actually started to have meaning and purpose.

On the way from the truck to the ramshackle building, the sky decided to open up. A wall of water hit us, soaking us all the way to the skin. Ten's pale hair clung to her cheeks and neck as she bolted for the doorway. Water ran down the back of my neck and made the ground slippery under my boots as thunder cracked with an alarming boom somewhere off in the distance. I put my hands on Ten's shoulders and used the momentum of her body to push the door open. The interior of the building looked much like it had the first time we trespassed on my past, but the ghosts and cobwebs of regret and remorse no longer clung to every surface. I'd cleared them out of my mind, as well . . . or she had. It was hard to tell, and I agreed with Wyatt. I wouldn't have made an effort to outrun the shadows I played tag with if it weren't for the woman in front of me.

I spun Ten around and continued to walk her backward toward the bed in the corner. The frame was wrought iron and old. The mattress was flat and entirely uncomfortable. But it was a flat surface and not the floor, so it would do in a pinch.

I used my index finger to push some of the wet hair off her face and gave her a smile I reserved for her and her alone, just like all the pretty words wanting to roll off my tongue whenever I was around her. "You and me, Ten," I sent her falling to the bed. She landed with a whoosh and spread her arms out on either side of her. She looked like an angel, except she had lived too much life to have an untarnished halo. Her experience and failures gave her a crown as sharp and pointed as a tangle of thorns. "We're going to have a beautiful life together. Every day, even when it storms, we're going to wait it out because we both know the sun's bound to show up again. There isn't anyone I'd rather run through the rain with than you."

She smiled up at me as she traced a water droplet cross my cheek and down the line of my neck. "I don't mind getting wet when I'm with you, Webb."

I chuckled and wiggled my eyebrows at her. "You like my pretty words. I like your dirty ones. It's like we were meant to be."

Her lashes lowered a fraction, and she lifted her chin a tad. "I'm glad I found you."

I dropped a kiss on her forehead, tasting rainwater and sweet woman. I dragged my mouth to her ear and flicked my tongue along the sensitive shell. "Didn't know how lost I was until you found me. I like knowing exactly where I belong." Far, far away from trouble.

Deep in my heart, I knew that I finally kicked the habit of falling into trouble when it came my way and understood it was my responsibility to walk away. Trouble wasn't some elusive, imagined thing. It was the easy excuse I used for all my poor choices. I always said I could never outrun trouble, that it followed me everywhere I went. It took some serious introspection and almost losing Ten and my brother to admit that I *was* trouble and trouble was me.

There was no getting away from myself, so it was time to make some changes.

I wasn't going to leave all fun and spontaneity behind, though. After all, there was something to be said for being able to surprise your girl at every turn. The smile on her face when I proved time and time again I couldn't get enough of her, any time, any place; that smile was my whole life.

She corded her fingers through the front of my hair, shooting water in a bunch of different directions.

"Where is that exactly? I'd like to know." She rubbed the pad of her thumb over my lips and cocked a golden eyebrow in question.

"I belong wherever you are. I want to be wherever you're happiest. I'd follow you to the ends of the Earth if you asked me. But, I'll stay in one place until the end of time if that's what you need me to do, as well. All you have to do is ask, Ten."

Her fingers tightened in my hair, and her eyes took on a serious cast, making them glitter like hard jewels. "I'm not the girl who gets what she asks for."

She was now. I kissed her below her ear and dragged my lips along the line of her jaw. I could feel her quivering underneath me. "You've obviously been asking the wrong guys. Ask me."

I watched her gather her courage, she bit her lip and moved her hands to my shoulders before the words came tumbling out. "Will you stay with me, Webb? Rodie offered me a job, and I want to take it. I want to work on the Search and Rescue team. I want to build a life in the place where I flourished and failed. I want Wyoming to finally feel like home, but I can't do that if you aren't there. I'll let you go when you need to, but I'll always expect you to come back to me. I love you, and I don't want to live this life without you in it."

I growled at her and used my teeth on the curve of her chin. "That was almost perfect."

I felt her frown, and I did a push up to lever myself up and over her. "Almost?" Her tone was snippy, and her eyes flashed with green fire.

"You don't ever have to let me go. If I need to be somewhere else for whatever reason, then I'm going to ask you to go with me, and if you say you can't leave, then neither will I. It's not a choice anymore. It's just the way it is, because I love you so much, I can't remember what my life was like before you." I lowered myself down, so the ends of our noses touched. "I love the idea of staying with you, Ten. I'm happy to do it. I never wanted to leave, but I wanted to make sure all your options were open."

She wound her arms around my neck and pulled me down so my body was stretched out along the length of hers. Our clothes were wet, and my dick was hard. Things were starting to get decidedly uncomfortable.

"This time I know it all the way down to my marrow, you are the right choice, Webb. Being with you is the right thing, and we *are* going to have a beautiful life together." She sounded as if she finally believed it and it was music to my ears.

"Even when it rains."

"Especially when it rains." She moved her head so our mouths lined up and kissed me until I stopped breathing.

I found the place where my past ended and my future began in this little shack, in the arms of this woman. I also found immeasurable pleasure and contentment. No one loved me the way she did, and I was going to make sure no one loved her better than I did.

The kiss turned heated, flames of desire evaporating the droplets of water still clinging to our skin. Clumsy hands pulled at clammy clothes, making the act of getting undressed way less sexy and erotic than it typically was. I almost fell off the bed trying to pry wet boots off my feet, and there was a moment where I was sure Ten was never getting the legs of her skinny jeans down past her thighs. Eventually, everything landed in a soggy heap on the floor, and Ten and I fell in a tangle of flushed limbs and surprised laughter.

Humor fled as soon as heated flesh touched heated flesh. We kissed again, this time it was aggressive and searching. Teeth bruised and nearly drew blood. Hands and nails left marks on skin as we fought to get closer, battling to become one. Her nipples pressed into my chest at the same time my knee pushed between her soft thighs. We moved in sync, bodies now familiar with one another. The chase for pleasure no longer a desperate need, but a leisurely journey with surprising twists and turns along the way because the destination was always breathtaking. We both knew how lucky we were to return to that spot over and over again.

I knew she liked it when I dragged just the tip of my very hard cock through her folds, nudging her clit with the wide head. She knew I lost my mind when she dragged her nails in a long line on either side of my spine.

All of it was good. Her heels digging into the small of my back. The way her nipples tightened against the sweep of my tongue. The quiver of her belly against my abs. The way her sighs and sweet sounds tasted on my lips. The bite of her teeth on the side of my neck. The brush of her inner thighs. The wetness between her legs, teasing every throbbing inch of my rigid length. Yep, nothing felt better than being tangled in and around her, at least nothing besides sliding into her supple, soft body and being surrounded by her life and her heat. She was the only woman I'd ever had this kind of connection with. The only one I trusted with every single part of me. She said she found me, but every single time I felt her heat pulse around my uncovered cock, I ended up lost in sensation. Luckily, Ten vanished into the feeling right alongside me, so while we were gone, we would always find our way back to reality with each other.

She lifted her legs higher on my waist. I sank deeper into the softness between her legs. The storm continued to rage outside the thin walls of my childhood home, but we paid it no mind. We had this beautiful, unbreakable thing between us, and when it was time to face the world after the storm was over, we would have each other. I'd learned over the years I was the kind of man who could wait forever for the sun to shine. I'd gotten used to the gloom; my days were filled with shadows and darkness. Ten brought all the light I needed to see exactly what it was I was missing, into my world.

I never asked for rainbows.

But I did need to find someone willing to wait out the bad weather, someone who understood the tempest sweeping through my life was the only way to wash the slate clean.

EPILOGUE

WARNER RANCH ~ 3 MONTHS LATER

I WATCHED FROM UNDER THE brim of my hat as the tan Blazer pulled to a stop in front of the large ranch house. When Wyatt called unexpectedly to say he was coming to Wyoming, I'd been unable to get off of work for the day, and no one besides the grumpy, begrudgingly helpful sheriff was available to go pick my brother up from the Billings airport. Ten was on a case. All the Warners were busy with stuff on the ranch and had their hands full with the guests visiting the property for vacation. And as much as I wanted to see Wyatt, there was no getting away from the duties I had for the day. Cyrus had already been so understanding about all the time away from work I missed, I was hesitant to miss any more days and have him view me as chronically unreliable. I figured it wouldn't kill Wyatt to spend a couple of hours trapped in a small space with his nemesis. My brother didn't agree, but it was the only option, so he sucked it up and accepted the ride.

It took me a few minutes to walk up from the barn where I'd been taking care of several of the ranch's horses to the car. It was one of my favorite tasks, and I'd added owning one of the big animals to my bucket list. By the time I approached the vehicle, my brother could be heard yelling at the sheriff who had pulled his door open and offered an arm to help Wyatt climb down from the tall all-terrain vehicle. Wyatt's rehabilitation had been a slow, arduous process, made even worse by his refusal to accept help. The few times I'd gone to the East Coast to visit him, he'd been sullen and withdrawn, still furiously angry about the loss of his job and easy mobility. His limp looked worse than it had after he initially left the hospital, and his hand was still a mess. Luckily, most of his memory seemed to be coming back, not that the small victory did anything for his overall sour disposition.

I wasn't above using a few of my old tricks to get my brother to visit so I could keep an eye on him. Now that Tennyson had gone to work full time for Rodie at the sheriff's office, we both agreed to find someplace permanent to call our own in Sheridan. I called Wyatt and told him there was no way I could make huge life decisions like buying a home, getting engaged, and getting married without his input. We also needed to have a serious heart to heart about what to do with the money from Bernard. Neither one of us wanted to touch it, but it was stupid to let it sit in the bank when we could use it for something good. There had to be a way we could reach out and help kids who ended up in situations similar to ours. I was determined to save the next Weston Jacobs from a similar fate. But I needed Wyatt's input and guidance. After all, he'd always been there for every big decision I'd ever made, and I felt like these were some of the biggest I was ever going to face.

It took some cajoling, some pleading, and some outright begging to get him to agree to come back to Wyoming. In the end, it had been Ten calling Wyatt to tell him she was worried about him and his progress, and her offer to move both her and me to DC for a few months to help him out. That got his cranky ass on a plane and back to the ranch. The fact she was willing to put her life and her job on hold for his well-being really broke through the impenetrable shell he'd enclosed himself in. Wyatt was on a plane two days later, and now he was facing off with the town's local law in a heated debate that looked like it could come to blows at any minute.

"Get away from me! I don't need your help and I did not ask for it." Wyatt's voice was a rough growl, and anger had twin flags of red staining his cheeks. He was still far too thin in my opinion. We no longer looked like mirror images of one another. My older brother looked every one of his nearly forty years.

The sheriff didn't seem bothered by Wyatt's outrage and bluster in the slightest. His tanned face was set in dispassionate lines. He only lifted a dark eyebrow as he leaned his big frame on one arm, blocking the doorway of the SUV.

"Oh, I read you loud and clear, city boy. You don't need anyone or anything. You've got everything perfectly under control." The sarcasm in Rodie's tone was so thick it was impossible not to feel it. I quickened my step, thinking I was going to have to intervene before one or the other lashed out with something more painful than words. "Only, I saw the way you nearly fell over when you tried to put your suitcase in the trunk. And I watched the way you turned green when you tried to text Webb we were nearly here. So as much as you want others to believe that you're perfectly fine, that you have the situation well in hand, the truth is, you're struggling. So, instead of shrugging off help when it's offered, why don't you take it, and be grateful like a grown-ass man would."

When he wasn't healing from nearly fatal injuries, Wyatt was a big, strong guy. But he'd never been as big or as physical as Rodie. With no preamble, the sheriff got an arm looped around my brother and forcibly helped him from the tall SUV. By that time I was standing at the front of the vehicle, watching the interaction with wide eyes under the shadow cast by the brim of my cowboy hat. Wyatt ended up on his feet mere inches away from the sheriff's broad chest. My brother looked wobbly and unsteady on his feet, but it was hard to tell if it was from his sudden ascent or the alarmingly close proximity to the other man.

They stood facing each other for a long, silent moment, eyes locked in an uncomfortably tense and intimate way. I almost wished I'd walked up on them a few minutes later. I almost felt bad for being witness to such a private and poignant moment.

Wyatt put his hands on the other man's chest and gave a hefty shove backward. Rodie took an obligatory step backward and lifted his hands in front of him in a gesture of surrender. Both were breathing noticeably hard and look flushed. It was a nice, temperate day outside, so there was no blaming the weather for the heat in their faces.

"Don't pretend like you know anything about me. I've always managed just fine on my own. It's just taking a little longer to adjust than I thought it would." Wyatt reached back into the SUV and returned with his cane in hand. He gave the needed device a dirty look and finally turned his head to look at me, open curiosity stamped all over my face. "Don't just stand there staring at me. Help me get my bags out of the trunk and show me where I'm meant to stay for the next few weeks."

I pushed the brim of my hat up with my index finger and gave my older brother a crooked smile. "It's good to see you, too, brother."

Rodie chuckled at Wyatt's disgruntled expression and I moved away so my brother could stalk to the rear of the SUV. I stopped next to the big man's side and gave him a knowing look out of the corner of my eye. "You push everyone's buttons like that . . . or is my brother special?"

The sheriff rubbed a hand over his bristly jaw and lifted a mahogany-colored eyebrow in the direction where Wyatt had limped off.

"That man has a million different buttons. They're all bright red with flashing warning signs on them. Who could resist giving them a poke?" Rodie lifted his chin in silent challenge. "You got a problem with me giving the city boy a hard time, kid?"

I shook my head in a silent no and laced my thumbs through a couple of my belt loops. "I don't mind you ruffling his feathers as long as there's a purpose behind it. He's been through enough. And no one can argue it's my turn to look out for him."

Rodie reached out a wide hand and gave me a solid thump on the back between my shoulder blades. I stumbled a little under the force and gave him another look out of the corner of my eye.

The sheriff crossed his arms over his chest as we both watched my brother pace agitatedly back and forth in short, angry lines by the rear of the vehicle. "There's purpose behind everything I do." Rodie shrugged and moved toward my brother. "You ever wonder what he would be like if someone came along and tempted him enough? If he could let go of even a fraction of the control he holds onto so dearly?"

Control was so deeply embedded in my older brother, imagining him without it was like imagining me without trouble nipping at my heels. I never thought it was possible.

"Wyatt is the brother who always manages to resist temptation." I watched the older man watch my brother and wondered what exactly I'd missed—and when I'd missed it—that was going on between the two of them. I was starting to speculate that Wyatt's reluctance to come back to Wyoming had something to do with the unmistakable tension radiating between the two powerful men.

Rodie chuckled softly under his breath as his eyes narrowed on Wyatt struggling to get the tailgate open. "There's a first time for everything, and the first taste of something tempting is always the sweetest, most memorable."

I tugged the brim of my hat back down to cast my face in shadows as I bit back a grin. As Rodie reached for Wyatt's suitcase, the two of them immediately started bickering back and forth once again. Wyatt's outrage and irritability seemed different as he squared off against the sheriff. It wasn't the same aimless, misdirected anger he'd been wallowing in since the shooting. He seemed focused and intent on not letting Rodie get the upper hand.

I was happy to see my brother. I could breathe easier knowing I was close by to give him a helping hand when needed. I was glad all my family was in one place. There were so many exciting things to look forward to. My older brother, I think, had finally met his match, and there was no way I was going to do anything but watch this all play out like a spectator at the world's biggest game. Hell, I might even offer Rodie a tip or two, because no one knew just how stubborn and difficult my brother could be . . . except me.

They were both trained fighters. Men used to being in charge. So I doubted the two of them going toe-to-toe was going to be anything but brutal.

But then again love wasn't love if it didn't leave a mark.

ACKNOWLEDGMENTS

THANK YOU SO MUCH FOR reading. Regardless if this is the first book of mine you've picked up, or the twenty-fifth . . . I appreciate both your time and attention so much.

This series opened a lot of new doors and brought around a handful of new readers, which is honestly so rad. It's always been my goal to write stories about all different kinds of characters, heroes, and heroines, and so many different types of love stories. Thanks to all of you awesome readers, new and old, I get to reach that goal with every new release. Seriously . . . every single person holding this book in their hands right now . . . YOU made me a better author and a better ME. Thank you for that, and thank you for being here.

Thank you to every blogger, reviewer, reader who helped get the word out about this book and any of the ones that came before and after it. Telling one other reader how you felt about a story is such a huge deal . . . I bet most of you don't even have a clue just how important and vital your thoughts on the books you love are. Trust me . . . taking two minutes to drop a review can make or break a book . . . so review to save an author today! I know it is often a thankless task . . . so here I am thanking you from the bottom of my heart.

I need to give a huge shout-out to my assistant Melissa and my amazing beta team. With each new book I put in their hands, I'm blown away by how much better it is when they are done with it.

Brutal feedback isn't always fun, but I have learned along the way it is necessary. So, Mel, Sarah, Traci, Pam, Karla, and Meghan, here is one of many endless thank yous for all that you do . . . even on those days when I want to throw my computer through a window.

If you don't know I have the best professional team in the biz helping me make these books beautiful, then you haven't been paying attention. I wouldn't be here at all if it wasn't for Mel, KP, and my agent Stacey. I want to quit life and reality pretty much twice a week. Luckily these ladies keep me on track and motivated pretty much every single day. I'm a mess, they bat cleanup.

Hang makes the best most beautiful covers . . . period.

Elaine is my most favorite editor in all the land . . . she's rad . . . it's a fact.

Wander is incredibly handsome in real life and knows how to take some of the sexiest, most alluring shots . . . end of story.

Beth is vicious, incredibly smart, totally cunning, and makes me look like a much more skilled writer than I really am . . . she's the best copy editor/editor I've ever worked with . . . no joke.

Christine is a peach. She works incredibly fast and is always calm and collected when I freak out over last-minute changes. She loves books and romance almost as much as I do. We're kindred spirits and my books are beautiful on the inside because of her . . . for really realz.

If you want the best book possible, holler at them when it comes time to publish!

Cover design by: Hang Le / www.byhangle.com

Photographed by and Copyright owned by: Wander Aguiar Photography / www.wanderbookclub.com

Editing by: Elaine York, Allusion Graphics, LLC/Publishing & Book Formatting / www.allusiongraphics.com

Proofreading & Copyediting by: Bethany Salminen / www.bethanyedits.net

Interior Design & Formatting by: Christine Borgford, Type A Formatting / www.typeAformatting.com

As for me, if you are looking for other places to find me. Here I am!

I highly recommend getting on BookBub and giving me, and all your must-read authors, a follow. The site is so good about sending updates about new releases and new titles. Way better, and way faster with the info updates.

Bookbub: www.bookbub.com/authors/jay-crownover
You can email me at: JayCrownover@gmail.com
My website: www.jaycrownover.com
www.facebook.com/jay.crownover
www.facebook.com/AuthorJayCrownover
Follow me @jaycrownover on Twitter
Follow me @jay.crownover on Instagram
Follow me @jaycrownover on Pinterest
www.goodreads.com/Crownover
Spotify & Snap Chat: Jay Crownover

I strongly suggest joining my reader group on FB. I hang out in there a lot and you get almost unlimited access to me: www.facebook.com/groups/crownoverscrowd

ABOUT THE AUTHOR

JAY CROWNOVER IS THE INTERNATIONAL and multiple *New York Times* and *USA Today* bestselling author of the *Marked Men* series, the *Saints of Denver* series, the *Point*, and *Breaking Point* series. Her books can be found translated in many different languages all around the world. She is a tattooed, crazy-haired Colorado native who lives at the base of the Rockies with her awesome dogs. This is where she can frequently be found enjoying a cold beer and Taco Tuesdays, as well as live music and terrible TV shows. Jay is a self-declared music snob and outspoken book lover who is always looking for her next adventure, between the pages and on the road.

GUYS!!! I finally have a newsletter, so if you want to sign up for exclusive content and monthly giveaways you can do that right here: www.jaycrownover.com/#!subscribe

CPSIA information can be obtained
at www.ICGtesting.com
Printed in the USA
LVHW021804040619
620112LV00015B/581/P